BOOKS BY ANNE MAYBURY

Radiance

RANDOM HOUSE  *NEW YORK*

Anne Maybury

Radiance

Library of Congress Cataloging in Publication Data
Buxton, Anne.
Radiance.
I. Title.
PZ3.M45438Rad [PR6063.A885] 823'.9'14
ISBN 0-394-50334-1 78-57129

Manufactured in the United States of America
2 3 4 5 6 7 8 9
First Edition

For
Henri, Kenneth and Siki

And both were young, and one was beautiful.

—George Gordon, Lord Byron, "The Dream"

Radiance

I

THE DOOR TO THE SALON swung softly open and a girl entered, walking with the flowing movement of long legs and supple body. Her footsteps made no sound, yet the women seated on the sapphire-blue sofas awaiting their call for hair appointments looked up. Conversation ceased, eyes were raised from glossy magazines, cigarettes hung poised from jeweled fingers, coffee cups were set down on their saucers.

Eve Thayer was passing through the salon.

Her eyes, gray or green according to the light that fell on them, glanced in a friendly way about her. She had been trained to greet all clients who came for beauty treatments to The House of the Contessa with the same interest, sociability and charm.

The salons of the Georgian mansion were like rooms in a club. A few women sat alone, but most were in small groups, friends and acquaintances who met at the great social functions both in London and on the Continent, and who enjoyed their meetings at the beauty salons where they drank coffee and exchanged scandals.

Eve was perfectly aware of what they whispered about her.

"Once she was made Contessa Girl of the Year she lost no time in marrying Regina's son." . . . "For love? Oh, my dear, all that romantic talk and the articles they wrote about her were so much sentimental rubbish. Money and position were what mattered."

Eve Thayer who came from nothing. The Cinderella Girl . . .

At first it had hurt to know what they said about her, but she gradually learned to live with gossip. It had become easy now to smile her charming, friendly smile as she made her way down the salon.

One of the Contessa Regina Vivanesci's hair stylists came out through the archway on the other side of which was the hum of dryers and the sound of voices. Lucien greeted Eve with the carefully practiced smile that had earned him a place among the jet set. He was a young man invited to chic parties and offered holidays in smart places because of his genius with hair styling, and also because his youth and his gift of making flattery sound sincere were important to his rich clients.

Lucien disappeared into the next salon, where the women sat in small bays, their hair plastered with their chosen tint. The room was decorated in a subtle shade of pink overlaid with a silver gloss that gave a shimmering effect, flattering to all skins. A subtle perfume drifted by as a woman with a new smoky blond hair color came out, saw Eve and greeted her.

"Oh, Mrs. Thayer, do please give me your opinion. Frederick tells me this is a new shade. Does it *really* suit me?" A woman, always unsure of herself, she watched Eve's face and then said quickly, shyly, "Oh, I shouldn't have asked you, should I? The

Contessa has such wonderful hair stylists. But Frederick is a new young man here and he persuaded me."

"Of course you should ask other people's opinion," Eve said kindly. "Why not? And I think it's lovely on you."

"I usually have Lucien, you know, but I couldn't get him this morning."

Eve said vaguely, "No, he's very busy, I believe." She didn't explain that Lucien was being held in readiness for a princess who usually had him come to her house to attend to her hair. But whenever a new color was needed, she came to the Berkeley Square salon because she liked to have Regina herself watching over the process.

The woman with the blond hair went happily toward the swing door that led to the elevator. Eve followed her, more slowly.

A magazine lay open and discarded on one of the low tables in front of a sofa. Eve glanced down and saw the full-page color photograph of her own face. It was an advertisement that had been enormously popular all over the world, and the wording on the bottom of the page said simply, "The House of the Contessa." But the portrait of Eve in profile held its own powerful message: "Beauty triumphant because you use Contessa Cosmetics."

Eve picked up the magazine and with a swift, impulsive movement ripped out the page and tore it in half. Then she crushed the pieces violently in her palm as if she were trying to erase herself.

Eyes all down the long room watched her, expressions incredulous, intrigue on every face.

Walking toward the door and the elegant hallway and elevator beyond, Eve was aware that her gesture had been quite unnecessary. She crossed to the velvet-covered wastepaper basket at the side of the appointments desk and dropped the torn photograph into it, then, turning and looking back, she had a swift picture of the reception room.

Regina had taken trouble with the robes her clients wore for their treatments. They were of beautiful sea-water green, pale enough to be flattering to every skin coloring.

Each floor of the salon was identical—silver-pink walls with niches lined with sapphire velvet and fronted with glass. In these Regina kept her unique collection of sculptured crystal. The pieces, specially designed for her by the best artists of the Tamarisk Glassworks Company and individually signed, glittered and sparkled in an amazing variety of complicated designs. There were ballet dancers and birds in flight, windblown clouds and intricate prisms, each facet gleaming like a small silver sun. The crystal sculptures were etched with stippling and lines drawn as delicately as cobwebs. There could be few finer examples of two thousand years of glass engraving than these exquisite pieces. Such was their beauty that on no salon floor in the Berkeley Square house was there any other decoration to spoil the effect.

Light, so important in displaying glass, was artfully concealed but focused in order to give each piece the necessary dramatic effect. Each niche was connected to a complicated burglar-alarm system, for Regina trusted no one, not even her richest clients.

"Millionaires are known to bribe professional robbers to steal art treasures for them," she had said. "No greedy connoisseur of fine crystal is going to gloat in private over anything he can thieve from me."

The telephone on the appointments desk had rung and Sidonie Lam, the receptionist, called Eve.

"Oh, Mrs. Thayer, the Contessa wants you in her office at a quarter to eleven."

The silver clock above the desk pointed to half past ten. Eve had fifteen minutes breathing space before the confrontation. It was the only word she could think of to describe any summons from her mother-in-law during working hours.

What this time? "You will fly to Rome. There is an important reception . . ." But that had been last month, when the editor of a new fashion magazine had given a great party there. "*Vogue* wants to do another feature on you." She doubted it. Eve decided that it was far more likely to be trouble—another clash of wills.

Ever since she had married Adrian Thayer, the Contessa's son by her first marriage, Regina Vivanesci had compulsively tried to condition Eve to the way of life she intended for her—complete dedication to Contessa Cosmetics—her business, her great, absorbing passion.

From the time Eve Fairfax had entered the fashionable church in Hanover Square in her white silk dress and with a coronet of miniature crimson roses on her hair, she had signed away her right to be herself. She was given her place, whether she liked it or not, as the third pillar of The House of the Contessa.

A middle-aged woman was waiting for the elevator and when Eve joined her, the woman's eyes brightened. "You are—you *are* the Contessa Girl, aren't you? I mean, I'm sorry if I shouldn't ask but—"

Eve said, smiling, "Yes, I'm Eve Thayer."

"Oh, then I must tell you." She held out her hands, her purse swinging from a gilt chain on her wrist. "Mrs. Van Francis told me about the wonderful new nails that you can fix on here. Mine have always been so terrible, I've been ashamed of them. But now . . . just look."

Eve recognized the beautifully manicured, natural-looking nails that were manufactured at the Contessa factory. They were semipermanent, guaranteed to last a year. Fine holes, almost invisible to the naked eye, allowed air to reach the real nail beneath, and a special solution enabled the wearer to slide the artificial nail down to the base as the real one grew.

"They're quite an innovation, aren't they?" Eve said, admiring them.

The elevator slid, satin-smooth, down to the ground floor and the woman sped happily out. Eve moved more slowly, waiting to speak to Vine, the commissionaire who manned the great glass door. Princess Daniella, the royal client, was coming for her appointment that morning and Vine must be prepared to make her entry easy, without outward fuss that could draw crowding spectators. Vine knew his job. He reassured Eve, and gave her the special smile he seemed to reserve solely for her.

She turned away, pausing to check the urns of yellow daffodils and golden roses. Facing her, set upon a pillar of ebony between the elegant double staircase that led to the first floor of the salons, was another of the famous crystal sculptures.

This one dominated the great hall—a head of Eve created by Tamarisk's chief artist, Vivian Mote. Although Regina had chosen its position and claimed it, it had been commissioned by Adrian soon after his engagement to Eve and had been unveiled at a small private party on the night before the wedding.

It was Eve exactly as she appeared in her publicity photographs, wearing the classic ancient Egyptian headdress Regina had selected for her. It completely hid her hair in order, Regina explained to the press, that Eve's marvelous bones would not be obscured.

Eve wondered, disinterestedly, how many cameras had been focused on her during that Year of the Contessa Girl. She remembered in particular the television advertisements, unique because they lacked the thrusting, vocal impact of the usual commercials. Before Regina would authorize her beauty products to be televised, she had stipulated that no words must be spoken, no seductive movements made. Only Eve's face would appear, flashed for a few seconds before the watching millions.

She felt a small longing for those early days when the excitement was at its most intense and her love for Adrian a thrill that made a rainbow of her life. She shook herself out of her mood of nostalgia, trying to summon all her strength of character for the coming meeting with Regina.

II

ON THE WALL of Regina Vivanesci's beautiful office was a gold-framed script. It read: "A woman who does not seek to make the most of herself is one whose spirit is dead."

That was the creed of The House of the Contessa, the lovely columned building in Berkeley Square that had for centuries been the home of the dukes of Lyre.

Seated at her carved desk, Regina checked the time by the fire-opal disc of her watch. She had ten minutes in which to calm herself before Eve arrived, and she had learned that if the relaxing exercises she practiced every day did not work, then the best way to ease tension was by thinking hard about something else.

Her reaction to her daughter-in-law sometimes frightened her, but she would quickly brush the emotion aside. She had weathered so many storms that a mere girl was not going to defeat her.

Unlike the great Helena Rubinstein who had held full-scale board meetings at her bedside, Regina rose at seven each morning and was dressed, impeccably made-up for breakfast and in time for the early meetings that were held in a very fine white-paneled circular room.

The meeting that morning had been attended by her chief copywriter and other executives. They had been summoned primarily to offer their suggestions for a name for the new range of Contessa Cosmetics scheduled for the late fall.

"A name . . . " she had said in her clear voice.

The men and women seated at the table had been leafing through the pages of reference books and legendary tales, wracking their brains for weeks in anticipation of this moment. Desperate to please, they poured out their suggestions.

"Arabesque" . . . "Sorceress" . . . "Divina"—this from Hugh Manross, her chief copywriter, suggested because it was common knowledge that "Divina"—the divine one—had been the nickname by which her second husband, Count Carlo Vivanesci, had called her.

"I think it's a fine name—" Hugh began.

"What *you* think," Regina had retorted, "isn't important. It's what the women will think of the name when they see my products displayed. It's the women I need to attract."

The meeting had ended with no flash of inspiration and no final decision.

She glanced at her watch again. Time seldom passed slowly for her and inactivity vexed her. She wanted the interview with Eve to be over, although she had no doubt about the outcome. Regina usually won.

There had been, of course, that occasion fourteen months ago when Adrian had openly defied her. He had faced her in their penthouse drawing room with a strength of purpose she had never before known him to have.

10

She had demanded, "You are going to marry—*who*?" Disbelief throbbed through her voice.

"Eve."

Dreams of duke's daughters and the sisters of earls crashed around Regina. A very handsome son with a great inheritance, a man of charm, losing his head over a girl utterly out of his own sphere . . . Adrian, who was magnificently eligible. And if there was a recklessness about him, an extravagance that sometimes went wild, well, any girl would close her eyes to that for the sake of such a marriage. And while she was alive she, his mother, could always keep him in check.

But now—"Eve Fairfax . . . " She breathed the name with scorn. "If this is some joke—"

"I have never been more serious in my life."

Regina had shivered. They were the exact words she had heard once before in that very room. It had been years ago but the thought struck terror in her tough heart.

"Adrian, dear, please. Stop and think . . . stop and remember . . . "

He had turned his back on her abruptly. "All that was many years ago. Anyway, this is different." His voice had a sudden strong, harsh note.

"Different? A girl *I* picked up at an art gallery?"

"For heaven's sake, Regina, doesn't it occur to you that for some men one girl can stand out above all the others? You don't know why; you even *ask* yourself why. But there it is. You meet her, talk to her, see her often—and suddenly she is in your blood. And there is no surgeon with a scalpel and no doctor with a miracle prescription who can free you from that."

"Bewitchment. That's all," Regina had cried. "Just plain, unrealistic bewitchment."

"It's neither plain nor unrealistic—and you know it. It's tremendous, and whatever you say, I am going to marry Eve."

"Darling, go away for a while—for three months, if you like. Give yourself a break from seeing her and you will return with a more balanced outlook. Eve isn't for you. Her world isn't your world, and she would never fit in."

"*Mother, I am going to marry Eve.*"

Adrian seldom called her "Mother" because she hated it. She was "Regina" to her son and to her executives.

In the end she gave in. She argued to herself that Eve Fairfax, with her beauty, could be an asset to the family. Whatever her background, the girl had a natural poise and she was highly intelligent. Regina even became gracious about the forthcoming marriage.

The beginning of their life together had been full of marvelous promise, but, very slowly, the enchantment had faded. Regina and Eve were two strong characters, and they pulled different ways. Battles usually stimulated Regina. But not this one. She sat very quietly, trying to contain the violent resentment she knew would flare up when she and Eve faced one another.

She reached out to a tray on her desk and picked up a tiny vial. Uncorking it, she tested the lotion on the back of her hand where the telltale aging spots were appearing. As soon as she applied the lotion, the brown marks disappeared. She waited a moment or two, then dipped a tissue in a small Chinese porcelain bowl of water and rubbed her hand. She watched and smiled in triumph. As she had foretold, and as the advertisement would proclaim, this covering cream for blemishes was waterproof and would be marketed in every known skin color. The aim was always to be one step ahead of competitors. Yet Regina never sacrificed the excellence and purity of her products—it was the sum total of her integrity.

In so many ways, Regina was fashioned in the mold of that last generation of beauty queens, Rubinstein and Arden, but in her personal likes and preferences she was entirely different. She never wore ostentatious jewelry or little bowler hats like Rubinstein, nor had she ever ridden a horse in her life and most certainly would not call them, as Arden did, her "little darlings."

She put the small vial back on the tray and flicked through a pile of photographic index cards left by model agents of their loveliest girls. But none of them had the special quality that Eve possessed. She tossed the photographs back on to the desk. It had to be Eve.

She opened a folder of Eve's publicity stills and stared at the top one. There had been no need to improve on it by the use of transparent veils over the lens or erasure of lines on the face or lights or shadows carefully tilted. Eve not only possessed perfect bones and lovely coloring; there was also a rare quality about her, a luminosity that seemed to come from some inner, almost spiritual, source. With her honey-gold hair and perfectly set eyes below winged eyebrows, Eve possessed what Regina could only think of by the one word that had struck her when she first set eyes on Eve Fairfax: radiance.

What angered Regina was that, given so much, Eve was also possessed of a fierce independence. Regina rose irritatedly and crossed the room to the floor-to-ceiling windows that looked out over Berkeley Square. Youth and middle age had long passed her, but her face and figure had warred against the years and had won. She was tall and well-built, without excess weight. Her hair, richly copper-tinted by Lucien, was worn smoothly and caught in a rosette of twists at the back of her neck. Against the ivory silk walls of her office, her profile was clear; her nose had a slight downward curve, and her lips were full and sensuous, the lower one protruding slightly.

She turned from the window and a great gilded mirror gave back her reflection. She glanced at her image without really seeing it. As if Eve had been manifested by Regina's own strong emotions, it was her daughter-in-law's clear undaunted eyes that seemed to look back at her.

The intercom buzzed. Regina went to her desk and flicked the switch. "What is it?"

Marion, her personal secretary, said, "It's Mrs. Thayer. You wanted to see her."

"Send her in." Regina sat back and watched the door. She was aware that her impressive, high-carved chair could be a daunting background to anyone sent for to be upbraided, censured or dismissed. But Eve gave no sign of nervousness.

"Ah, my dear. Sit down."

Eve did so, remembering one of Regina's lessons: "When you sit, try always to cup one hand in the other, with your fingertips uppermost. It releases tensions."

Eve found that it didn't always work; it wasn't working on this particular morning. But she looked her mother-in-law straight in the eyes and waited.

"I thought at first that it would be best if Adrian joined us for this talk, but I have decided to have him come in a little later." Regina fingered a silver note pad. "You know that the princess will be coming at half past eleven? You have checked the flower arrangements in the hall and warned Vine to telephone Marion?"

"Everything is organized."

"Good. Then we have plenty of time for our talk before she arrives. I shall, of course, sit with her while she chooses her tint, and I must not be disturbed."

"Of course," Eve said calmly, and wondered about Regina's unnecessary preamble concerning the princess, since everyone working at The House of the Contessa understood the procedure and protocol necessary even for minor royalty. This unnecessary scrap of conversation could only mean that Regina was stepping cautiously into battle.

"Adrian and I," Regina said, "have already had a talk about the matter and we have agreed, Eve, dear, that it is time you took a more active part in the business." Her voice, as always, was rich with measured cadence; the sting was in her choice of words. "And now," she continued, "I want to go into more detail with you." She paused and smiled, but her eyes were hard. Both knew that the swords of battle were about to be drawn.

Eve said quietly, "Everything is so beautifully ordered here that I doubt if anyone could find much for me to do. I only wish they could. I wish . . . "

"Your place here was made very clear to you the moment you

married Adrian. The sad thing is that you won't see it. Whether you like it or not—and I refuse to believe that you could either dislike or be blind to it—Contessa Cosmetics is your heritage now as well as Adrian's, and that necessitates that you take your rightful place and do your duty as it is laid out for you."

"My . . . duty, if you choose to use the word, is to Adrian."

"Of course. And also to me, because we are one—the three of us here in this house."

This house over the shop . . . Eve tensed and only the faint sound of distant traffic heard through the heavy storm windows broke the stillness.

Regina allowed the sound to hang between them like a threat. Then she said in a changed tone, meditatively, "When Adrian came down from university, he had a spell of rebellion, too. But I dealt with it. I made him realize that the honors he won in mathematics proved his great ability in that side of business affairs, and that, for his own sake as well as mine, he must not fritter his life away on . . . on flippant, youthful interests which would be of no use to him in later life. My efforts to train him have paid off. You know how absorbed he is in the business; how deeply it matters to him. He loves it, Eve, just as I do . . . and as you must. He serves it as I do and as you must."

"If I have any small gift it is for understanding modern art and design. But that doesn't help here."

"Your place here lies in your looks. You know that you are beautiful," replied Regina.

"That would only serve if I were a model. I'm not."

Regina watched her. Then she said, "Don't you believe in my products, Eve?"

"Yes, I do."

"And you should, because they are important. One of the saddest things an old woman can say to herself is, 'I was never good-looking, but I could have made more of myself if only someone had told me what to do.' That is why my clients never leave me. My creams and lotions and treatments defy the worst ravages age can bring but, unlike indifferent cosmetic surgery which can strain every wrinkle out of a face, my treatments give touches of youthfulness and yet leave a woman with certain faint lines that mark character."

Eve sat quietly. She had heard it all before, but this amazing, intelligent, dynamic woman had a weakness for repetition where her favorite subject was concerned.

"Success is a demanding mistress and I had to achieve it without help from anyone, not even from Adrian until I took him firmly in hand. Thank God, he listens to me, and he is gifted in his own way! Figures to him are like notes on a piano to a fine musician. He thinks *my* way now. And so, my dear, must you."

Eve said with spirit, "Can't you see, Regina, that I really have tried to give? But I'm a person, too, with the right to some say in my life. You must know, surely, that Adrian promised me, just before we were married, that we would have a place of our own."

"Then he promised out of a foolish impulse. *This* is your home and there was never any question of it not being so. But, of course, if you don't appreciate beautiful and rare things, you won't appreciate this house."

"I do. But it isn't *ours!* Nothing has been chosen by us, nothing is mine except the clothes I wear and the few small personal treasures I brought with me—and which are shut away because none of them would fit in with your perfect decor. Regina, *can't* you try to understand? But you don't. You didn't care how hurt I was when you made me take down that portrait of my mother and father I had hung in our sitting room. It wasn't a good painting, I know, but it was done by an artist friend of my father's *with love*. You made me take it down because it offended you. It didn't 'go,' you said, with the Louis Quinze furniture. So I took it down to please you. And *so* I live your life, in your world 'over the shop'—*your* shop." She watched the cold, disinterested face, hoping for a glimmer of compassion.

"Adrian had never complained about living with the beautiful things I have collected here, nor should you. You are involved here." Regina's eyes narrowed. For a moment she watched Eve without speaking. Then she said, "Be careful, my dear. Adrian is thirty-five. It's an interesting age for a man, and you aren't the first woman in his life."

"I'm quite certain of that!"

Regina looked away over Eve's shoulder, her eyes suddenly curiously remote. "They weren't important—except one. And that was long ago. But be careful, Eve."

"You mean—women and Adrian? Oh, I've seen it all—the way they look at him, the way they look at me. Adrian is a woman's man as well as a man's. But I don't go around watching for warning signs. I trust him. And if we find we have made a mistake and there's someone else more important to him than I, then we'll break up."

"Dear heaven, you don't understand!"

"What don't I understand?"

Regina didn't answer her. Once again her eyes held a strange expression, as if she were looking beyond Eve, back into a memory. In those swift moments Regina had obviously forgotten Eve. Then she pulled herself together with a distinct effort.

"Let's stop all this argument, because it is merely a waste of my time." She reached forward and selected a small bottle of nail varnish from the test tray. "I want you to try this. You haven't got color on your nails, have you?"

"No." She held out her hands, watching Regina, wondering what it was that haunted her and made her forget, for those few moments, all the argument that had seemed so important before.

"You know I like you to have color on your nails. It's good for business. But never mind now. This is part of a new range. Try it."

Eve sat down at a small table, spread the tissue Regina had handed her and opened the tiny bottle.

"It has gold in it!"

"Yes. I think it will be popular for evening wear." She watched Eve brush the liquid onto her nails. It was a pale cyclamen studded with tiny gold specks. She finished painting the nails of one hand and held them out for Regina to see.

"As I say, it will be popular. Personally, I don't care for it, but

17

many of my clients are always looking for something different. I know other nail varnishes on the market with gold in them, but none of them are as strongly defined as this. I can see it only on a very beautiful woman with dark hair, wearing a perfectly cut simple black dress and gold jewelry. Oh well, it's for the public to decide."

As Regina studied the new varnish, she was remembering another girl in her son's life. The girl who would not do as she was told and the tragedy it had brought. She had forgotten it for so long, and she knew she must put it out of her mind again. Eve was a very different character. The long-ago drama could never happen again, please God.

She relaxed her hands and smiled. "Now," she reached for a writing pad, "to business again. I've been talking to Josh Carter. He agrees that Adrian and I are right. You, and only you, must be the Contessa Girl again this year. I'll call a meeting next week and we must plan the publicity shots and work out the promotion. As yet no one has come up with a suitable name for the new range, but one thing I am determined about—this is going to be the biggest campaign Contessa Cosmetics has ever known. And you—"

"Regina, please understand. I can't do another year. I need work—you know that and so does Adrian. Cassius More, for whom I worked when you first met me, has hinted that he may have a job for me in his gallery. It's work I love and understand because he deals only in modern art."

"And now that you are Adrian's wife, you can forget it. Just remember, instead, that *I* trained you in all the things that models pay heavily to learn. I trained you and made you famous."

"I can't go through all that again!"

"I didn't notice that being on exhibit made you miserable," Regina said tartly.

"It was fun to begin with; it was different from anything I had ever known and—" She stopped speaking as the doors opened and a small, quiet man entered.

His appearance gave no indication of his curious ability, his flashes of inspiration as director of advertising.

"I gave orders that I was not to be disturbed," Regina snapped at him.

Alan Patterson said humbly, "I'm sorry. I didn't know. Marion was not in her office when I came through."

"Well," Regina's tone was as ungracious as she could make it, "now that you are here, what is it? No, Eve, don't go."

"I have an idea for publicizing the new range of products," Alan said.

"What idea?"

"Kites."

"K-i-t-e-s?"

A man without courage would have turned and fled at her tone. Alan stood his ground.

"They could be designed very artistically with The House of the Contessa colors. And there are now fantastic ways of flying kites. It's like a new art and . . . "

"How long have you been working for me?" Her voice was quiet and deadly.

"Fifteen years, Contessa."

"And you still bring me some vulgar suggestions for my publicity?"

"It would be . . . "

She cut him short. "I have forgotten more about publicity than you will ever know," she snapped back. "Cosmetics aren't a brand of sausage, nor are they sold in street markets. If you can't come up with something better than that—"

"But—"

"But nothing!"

Alan insisted, with nervous bravado, "It is said that it isn't elegance that women want; it's to be noticed, to be told in startling terms *what* they want. And these kites . . . "

"They don't want elegance?" Regina drew in a long, hissing breath. "So *they* think! Isn't that what I'm doing—*making* the public want elegance? Must I din it into you as if I'm giving a lecture? Everything in life is a cycle—fashion, beauty . . . We had the Georgian charm and the Victorian stiffness and the Edwardian overdressing. We've had the utility rubbish and unwashed hair. And now the idea of beauty has come full circle and the next stage will be elegance. They'll have done with not bothering with their lipsticks and their hair styles. You can't stop rotation. Charm will return for the girls in the high streets of the surburbs and the secretaries at their typewriters. And I intend to be leading the field in the cosmetic world. Now, Alan, I have things to discuss with Mrs. Thayer." She dismissed him with a brief wave of her hand.

In spite of her own resentment, Eve had the sudden hilarious thought that Alan Patterson should be walking backward out of the room as if Regina were living up to her name and were a queen. If only there was someone in that great house to laugh with—but laughter was alien to the two most important people who took everything so seriously. It was like being told that you must never laugh loudly in church . . . as if God would mind. Regina would.

The door had scarcely closed behind Alan before the interrupted conversation began again.

"And now, Eve, you have had a little time to face up to your role here, so let's have no more argument and get on with our plans."

"However much you want me to, I can't change my mind. Please, let me be useful in some way or other here, let me work with you on some project, but don't ask me to spend another year on modeling and promotions."

Once again there was an interruption. Adrian walked in.

"I'm sorry if I'm late. A call came through from Rome."

Eve swung round on him. "You knew about this plan that I should return for another year as the Contessa Girl?"

"Yes, of course." He gave her his charming smile. The sun slid from behind a cloud and shone on his hair, turning it to corn gold. "You loved it before. And you were perfect in the role."

"And then I got bored with it," she flashed at him, half turning her back on Regina. "Probably Cinderella would have got bored with her glass slippers if she had had to wear them all the time." She sensed a tension in the room and her flippancy fell away. She said very seriously, "People change, you know, Adrian. Perhaps sometime during my role as the Contessa Girl I grew up. All I know is that there came a time when it wasn't fun any longer; it was just very hard work and embarrassing, always being stared at and answering the same questions over and over again. I *want* work. I've explained that to Regina, but it must be my kind of work, something that I understand and enjoy doing."

She glanced at Regina and saw the impatient shake of her shoulders. "You're very argumentative, aren't you, Eve? I suppose in your peculiar previous life, you've always been allowed to have your own way. But it's different now. Your life is not entirely your own to do as *you* want. Our plans are made and you will fall in with them."

"Mother, please—" In his agitation Adrian forgot her dislike of being called "Mother." He was seeing her as such in these tense moments of argument—his mother, his employer, the very lifeline by whose grace and brilliance he received his splendid salary; by whose business acumen he lived in supreme luxury and from whose approval he drew emotional sustenance. "Somehow," he said, "we must compromise." He shot a glance at Eve, loving her to the point of his obsession. "If Eve could work, say, twice a week at something she enjoys doing—in an art gallery, perhaps—then she would be happier and could carry on as the Contessa Girl for the rest of the week."

"No," Regina said sharply. "What I have planned is a full-time occupation."

Adrian ran a hand over his crisp, shining hair. "Something has *got* to work. For heaven's sake, we can't go on warring like this. Don't you both see that between you you are tearing me apart?" His voice rose sharply.

The room seemed charged with the violence of conflict. Then Regina said in a slow, calculating tone, "If a house is divided, it falls. History has proved that over and over again. There is only one alternative if you fail us, Eve. The business will eventually cease to be private and become a public company."

"For God's sake, no!" Adrian cried. "It's ours; it has always been ours. We can't have strangers in a boardroom, shareholders always at our heels over profits. And I don't believe that you would do such a thing merely because of a silly quarrel with Eve. Regina, you couldn't!"

She said, looking steadily at her son, "You and Eve are supposed to love one another. Therefore, both of you should work to the same end, if not for my sake then for your own. You know what profits were last year, and this year they are increased by twenty-five percent. This, in these tricky times, is excellent, but it takes constant effort. That's why I must have the finest promotion for my new collection. It's not going to creep gently onto the market, it's going to blaze. And, for that, I want quality."

Eve had heard enough. She got up and walked past Adrian to the door.

He called to her, pleading with her. "Darling, stay. We must talk this out."

Eve thought to herself, "Round and round we'll go, with the same platitudes, the same pleadings, the same urges toward compromise! And all the time it will be merely a matter of wearing me down until I say 'All right. I'll do it. I'll be the Contessa Girl again.' But I won't . . . ."

She was through the door as the intercom buzzed. Marion was at her desk speaking to Regina.

"The princess's car has turned into the Square. I've called the elevator and warned Vine."

Regina's clear voice came through the doorway. "I'm coming now. And go down and see that the hall is clear of people."

Eve avoided the elevator and climbed the flight of stairs to the penthouse. Because of her love for Adrian she felt a stirring of guilt that she was defying him. By marrying into the family she enjoyed the riches and the position they provided and they had a right to expect some kind of cooperation from her.

Yet she did cooperate in a way she had hoped pleased them both. Since she had no home to look after, no meals to shop for and cook, she had made it a practice to spend a great deal of time each morning and early afternoon in the salons, moving from one to the other, talking to clients, giving help where she could, but always careful not to obtrude between the client and the particular hair stylist or beautician she was waiting for. Her self-imposed task needed tact, but tact had been one of the requisites necessary during her year as the Contessa Girl.

What she had found as the months of her marriage went by was that Regina saw her as a "commodity," as someone whose whole way of life must be geared to the glory of Contessa Cosmetics. And although Adrian adored her, he, too, could not separate her from the business. It was like a vast magnet drawing her into it so that, if she did not resist, she felt she soon would lose every scrap of individuality she possessed. Nothing in her life would be her own choice; every hour of her day would be geared to the glamorous "shop" over which she lived.

She thought rebelliously: *I married Adrian, not a beauty empire.* But she knew now that that was wrong. She had indeed married a business, only she had not fully realized the extent of the price she was having to pay for loving Adrian.

III

PRINCESS DANIELLA WAS THE DAUGHTER of the Earl of
Camberay and had married a European prince. She was
spoiled, self-indulgent and known to be "more royal
than the royals."

Regina was waiting for her as, followed by a maid carrying a
white Pekingese, she swept into the columned hall. Vine bowed
to the princess; Regina came to meet her and made a very faint
movement of her body which was neither a curtsey nor the familiar greeting of acquaintances. It was an in-between acknowledgment that Regina had managed to perfect of a woman of the
world to a member of the lesser royalty.

"It's a great pleasure, Princess." Her tone was honeyed and so apparently sincere that she might have been the charming twin sister of the autocratic and harsh woman her staff knew.

The princess extended her hand in what was known by royalty and in embassy circles as "the diplomatic handshake"—palm turned downward so that guests could only manage to touch the tips of royal fingers. It was a way in which those who had to shake hands a hundred or more times at receptions guarded against too exuberant handshakes. After the light touch of fingers, the princess entered the elevator, Regina and the maid following.

The small retinue left the elevator on the second floor and walked through the arched doorway into the hair-styling salon. The women seated at the mirrors in the rows of bays that lined the room glanced at the small, regal figure in the Givenchy suit with the ruby brooch on her lapel. The thought in most minds was the same: What color is she choosing this time? For the princess was known for her passion for changing her hair tints. She had been light blond and titian, nut-brown and ash blond. In between the various tints she wore beautiful handmade wigs that covered her head until the latest shade had grown out.

The cubicle to which the group made their way was enclosed by silk curtains. It was one of the few small rooms where those clients who insisted on privacy were taken, and where they could hear the chatter from the main salon and at the same time enjoy their privacy.

The princess sat down and waved her maid to a corner chair. "Just watch closely, Sabine, because when the tint is complete I want Lucien to restyle my hair and you'll have to learn how to do it." She turned to Lucien. "I want a much brighter tint than the last. Show me the swatches of hair."

Lucien had them ready and laid the soft swirls of color, from black to silver blond, in her hand. She flicked through them and suddenly stopped at a brilliant sunshine yellow.

"That is the color Madeleine d'Avergne has had her hair tinted, and everyone is saying how gorgeous she looks. Well, that is what I want. My husband thought it marvelous."

Bending over the swatches of hair, Regina thought: You want it because you know that Madeleine d'Avergne would snatch the prince from you tomorrow if she could . . . *And* she could. But that yellow!

She said, choosing her words carefully, "I saw her, too, but I thought the color overly bright. It has a metallic look about it, and we have never used it except on one or two dancers who need the brightness for the stage. Forgive me, Princess, but I know you always ask for my opinion; otherwise, of course, I would not give it."

The d'Avergne girl's hair was tinted and styled by a couple who were fast making a name for themselves among the young jet set, and although Regina knew she had no need to fear them as rivals, neither did she wish to praise their slightly outrageous efforts.

"What is the color called?"

"Sunflower," Regina said reluctantly.

The princess held it against her cheek. "It will go beautifully with my new Givenchys."

And badly with your sallow skin, you silly woman . . .

"Perhaps, Princess, if you will tell me your color choices for this spring," Regina said charmingly, "we could find a really perfect tint for your hair. In fact, I'm sure we could. I keep a very large stock of colored silks for testing for makeup and tinting, as you know."

The princess became regal. "There is no need to waste time. This is the tint I want."

Regina refused to meet Lucien's eyes. She knew perfectly well that he would be prepared to protest, and he must not. A customer with the influence of Daniella could never be crossed. Behind her smiling charm, Regina was furious. To have the princess openly announcing to her friends that Contessa Cosmetics had given her that bright, metallic yellow was a bad advertisement. But she comforted herself that Daniella was already known as "the chameleon princess."

"By the way"—the princess sat back and closed her eyes, holding out the swatch to Lucien—"I would like you to advise me on the new styling, Contessa, when the tinting is completed and I am ready."

"Of course. I'll come back in about an hour, Princess." Regina had recognized the inferred dismissal and rose.

She managed to hold onto her graciousness as she walked quickly along the carpeted reception room, smiling greetings at the clusters of clients. She paused once to speak to an actress starring in a current West End show, congratulating her on her performance. Two women in their silvery green Contessa Cosmetics gowns were wandering toward one of the niches where a crystal phoenix spread illuminated wings. Another client, who had come for one of the famous reducing classes, was crossing to friends, her gown flying open to show the leotard they all wore for the exercise session.

Regina moved on, passing through the door to the elevator. Once out of the public eye her face returned to its harsh lines. She had lost a battle. It was bad for business when a client insisted on a style or a tint that didn't suit her.

Regina, with no more need to be ingratiating, saw Eve as she left the elevator. She glowered and called, "Have you made that appointment for the photographer?"

Caught between the elevator and the executive offices, Eve paused. "I've just been to have a manicure. Lesley was free and I seized the opportunity." She held out pale tinted nails, a far cry from Regina's gold-flecked test polish.

"So now you can go and make that photographic appointment," Regina retorted. Her eyes were cold as steel. The princess would scarcely have recognized the charming Contessa Vivanesci.

Eve shot her a calm look. "Not now," she said and started to walk toward the staircase that led from the salon to the executive offices on the floor above.

"I have a question to ask you." Regina's voice was soft, but the words carried because of the inner force behind them, like a stage whisper.

Eve waited without moving. Everything seemed very quiet, as if both clients and staff all over the building were frozen in their places, listening.

"Where are my grandchildren, Eve?"

The question was so unexpected that Eve, too, froze. Then she turned and said, quietly, "Surely that is a matter for Adrian and me?"

"And also very much for *me* . . . for the continuance of the business. Or do you want strangers to run this place after I, and then Adrian, are both dead? And don't look at me in that shocked way. We are all mortal. Well?" She waited. Then, as Eve said nothing, she continued, "Over a year of marriage—and I am still awaiting my first grandchild."

Indignation whipped Eve to a hot, angry retort. "I want my child—my children—to be born for *their* sakes, not for mine or . . . or for Contessa Cosmetics. I hope—and believe—that Adrian feels that way, too."

"In the matter of a great business such as mine, where there are so few to inherit, the next generation need to be born, not just for the sake of their parents or for themselves, but for that inheritance. Duty, Eve . . . "

"Oh, no! Not with children. They must never be born for that."

"Without it, very little would be achieved."

"And what would be achieved that way is the coldest success in the world." Eve turned and walked up the stairs without looking back.

IV

THE HUGE GEORGIAN MANSION had ample room for both the business and the family. A double staircase, known since the time the house was built and kings and princes walked up it as the Grand Staircase, led from the circular hall with its marble columns to the first floor on which were situated the hair styling and facial treatment salons. At the top of the staircase, to the left, was a huge and splendid room with one of the painted ceilings for which the house was famous. The dukes of Lyre had used it as a ballroom; Regina held her formal receptions there, and next to it was a smaller paneled room known as the Meetings Room. A conservatory rich in tropical plants and with a little fountain led off the main room, and a doorway led onto a twisted outside staircase that ran down to the walled garden.

Whenever Regina held her formal parties in the former ballroom, double doors of opaque glass and gilded curlicues were used to close off the salons to the right so that any guest who did not know the layout of the house would not realize the world of business and beauty that lay beyond the beflowered gallery that led to the ballroom.

Above that floor was a second, given over entirely to massage, skin treatments and expert advice on a myriad of clients' problems.

Above, again, were the executive offices. From the center of these rose a semicircular staircase of delicate wrought iron. It was one of the most beautiful and elaborate of the famous wrought-iron staircases of Georgian Mayfair. The gilded fleurs-de-lis were interspersed with the spreading wings of the legendary phoenix, all cast in slender curves of iron, a marvel of the craftsman's art. This staircase led to the two-floored penthouse where the family lived. It was said that an eighteenth-century Duke of Lyre had had the top floors decorated with treasures from the East, and that he allowed only his closest friends to climb the staircase to his special rooms.

The house itself was one of the last of the great Mayfair mansions, which, to Regina's credit, had retained its original lovely proportions and interior beauty.

As Eve walked up the staircase to the penthouse, quick, light footsteps sounded from the top floor. Shari, Regina's fourteen-year-old adopted daughter, came down to meet her.

Shari was very thin and awkward in her movements in spite of all Regina's efforts to teach her grace. Her hair was dark and straight and her small face had an avid look about it which was unyouthful and faintly disturbing.

She held out the small object she had in her hand. "Look, Eve."

It was a lipstick. Eve took it and uncapped one end. The color was a startling red.

"Now turn it upside down and take *that* cap off," Shari said.

At the other end was a lipstick of purplish pink, as difficult to wear, except theatrically, as the vivid red. The casing of the lipstick, however, was of silver and blue enamel, beautifully and intricately worked with small aquamarines, like tiny droplets of glittering blue water.

Eve recognized it as one of the new and expensive gimmicks Regina had manufactured for her most extravagant clients.

"Mama told me I could choose one. Didn't you?" Shari glanced over Eve's shoulder.

Regina was standing behind her.

"Let me see it." Regina held out her hand and took it from Eve. Then she looked from the lipstick to Shari's overbright mouth.

"My darling child, haven't you yet learned what colors are suitable for both your skin tint and your age? This is most certainly ridiculous for you." She thrust it past Eve into Shari's hand. "The case is very expensive and I won't have it just lying around unused. You must return it to the stockroom and get them to insert much quieter colors. You know perfectly well which ones I have told you to use."

"But Mama—"

"No 'buts,' darling. Just do as I say." She reached out as Shari came down the stairs and patted the girl's sallow cheek.

The telephone extension on the small gilt table at the end of the gallery rang and Eve went to answer it.

"Oh, Mrs. Thayer, Miss Tamsin has just finished her massage and wants to see you before she leaves. I believe it's about a charity show she wants you to help her with."

"I'll come straight down." Eve replaced the receiver and explained to Regina: "Joan Tamsin wants to see me."

Running down the stairs, Eve had Shari in her thoughts. Fourteen years ago Regina had startled her acquaintances by announcing that she was adopting the child of a great friend who had died in childbirth and whose lover had deserted her.

"It's a legal adoption," she had said, "and from now on she

will look on me as her mother. I want her to feel that she is one of the family like any other child." And, to Shari, Regina had said, "You will call me 'Mama' because, darling, you belong to us, to *me*."

For the first three years of her life Shari was looked after by nurses at Regina's Cotswold manor house in the West Country. Then, quite suddenly, she was brought to London and remained at Berkeley Square. She had been christened "Shirley," but the name had been difficult for her to pronounce when she was very young. She had called herself "Shari," and Shari she remained.

Because of her size, she looked less than her fourteen years, but such was the unnaturalness of her life at The House of the Contessa, that she was a mixture of childishness and sophistication. It saddened Eve, whose own youth had been very happy, to see Shari so unlike a normal child. She had been geared, as had Adrian for many more years, to being the daughter of a huge empire whose empress treated her, according to her whims, as a child or as an adult. Shari, living her luxurious and yet lonely life, was completely out of her depth. She felt that the few girls who were her friends were being used by their own mothers as a way of getting a foothold into the high social life of the Contessa Regina Vivanesci, and it was Regina herself who had conditioned the girl to suspect the motives of others. In fact, the reason Shari's acquaintances were not sincerely her friends was due to her own cautiousness and reserve.

Joan Tamsin was waiting in the third-floor salon where, behind a door, was the sauna which Regina hated. Some years earlier there had been a fire, and she had decided to close the whole solarium. Repeated requests from clients, however, induced her to change her mind, but she herself never used the facilities and none of the salon's fitness programs included sunlamps or steam baths or the sauna.

Seated with Eve on one of the deep sofas in the reception lounge, Joan said, "I wanted to speak to you about an idea I have about giving fashion shows in hospitals. I think it would be good for the patients. They can think out ways of modifying what they see to suit themselves. It must be so boring for them just lying in bed, and I know they would love to see you in person because your face is so well known. Would you join us if I can plan it? The hospital authorities like the idea and I thought of getting about six or eight models, with you, of course, as the chief attraction."

On show again . . . but this time for a cause that was good. Eve promised, and after Joan Tamsin's thanks, they walked down the stairs together, parting at the door.

Eve paused on the steps for a moment or two. And then the lovely April green drew her out, and she went into the Square.

The light had the brief brilliance that so often comes before a storm, and she saw the clouds already massing over the rooftops. The rough elements of storm and wind always seemed to soothe her when she was anxious or upset. Crossing the gardens of the Square she felt the first rain on her face, cleansing the air and cooling the anger that still burned inside her at Regina's efforts to control her life.

Adrian's involvement in it all troubled her. She knew that he loved her, but she had learned since her marriage that, putting aside filial love for his mother, it suited him in his position as heir to an empire to make efforts and sacrifices to please Regina. This meant that he had constantly to face a powerfully dominating mother and a strong-minded wife and try somehow to avoid battles between them. Such a position, as Eve saw it, was insoluble, and would only bring despair to the three people concerned.

She walked twice round the Square and then, passing the house a second time, recognized a man coming toward her from the big garage at the far end of the walled garden. Certain of Regina's executives and high-ranking staff were allowed to park their cars at her garage entrance if Regina should summon them for a meeting.

The man was Regina's chief chemist, Scott Somerset. He came very seldom to Berkeley Square and was the least known, although one of the most important, of all her employees. In many ways a secretive man, he received both respect and devotion from his staff; he was also one of the few who did not fear to contradict or oppose Regina.

Most of the company's executives kept themselves free, even during the hours when the office was closed, to obey a summons from Regina. But not Scott. He went his own way, and only something extremely important would bring him to Berkeley Square at those times he had decided were essentially his own.

Regina had known his parents, and when Scott had come down from Cambridge with a first-class honors degree in science, she had offered him a place in her laboratories. Scott refused. He wanted to do research in medical science. Regina argued, cajoled and at last won him with a promise.

"You are young. The experience in a commercial laboratory will be interesting and will give you a good financial base. You shall have a three-year contract with me, and it will be invaluable. When your contract with me ends you will still be young and free, either to remain in my laboratories or leave. That is surely a fair offer."

Scott accepted, and had now been with Contessa Cosmetics for eight turbulent years. He was a fine chemist, and when he knew he was right he did not give in—he had rarely lost an argument with Regina.

Conjecture was rife about him. No one, not even the colleagues with whom he occasionally had drinks, knew what he did in his spare time. When he was not at his laboratory, his life was entirely private. One thing he made very clear, however: that social scenes, which on occasion he could not avoid, frankly bored him.

Eve watched him approach and thought with amusement that they were on a collision course right outside The House of the Contessa. He saw her and stopped. His eyes, as gray as the clouds lifting and sweeping away over the rooftops, narrowed with amusement as he looked down at her.

"You never cease to surprise me."

"Why?"

"You should be seeking sun—I thought that's what all little rich girls did. Instead you go walking in the rain. But I seem to remember you once told me you loved 'the winter and the winds and the racing clouds'—your own expression, I think."

"Probably. It's true, anyway. It's a joy—probably a perverse one to you. And when I'm angry it soothes me."

"*Are* you angry?"

"It's not important."

"Anger is always important to the angry. So why?"

She said, vaguely, "Oh, because I'm being asked to do something I don't want to do."

"Then say no. It's quite easy."

"I *have* said no." A tiny jewel of a raindrop fell onto her face from the plane tree under which they stood. She put out her tongue and tasted its softness.

Scott asked, laughing, "You also drink rainwater?"

For the first time that morning she heard her own laughter. She said, "One of these days I'll startle Adrian by asking for a gin and rainwater when he takes me out. But I suppose it would be a case of 'first catch your rain.' " It was silly and lighthearted, but it did her good to be able to be that way.

She was aware of Scott watching her, making no effort to be on time for whatever appointment Regina had made with him. He said, "You're full of opposites, aren't you?"

"Am I? But do go on, I love talking about myself. I suppose most people do."

"Very well, then. You have the look of gentleness and yet you are full of spirit; you are surrounded by the trappings of glamor and yet you choose to walk in the rain."

"Deep down," she said, "perhaps I'm not really civilized."

He considered her. "Perhaps you aren't. Come to think of it, we're probably both ill-starred with contradictions. I should be letting the sun burn through my soul in some desert or climbing a devil mountain, defying death and rather liking the challenge. Instead of which, I'm tied to all this paraphernalia just as you are, working on experiments to make women younger and prettier. The difference between us being that you enjoy it."

"We'll let that pass. But I think you must like your work. If you didn't, you'd get out."

"Ah, that's the crux of it all, isn't it, Eve?" He made a gesture of impatience with his shoulders. "But I don't think this is quite the time or the place for delving into the psyche—yours or mine. Let's leave it. Anyway, much as I would like to stay out here and smell the rain in the streets, I have to see Regina. Do you know why?"

"No."

"I thought you were a part of the business."

It touched the sore, angry point. *"No, I'm not!"*

"All right! All right! You don't have to be ferocious about it."

She turned quickly from the narrow eyes laughing at her. Scott said, "Regina wants me to go to New York to sack Jeff Mackerson."

"Her chief laboratory assistant there?" Eve stared at him. "But why? And why you?"

"She doesn't think he is pulling his weight. He is, of course, but if Regina decides against it—"

"And why do *you* have to participate in who is or is not to be dismissed when there are her own executives over there?"

"Because they're hedging; they don't want him to go. I understand the work he does, so I can dismiss him on technicalities. At least, that is how Regina has explained it on the telephone. But a telephone conversation isn't as satisfactory as a face-to-face one, and so I've come in person to refuse."

"She won't like that—"

"Any more than I like being asked to fly thousands of miles to do such a job. So, we fight with equal weapons—psychologically, I mean."

She turned toward the steps that led to the doors with the two initials "C.C." intertwined in gold on each pane, and felt Scott's sideways glance.

"You are much more beautiful without all that makeup."

"And much more comfortable. I never enjoyed feeling iced all over like a cake."

He laughed. "And that's something you dare not admit to the world. If you did, you'd stop being Regina's product."

"Oh, I'm not . . . not anymore. I'm myself."

"Are you?"

Once again she was aware that he was questioning her understanding of herself. And this time she had an uncanny feeling that he saw her too well, that trying to hide her thoughts from him was like being behind clear glass. She heard herself say, without the words seeming to have come from a desire to say them, "I envy you, Scott . . . being strong. I am, too. But not strong enough."

"And for what particular battle do you need more strength than you have?"

"To hold on to what I am." She turned to him as she spoke, and felt embarrassed by his steady, silver-gray eyes on her.

She said brightly, "Margaret will be home soon, won't she?"

"I believe so." He laughed. "But I never quite know. That sister of mine comes and goes, free as air, but she usually manages to bring back some ancient dust from one of her 'digs,' and it's like a magnet drawing her back again. I think this archaeological expedition to Peru hasn't yielded much—no marvelous new civilization or Inca treasure-trove."

"It will be lovely to see her again. I had a card from her a few days ago."

"You're lucky. With me, she doesn't write, she just appears," he said affectionately. "As sister and brother we get on well— that's because we let each other live our own lives."

"I envy you."

He said in surprise, "Do you? I wonder why?" But even as he asked, there was a clear, penetrating look in his eyes that conveyed not puzzlement at all, only compassion. " 'She has a lovely face;/God in his mercy lend her grace . . . ' "

"Tennyson's 'Lady of Shalott,' " Eve said. "But she drowned, floating down to Camelot."

"Well, I just hope you can swim."

"I don't get the connection."

"Don't you? Never mind. Are you coming in?" He paused, waiting for her at the bottom on the steps.

"Not yet. I want to walk."

She smiled over her shoulder at him and crossed the street, walking once more round the Square. She passed No. 50, Mayfair's haunted house, then No. 49, which was now redecorated back to its original lovely eighteenth-century style. She knew every building, every statue set among the trees, and she loved them all. She could even enjoy the great modern blocks that now stood on the sites of the historic mansions because, in some strange way, they did not offend.

Her thoughts were of Margaret Somerset, Scott's sister, whom she had met when she first came to work for Regina. Scott, arriving for some meeting, had been driven by his sister in her car. It was the happiest of introductions, for it led to a real friendship. The slim, red-haired young archaeologist and Eve met often until Margaret left for the exploration of a site in Peru.

The thought that she would be seeing Scott's sister again soon gave a lightness to Eve's walk under the shining, rain-wet leaves of the Square. Eve's friends from her pre-marriage days lived a considerable distance away, in artists' colonies around Chelsea and Fulham and new-old parts of London like Islington, but Margaret and Scott Somerset's house was nearby, and this had cemented their immediate liking for one another. She could "drop in" on Margaret for a stolen hour and a release from her grand and unhomelike home.

V

THE SCENE WITH HIS MOTHER and Eve that morning had so upset Adrian that, despite his usual love for his work, he had the urge to sweep the papers on his desk to the floor in a passion of frustration. He wondered how another man would handle a situation where feelings were equally divided between two strong women.

Glancing down into the Square, he saw Eve walking in the street below, her fair head raised so that the cool beads of rain dripped onto her face. He watched her pass under the shelter of trees and out again. Then, as she drew near the house, she stopped.

Scott Somerset had appeared, and Eve was talking to him. But as Adrian watched, he felt none of the jealousy that tore at him when men at social functions hung round her. They were usually rich, socially important, titled—and ruthless. Scott Somerset possessed none of the first qualifications for that jealousy and, as far as ruthlessness was concerned, it would be a losing game for him, for Eve had now been so conditioned to luxury, to glamour that however much he might try, Scott would never stand a chance.

Somewhere in the house Regina would be making her plans for Eve to be the new Contessa Girl, and knowing his mother, Adrian was quite certain that, to her, Eve's refusal was nothing more than an irritating speck on the horizon. Regina always got her way and would expect Eve to conform. Yet, as he looked back over the year and a half of their marriage and recalled how many times Eve had capitulated, he knew perfectly well that she had done so only because she loved him. But for how long could such a state continue?

Somehow, he must persuade her. Regina was his mother and her empire would one day be his. It was his crock of gold beyond the rainbow, his Golden Fleece. It was, in fact, half the meaning of existence to him. The other half was Eve. He had to reconcile the two parts of his life, and the commanding factor was a truce between his wife and his mother.

He turned and crossed the room to a Marc Chagall painting, pulling it aside to reveal a small safe. He manipulated the lock and opened the steel door. Inside were two shelves. One held personal papers, carefully documented and tied with tape. On the other, deeper shelf was a large casket richly ornamented in silver gilt, pearls and turquoise. Adrian set the casket on the walnut table and unlocked it. A glitter of jewels lay on the soft padded velvet. He dipped his hand in and scooped up a necklace of small diamonds and a star sapphire ring. There was a blaze of other jewels lying on the velvet—a tiny watch with a golden face studded with rubies; earrings and matching bracelet of aquamarines encircled by diamonds. Treasures . . . treasures for Eve that as yet she knew nothing about. Two additional small leather cases lay at the bottom of the box, but Adrian didn't open them. It

40

scared him even to see them. They had been bought at an auction by an agent bidding on his behalf, but the prices he had paid had been far outside anything even he, in his rewarding position at The House of the Contessa, could afford. He knew that he had been mad to declare so airily to the agents that the price was unimportant, he wanted the jewels.

Ever since their marriage Adrian had been quietly buying. Payment for Eve's love . . . a treasure chest like Faust's gift to Marguerite. But he was no Faust. He was not bargaining his soul for a woman, only his money.

Regina had once said to him, "Money buys everything except health—always remember that." He believed her—the people with whom he was surrounded socially proved her point.

By normal standards, Adrian knew that he was very rich and he never stinted himself. He had a passion for spending money, for acquiring things, many of which he might never need. It was a compulsion, like gambling.

There was the great yacht off Chichester Harbor with its full complement of crew paid, most of the time, to idle on the ship; taking her to sea only occasionally to keep her engines in running order. Although he used it very seldom himself, he liked to be able to lend the yacht to friends, and dreamed of the day when he could take a glorious voyage with Eve—as soon as he could tear himself away from the business for long enough. There were the horses stabled at the country house in the Cotswolds, exercised almost exclusively by grooms. And there were the two plays he had backed and lost on heavily when both turned out to be flops.

One day, Regina's millions would be his. Adrian spent now as if they already were, aware that so far Regina had closed her eyes to the extravagances she knew about. But she did not know about the jewels, and he did not dare tell her.

Where Contessa Cosmetics was concerned, Adrian's head was hard and shrewd. But the jewels . . . that was different. The passion and the turmoil of loving Eve and the dreaded knowledge that he could not be absolutely certain of always having her, possessing her—that was the thought which was like a vulture's wing hovering over him.

There was, of course, another way by which he might hold her—a different sort of bribery.

If they had children . . .

He knew that Eve wanted them eventually and that Regina was impatient because Contessa Cosmetics must have progeny to carry on. Through her grandchildren and great-grandchildren she, Regina Vivanesci, would endure.

Adrian himself didn't want a family yet. One day, when he felt that Eve's differences with Regina were resolved and they were living contentedly and in harmony in the same house, he would feel more sure of her and more ready to have children. For the immediate present, however, there was the terrifying risk that Eve might defy them all and go back to her old life with her artist friends. He couldn't even be sure that having children would hold her, nor was he certain that he was prepared to share her with them. His passion for possession was so strong that he felt he could not face even a minuscule of Eve's love to be given elsewhere. He was not at all sure how he would react to watching a child demand her kisses, her soft face against its softer skin, her body bent over a sleeping infant, forgetting Adrian in her love for another life.

He picked up the jewel case and went quickly up the stairs to the penthouse.

In the small anteroom between Eve's bedroom and his, there was another safe set in the wall above a fine bronze group of galloping horses. He unlocked the safe and laid the box inside. Placed there, secure and hidden between their two bedrooms, he felt it was like a link binding them secretly and strongly together.

Then he stood for a moment looking into Eve's beautiful bedroom with its Louis Quinze furniture, the bronze-doré chandelier, the exquisite Russian malachite clock. Regina's taste, Regina's possessions. How could any young woman born into the middle class resist the thrill of living in such surroundings? After over a year of marriage, he still knew Eve so little that he could not imagine her leaving such beauty—or so he told himself between moods of terrifying doubt.

Down in Berkeley Square, in the clean, rain-washed air, Eve continued her walk, and as if her feet chose the way to go, she found herself in Curzon Street and within a few steps of Cassius More's art gallery.

She paused, looking at the single picture in the window. It was a fine painting of a wild sea, the spray flying like unruly white hair.

Eve pushed open the door and walked in. The large room with its perfect lighting and cleverly hung paintings, the pile of catalogs on the big yew desk, was so familiar to her that she felt an overwhelming sense of nostalgia for the old days when she worked there.

Cassius was talking to a woman and Eve went quickly to a corner, turned her back and examined a painting. She heard the scrape of a chair as the woman rose, heard her footsteps to the door, the click of a catch.

"For all that's wonderful! My favorite beauty!"

Eve turned and two arms enfolded her. She felt a smacking kiss on her cheek and then heard the gallery owner saying, "I know. I know. You are now so rich that you want to buy my paintings because you know that anything I choose to exhibit here will increase enormously in value. I'm the best judge of modern painting outside the big public galleries, and you know it. Now which ones have you got those gorgeous eyes of yours on?"

"None," she laughed.

"Oh, my dear!" She saw his face fall. "And there am I almost on the breadline because the public just doesn't want good art and—"

"And, Cassius, you are forgetting I once worked for you and I can't help knowing the size of your beautiful bank balance."

He looked like a little gnome and his wide, rather gentle eyes hid a shrewd brain. "So, Eve, you just came in out of the cold, is that it?"

She shook her head, "Have you any vacancies here or in your Mount Street office?" she asked.

"Which means, Eve darling, that you have some penniless little protégée you want to find a job for. Well, tell me about her—I trust your judgment. Because I need an assistant here and you should just see the type of girls who come hoping I'll take them on! They wouldn't know a Van Gogh from a Modigliani."

"I'm the girl." Eve said. "And I need an outside interest."

"That, darling, is something I foretold would happen sooner or later if you married into that gorgeously rich, overstuffed family."

"You make them sound like Edwardian sofas."

Cassius feigned dismay. His eyes looked at her with the plaintiveness of a spaniel. "I didn't mean to insult your family, darling. I meant overstuffed coffers." He brightened. "But if you really mean that you'd like to work here, I'd jump at the chance to have you back, only—"

"Only . . . ?"

"Regina."

"I know. But it *is* my life and I need a good, solid occupation. Please, Cassius. Money isn't important. I would donate whatever you paid me to any charity you chose."

She heard his sigh. "I wish it could be. You're so decorative that I'm afraid the buyers would end up just by wanting to buy *you* and not my wonderful pictures."

"Oh, shut up!"

She heard his little giggle. "You defeat me, Eve. Yes, oh, dammit, I need someone with your qualifications and I would rather have you than anyone else. All right. You win."

"When can I start?"

"Monday, at ten o'clock."

"Cassius, I love you," she said and kissed his cheek and fled. She walked home on air. To have told the family that she wanted outside work was true but would have been ineffectual. To be able to tell them that it was a *fait accompli* was decisive.

Two bronze lions guarded the double doors of the penthouse. It was ironical to think that the great immobile beasts stood guard when nothing could protect, in this house that was geared to a great business, the privacy of two people in love and loving.

Marble Corinthian columns flanked the doors to the room leading off the hall. There were no windows, and a Louis Quinze chandelier hung on a long chain from the frescoed dome. On the round table under it stood some rare snuffboxes, gilded and jeweled, some of the deepest blue-and-green enamel, some gold and embossed with scrolls and miniature paintings. A lovely fifteenth-century madonna stood against a purple velvet curtain.

Eve pushed open the double doors on the left and the bright April sunlight pierced a high-ceilinged inner hall hung with cream silk wall panels woven in France. More double doors led from here to the drawing room and dining room and a few stairs to the right and left led to the top floor of the penthouse. This floor contained Regina's luxurious suite and the suite she had arranged for Eve and Adrian. Farther off, in what was called the east wing, Regina's personal staff lived.

A sleek-furred cat appeared from nowhere and leapt up the stairs in front of Eve. She called his name, softly, "Dalua," knowing that he didn't hear her for, like so many white cats, he was deaf.

They entered the bedroom together, Eve and the cat, and he immediately leapt onto one of the elegant Louis Quinze chairs and curled himself up, purring.

Eve went straight to the west window and looked down on to the garden, a small, high-walled oasis of bursting green leaves, grape hyacinths and yellow daffodils. At the end of the garden, opening onto the side street, were two garages. The larger, at one time the stables and carriage house, now housed Regina's Rolls-Royce and Adrian's Bentley. It also contained a workshop for Sanderson, the chauffeur. Beyond the main garage was a smaller one which, in Georgian times, had been the livery room and this was where Eve garaged her own dark-green Volvo. Both garages could be reached by going through the garden, Eve's by then crossing the large garage and going through a door into her own. This garden route was one the family chose to use rather than to go round by the street.

Below her as she stood at the window was the gnarled and twisted trunk of a very ancient walnut tree, and against the sunny south wall a magnolia was almost ready to burst into snow-white bloom. Flowers blossomed early in that small sheltered garden, one of so many tucked away behind high walls in Mayfair and little dreamed of by passers-by.

Alone and quiet, Eve leaned against the window frame and thought back to the days before her marriage. Most of that life had been spent with a happy, united household of parents, two brothers and a sister in an old Victorian house overlooking the Thames at Richmond.

Gradually, the pattern changed. The family grew, spread wings. Her brothers came down from their universities. Jack, her favorite, returned with an engineering degree that brought him a good job in Saudi Arabia. Her younger brother, a botanist, was—as he put it—"with friends in South America having a look at the Amazon." Her sister, who was interested only in horses, was helping to run stables in the West Country.

Five years earlier Eve's father had died, and her mother had later married his closest friend. After the wedding they had gone to live in Paris, where Eve's stepfather had a diplomatic post in the British Embassy.

Eve herself had taken a diploma in art history and had gone to work for Cassius More. Her ambition, after a few years of experience in the art world, was to work on designing. Exactly in what field of design she hadn't made up her mind. Mosaics fascinated her, as did lacquer, but they were both risky and very specialized and she needed to earn her living. So she played for safety, working for Cassius in his gallery to earn money and studying at night school. She got to know a great many young artists and sculptors and she was entirely happy with her life, loving art and learning fast to understand it.

It was at a party given by Cassius More to open a new gallery in Curzon Street that Eve first met Regina Vivanesci. Cassius had pushed through the crowds clustered in groups in his gallery, looking more at each other than the pictures on exhibition.

"Eve darling, the Contessa Vivanesci wants to meet you."

Eve had laughed and said, "I don't believe that. You're just trying to mix your guests and I'm certain I won't have anything to say to her." Then, glancing between the crowds, she had seen Regina watching her and knew that Cassius had been right and that the Contessa, in her suit of bronze-colored silk and her gleaming hair, was waiting for her.

The meeting was brief and impersonal, and so far as Eve was concerned, forgotten the moment the gallery closed its doors on the last of its guests.

It was soon after this that the letter came asking her to call at 500 Berkeley Square. Eve had no idea as she walked under the striped awning how that interview would change her life. Looking back, she knew that sitting in the lovely room which was Regina's office she was overcome by the personality of this woman "queening" it in an historic house. Eve was twenty-four, and the world of cosmetics seemed strange and compelling and glamorous. She was human enough to be flattered by the great woman's compliments.

As she sat at her desk, Regina's eyes had watched Eve's every movement across the room to the chair where so many had sat dreading the minutes to come. Eve felt no fear. She had her work, her life, her friends—she had nothing to lose by coming to see what the Contessa Vivianesci wanted of her.

"I knew it!" Regina's voice held triumph. "I knew it as soon as I set eyes on you, Miss . . . Miss Fairfax, isn't it?" She glanced at the writing pad in front of her. "Well, Miss Fairfax, I need you here." It was the firm, uncompromising statement of someone who had every intention of getting what she wanted.

For a moment, silence hung between them. Eve waited for the

Contessa to explain. Regina anticipated a dazzle of excitement in Eve's eyes, but it never came.

Eve merely said, "I don't understand, Contessa. What could you possibly want me for?"

"As my Contessa Girl."

"You mean, to have me *work* for you?"

It took a few minutes for Eve to comprehend exactly what that meant. In a kind of daze she heard bits of sentences, each interspersed with her own almost hilarious thoughts. It isn't true . . . someone is having a joke at my expense . . .

" . . . groomed for real beauty . . . you have the basic features . . . quite perfect . . . beautiful bones and a clear jaw line . . . "

Eventually, Eve came out of her daze and interrupted. "It's very nice to hear flattering things said about one, Contessa, but I'm afraid I still don't know why you have singled me out. There are thousands of girls more beautiful than I . . . "

"Oh, thousands *as* beautiful," Regina had conceded. "If that were all I am looking for, it would be easy. But I have known for a long time that I need to find a girl with a quality that is difficult to define. Luminosity . . . radiance . . . I suppose either of those words could describe it. But in all my years, with the mass of lovely girls I have seen and had photographed and used for my products, I never found that quality until I saw you at Cassius More's party."

Eve, with nothing to lose, was prepared to argue."I'd have said that actual looks were the most important point in a beauty business."

Regina had retorted, "Fashions and concepts of beauty change. Whatever girl I have chosen in the past—and I have chosen many—there is always someone who will say to me, 'but she's not really beautiful, is she?' The eye of the beholder varies. Every century has its own idea of beauty, and the following generation could think her plain. No, it isn't just beauty I'm looking for, it's an ageless, timeless thing—and you have it. And so, I need you here to work for me."

As Eve moved her head, a wing of honey-gold hair fell across her face. She laughed and pushed it away. "That's one thing that isn't my best point," she said. "My hair. It won't wave, it won't even stay where I want it. No hairdresser can do anything but let it fall as it wants to."

"No," Regina agreed. "It's so fine. Baby hair. We will get my top hairdresser to graduate it and devise a way of setting it to show off those fine bones of your face." She frowned as she saw Eve's unbelieving smile. "All looks can be improved, Miss Fairfax. Why do you think I have *this*?" She spread her arms to encompass her beautiful office. "It's because so many rich clients come to my highly trained staff to do what women fear is impossible—to beautify, and if not, then at least to improve enormously."

Eve put up her hands and pushed her hair tightly back. "This is what I do with it when I'm working."

"Never mind about your hair. It isn't important for the photographs. I want your *face*—your profile particularly—and no pretty-pretty hair style to spoil the effect. You had the right idea when you dragged it right off your face." She sat for a moment, thinking. Then she smiled. "I know what we will do. Have you seen photographs of the Egyptian Queen Nefertiti—a sculpture of her head was found after three thousand years, and is in the Berlin Museum? The headdress hides her hair so that one can concentrate on just the beauty of perfect bone structure, the pride and poise of her head. If she really resembled that head of hers, then she must have been the most beautiful woman who ever lived. Well, I shall have you photographed as she looks in that headdress." Regina gave a great, satisfied sigh. "So it's all settled."

Eve had a moment's rush of spirit. *Oh, no it isn't!* She opened her mouth, ran her tongue round her lips and prepared to say so.

But Regina was talking again. There was to be a year's contract, and she must understand the conditions of employment which would be laid down clearly. And salary . . .

Suddenly Eve's bemused state completely vanished and she sprang to interrupt. "I'm sorry, but I'm afraid I have to turn your offer down, Contessa. You see, I have a job and one I enjoy. I study modern art and I work in Cassius More's gallery in Curzon Street, where you met me. I love it there and I could never be a model. I'm not trained for it. I don't think I like the idea of being part of a publicity drive, being stared at and interviewed. I'm sure I'd say all the wrong things and—"

"You aren't modeling *clothes,* my dear. And when you travel you won't be traveling like models do—gypsies that they have to be! When I send you to New York or Paris or Rome, you will go comfortably, in style. I will give you the training you need, and that is very little. There'll be none of the search through agencies and cat-fights with other models. You will be *my* model for that year. And one good thing: you already walk well, Miss Fairfax— though I don't intend to call you that. What is your first name?"

"Eve."

"Well," Regina said doubtfully, "I suppose that will do. Tell me, did you have a chance to look round my salons before you came in here?"

"I went through one, yes, because I thought I had to see the receptionist first. But I was on the wrong floor." She laughed. "I can't imagine how for generations only one family lived here— unless of course all their relations came too!"

Regina had no time for society history or dead dukes, and she dismissed the faint disturbed sensations she felt at Eve's complete ease of manner. She said with a forced smile, "I doubt if you can imagine working in more beautiful surroundings."

Eve nodded. "Oh, you're right, Contessa. But I really love the work I'm doing now."

Regina ran a hand over her luxuriously tinted hair. "I will make your face famous, and not only in Britain, and you wouldn't be human if you weren't prepared to love *that* perhaps even more than this work you are doing now."

"I think I'd be scared, too," Eve said honestly, "because fame is something that dies quicker than most things. I could see myself sinking without trace and then I'd feel such a failure."

"You are too cautious for someone so young. Forget caution. Take the brightest and best that life offers you. As I say, I will have a contract drawn up and you can come tomorrow to sign it."

"You may be wasting your time, Contessa. I may not come tomorrow. In fact I—"

There was a sound behind her. Someone had entered the room and Eve turned to look.

He was of medium height with richly growing fair hair which, when it caught the sunlight, had silver tints in it; his eyes were very blue. He hesitated, glancing at Regina. "I'm sorry. I didn't know you were engaged."

"Stay." Regina introduced Eve, " . . . and this is my son, Adrian Thayer. His father was my first husband." She added, with a smile that gave the first touch of lightness to the interview, "I'm English, but my first husband was half Rumanian and my second an Italian, so I suppose I've become cosmopolitan."

While she spoke, Eve was facing the fact that she would have to make this woman understand that she was not to be cajoled or bullied into leaving work she enjoyed for a beauty business in Berkeley Square.

And then Adrian Thayer smiled at Eve and held out his hand. In that moment willpower failed her—or, she decided later when she thought about it, physical attraction took over from every other emotion whirling inside her. It was as if these two strangers had exchanged a silent message: *I must know you better.*

But there was no meter by which Eve could gauge what had flashed between them. It had happened as it had done to thousands of couples—a powerful, inexplicable and invisible urge that could not be argued by logic or reason.

Regina, sensing nothing, had turned to Adrian and plunged into a list of commands. Eve sat listening. Somewhere at the far side of the daze that misted her mind she knew she would sign whatever contract the Contessa Regina Vivanesci would put before her.

Take this job . . . know this man . . .

She heard Regina asking if everything was arranged for the executive dinner the next day; heard Adrian assure his mother that Marion had taken care of it all.

Regina asked. "And Ferrand?"

Adrian nodded. "I coped with him. I used every argument under the sun and a few threats thrown in. He capitulated."

Regina looked pleased. "That's wonderful. Adrian, you are becoming a master at persuasion. Remy Ferrand has always been troublesome." And then she added softly, "My French rebel public relations boy! So brilliant and so conceited. And Adrian, remind Marion that this is one of the occasions when cocktails must be served before dinner, not whiskey."

Adrian, looking at Eve, answered his mother. "It's all arranged."

Eve listened as they quickly discussed business affairs. "You see," Adrian was saying, "We can afford to double our expenditure on the new promotion or even take one great gamble and treble it. If it comes off . . . "

"*If* it comes off, Adrian, then we would make headlines in the financial world. But if it didn't—"

He laughed. "Then we'd have failed. But the new range of products is sensational and—"

"There is much more to trebling a fortune than merely being sensational, my dear, as you perfectly well know. You are too reckless. Thank heaven you aren't as reckless with figures as you are with your ideas, otherwise our auditor would have something to say." She shook her head as she remonstrated with him.

"It's *because* I have to be financially cautious that I let myself go when I think I have any bright ideas for Contessa promotions," he said.

Sitting very still, fascinated by all she saw and heard, Eve thought: *Working here at The House of the Contessa—what have I to lose? If I hate it, I don't have to stay. And it might be fun.* To herself she acknowledged with honesty that "fun" wasn't quite the word she meant. She looked at Adrian.

He said, with his smile kind, "I think it's a wonderful idea of yours that Miss Fairfax work for us—always providing she wants to."

All Eve's plans for herself and her future did a somersault. She had a moment of heady excitement, and because of it, missed part of Regina's next sentence.

" . . . —public glamour is too easy, too dependent on props. I want no props for this child except a headdress to cover her hair completely. It's her lovely bone structure that must be stressed."

This child . . . Eve Fairfax . . .

VI

EVEN NOW, TWO YEARS LATER, the memory of that interview and its fantastic result was still vivid in Eve's mind. Standing quietly in her room, she could recapture it as though there was no intervening time.

Regina had been delighted with her from the first set of photographs, had watched her at press parties, at receptions in London and New York and Paris. And every product that was launched with the Contessa Girl label was a riotous success.

"The Contessa Lotion No. Eight has sold very well this month, a fifteen percent increase over last month . . . " Contessa eye shadow . . . Contessa blusher . . .

Rich, sapphire-colored bottles and boxes poured out of the

factories in the various countries, and Eve's face appeared in a hundred magazines and expensive flyers.

Her days were full. For the first few weeks she had been taken over by Lynne Carstairs, whom Regina called her "poise mistress." Eve learned to walk into a room with as little flurry as possible.

"Always enter looking confident," Lynne told her, "but neither exaggerate your movements nor enter with your head sticking out like an anxious tortoise—not that I have to tell you that," she added, smiling at Eve. "On the other hand, don't hold your head up too high or it will make you look snobby. Keep your chin parallel with the ground." . . . "Always stand with one foot in front of the other." . . . "When strangers come up to speak to you, have something pleasant ready to say so that you put them at their ease. Remember a lot of them will be shy of someone beautiful and famous so, even if you hate the sight of them, be charming."

It was Lynne who told her how Regina insisted that all her clients must enjoy whatever treatment they were having at the Berkeley Square house, that none must leave feeling crushed by any superciliousness. Not that Regina cared what people felt about each other, but charm was good for business.

After the lessons and the grooming, the real work began. Eve was Regina's living example. Because of her, new people came to the salons all over the world in an effort to fight off age, hoping for minor miracles, drawn by the beauty of that much-publicized face, and seized with immortal longings to be ever young.

But the glamour was only superficial. Behind it was the reality—hard and tiring work, with Regina always at hand to demand and command. The photography sessions were endless, the meetings with the press, the everlasting waiting at airports because Regina refused to allow the private plane to be used just for a girl doing a regular job. Eve found it tedious and exhausting, particularly as all the questions put to her by the press and the public were the same, and all too often she found her polite smile frozen on her face.

She had become familiar, also, with crazy letters—either protesting love or threatening: "You are too beautiful to live." Or, "Your luck won't last, so make the most of it, my beauty!" Envious or sick or plainly mad letters that had upset her badly when she first received them, but which Regina had taught her to ignore. Telephone calls to her were monitored by the house's switchboard, so she was saved those.

She was within a few months of finishing her year as the Contessa Girl when she became engaged to Adrian.

Watching the birds fluttering across the lawn below, Eve remembered her wedding.

Although her mother and stepfather had met Adrian twice, it had been the first time they had met the Contessa. The elaborate wedding was what Regina had demanded. It was only later that Eve learned that when her mother had written she wanted her daughter married from her home in Paris, Regina had answered that—as she put it—the house in Paris wasn't strictly speaking Eve's home, since her mother had moved there after her second marriage. And more importantly, since Eve would one day be "the chatelaine of the great Berkeley Square house," as such she should be married from there.

She had added in her letter, "This is what Eve wants," which was not true. But Regina had her way.

During the reception, Eve had stood for a few moments alone with her mother, and had explained. "Regina? Oh, she likes me to call her that—Adrian does, and so do her business associates. She's an amazing woman, isn't she, to have built all this from nothing?"

Eve's mother had said softly. "She reminds me of Medea," and then turned quickly to speak to someone who had been brought to be introduced to her.

Eve had never asked her mother what she had meant. But now she knew. Regina was the sorceress in whose hands everything turned the way she wanted. Now, in her quiet room, Eve faced the fact that she had to fight Regina's powerful will.

She remembered at the wedding Regina's clear voice saying,

with pride, "Yes, I found her. And now she is part of the family. My dear daughter." Regina had bent and kissed her cheek. "Have a lovely honeymoon, darling."

They flew to Mexico, where Regina had friends. "It's a market that I need enlarged," she had said, "and with Eve there to show what Contessa Cosmetics can do—" she smiled at them benignly. "Well, just mix a little subtle business with your honeymooning, like good children."

They made a few important contacts while in Mexico City and then flew to Acapulco, where they swam and sunbathed and loved through the star-glittering nights.

After the first week, a faint shadow seemed to fall over them. It was nothing tangible, no diminution of love, no lessening of their joy in one another. Yet, behind the fever and the sweetness, Eve sensed a restlessness in Adrian. She knew that if she asked him what was wrong he would try to reassure her—she had had time in which to experience his passionate need always to please her. But puzzling it out for herself, deliberately tilting the conversation to help her discover what the shadow was, she hit upon the truth.

Adrian was fretting for London and 500 Berkeley Square, and the excitement and challenge of his life there. She suspected, also, that he missed the stimulus of Regina's powerful personality.

He was an easy and charming companion, and although Eve was surprised, she accepted on that honeymoon his one idiosyncrasy: even with his great passion, he could not share a bedroom with her. He had explained this before they were married.

"Please understand, darling. It's an oddity I've suffered from all my life. I cannot sleep if there is someone else in the room, and loving you as I do makes no difference, I'm afraid." He had continued, with apologetic laughter, "I think in some previous incarnation I must have been murdered in my bed and so I'm afraid of anyone being around while I'm unconscious with sleep. Or maybe, darling, I'm just neurotic."

Eve didn't mind. Adrian was a wonderful lover, sensual and thoughtful. She became used to the loving, to the "Good nights."

She was a completely satisfied woman and later, alone in her bed, she slept in happy peace.

At the time of their engagement, Eve had said, "We must find somewhere to live. A small house, or an apartment near enough to Berkeley Square for the journey not to be too tiring for you when you have to stay for late meetings. And it would be so nice to have a garden or terrace."

"Of course."

"When shall we start looking?"

"Darling, not yet, please. We have a very busy few months ahead of us at the office. Just leave house-hunting for the moment."

She had left it for a few weeks and then, when she mentioned it again, Adrian had protested. "Eve darling, you really are impatient! But I forgive you because you are beautiful and I love you. Just wait."

Eve had waited, caught up herself in the last months of her work in the Contessa campaign, making journeys to America and Europe. Then, her year as the Contessa Girl coming to an end, there was a constant influx of foreign executives and Adrian had to make short, swift trips to several European cities.

Regina's surprise came two days before the wedding. She took Eve up to the top wing of the penthouse where a door closed off some rooms that Eve had not even known were there. Regina had unlocked the door dividing the wing, spread out her hands and said, "This is part of my wedding present to you."

Three rooms, each furnished with rare and lovely pieces, mostly Louis Quinze and French Empire furniture, were to be her home. Eve had walked through the sitting room and the two bedrooms in a stunned silence that Regina either did not or would not notice. She had carefully guarded her secret behind that locked door, a secret splendidly kept, but kept with a deadly purpose. *You will live here . . . in my house among my possessions. You will be part of Contessa Cosmetics.* Eve had faced the fact, then, that they would have to live there at least for a time.

But gradually she saw that there was to be no separation, no life apart from Berkeley Square. And too much in love with Adrian and bemused by the riches surrounding her, Eve had not made the stand she should have. She had acquiesced, still hoping vaguely that the whole idea was a temporary one.

She had only too quickly discovered that Adrian's life was dominated by his efforts to please his mother, and like a crown prince he was dedicated to serve an empire that would one day be his. Eve's effort at breaking the steel cord that bound him to Regina failed.

Often, in those early days, Eve's swift protest would rise and flood over Adrian. "We can't go on without some life of our own. All right, so the business is all-important. But *we*, together, are important, too. We've got to have a certain freedom to live our own lives—that's what we agreed before we married. The house overwhelms us . . . Adrian, please let us have a place of our own."

The pleadings led nowhere. Always at the end of them were the same arguments, the same protests.

"We are like a triangle—Regina, you and I. We *are* the business."

Once, Eve had exploded. "Heaven help you! Your mother has completely conditioned you."

"Oh no," he had replied. "It's just that Regina and I feel and think alike. And you, too, when you've got used to it all, will think and feel as we do." His voice had softened. "Darling Eve, try to enjoy it. You and I on our own could never have such a beautiful life in such surroundings."

She had slid out of his arms. "A houseful of treasures. But also a houseful of beauticians, of executives, hair stylists, secretaries and accountants. Adrian, can't you *see*? The business overwhelms the house—and the business *is* Regina."

"But *you* overwhelm me." He stopped her protests and made love to her so beautifully that she was caught up again in her passion for him.

The arguments, however, continued.

"Just a small house, Adrian, or an apartment . . . I don't care as long as we are in our own home."

But every time she pleaded she lost. So far . . . Now, it was different. With her old job back she had the opportunity of a life that was, for some part of the day at least, her own. She would be content with that.

VII

REGINA HAD RETURNED to the cubicle where the princess sat, the Pekingese on her lap. As she pushed aside the heavy silk curtain Regina stifled a gasp and glanced at Lucien. He didn't meet her eyes, but there was a small smile curving his mouth.

The princess did not have hair the color of sunflowers. The tint was softer, gentler, like pale sunlight.

The man is a genius—I have always known it, Regina thought triumphantly. She was impatient to ask him how he had managed to turn the princess's mind from the vivid yellow she was so intent upon having, but she would have to wait until the semiroyal client had swept out of the salon.

"Well?" The princess turned to Regina.

"Wonderful . . . And the new hair style, too!"

When approval and flattery had reached its peak, the princess glanced at her watch and rose to go. The little white dog was handed to her maid and the small procession wound its way to the elevator. Regina escorted the princess to her car, then she returned to her office.

Once there, she was fully back into her own difficulties. She stormed around her room, seeing nothing of the fine Italian furniture and the Flemish tapestry on one wall. Nor did she see the tops of the trees outside her windows, waving in the wind like plumed kings.

Part of her fury was with herself, or rather with the circumstances that had drawn Eve into her orbit on that fateful day when they had met at Cassius More's. The other part of her anger was directed against herself. She was furious that she had not read Eve's character correctly, and listened to the faint twinge of warning that had crept into her mind when she had interviewed her.

All her life Regina had worked and planned and schemed for what she wanted, and she had no intention now of being defeated by a girl whose face she had made one of the most famous of the year. To reassure herself, she took stock of her life from the time she was a young and highly promising chemistry student. Often, in quiet moments, she found herself returning to the past, reviewing her life with triumphant satisfaction. Everything might have taken a far less exciting turn had she not met Victor Thayer, a brilliant lecturer in chemistry who had an English father and a Rumanian mother. His parents had both died within a year of one another when he was six years old, and he had been brought up by his Rumanian grandparents.

Regina had met Victor in Paris, where she had gone after taking her degree in chemistry. He was on the point of returning to Bucharest and a laboratory that had been offered him there for his work. After a brief love affair, they married. Victor was interested in the medical side of chemistry, but Regina dreamed of beauty products and she was determined to lure Victor away from the medical side of research to the more remunerative cosmetic aspect. She hoped to get him to convert a healing cream he had perfected into a beauty cream, but before she could persuade him, Victor was killed by a car with failed brakes.

It was, however, this idea of Regina's that started her dreaming of a beauty business—a simple cream that could perhaps be a basis for a new career. The only difficulty was money, for Victor left very little and Regina had none of her own. She had longed for some time to return to western Europe, where she would be more at home—she had never mastered the Rumanian language, anyway.

She made her plans quickly. She packed the most important items of Victor's laboratory, bundled Adrian into warm clothes and took off for Rome.

With the little money available to her and her extensive knowledge of chemicals, proteins and hormones, Regina opened a small laboratory on the Trastevere part of the city. She worked hard, not just in the laboratory but in an effort to meet the people who could help her. She made social contacts, using her lively mind and attractive face, her dress sense and her wits. But none of these opened up the world as she had dreamed it might. She saw herself as struggling with a small business for the rest of her life, and she hated the whole dreary thought.

In later years, when she looked back, she was quite certain that her own will to succeed somehow or other had driven her in the direction that brought her final success. Her creed became: "Want a thing badly enough, *will* it to happen with every ounce of your power, and you'll get your dream."

Regina's came to her in a way that was at once miraculous and at the same time wounding.

Two years after leaving Rumania she met Count Carlo Vivanesci. She was in her late thirties, her hair as richly bronze as a young girl's, her violet eyes brilliant with animation, her figure perfect. She was also very strong-minded and that in itself was a quality irresistible to weak men. And for all his good looks and delightful ways, Carlo was weak.

When Regina first knew him she was only vaguely aware of that side of his character. Unlike Victor, who had been grave and serious, Carlo was like sparkling water from which Regina, a little starved of the lightness of life, drank with greed. She bathed in his determination to enjoy life at all costs, was stimulated by his gift of laughter and enjoyed the lavish hospitality of the parties at his *palazzo* where she met people whose names figured in the jet-set gossip paragraphs. She believed fervently that this time she was in love with a man and not with a brilliant brain, and for a while she was supremely happy with Carlo.

His seventeenth-century home was like nothing she had ever seen before, treasures crowding great rooms with painted ceilings, tapestries, bronzes and rare furniture. The days of her childhood as the only daughter of a London civil engineer, through her years at a northern university and those of her marriage to Victor and the spartan life they led in Bucharest, had left her unprepared for Carlo's luxury world.

Carlo, for his part, was intrigued by this very attractive and highly intelligent woman who flung herself into his life as if she were enchantingly drunk with it. He had no idea that what he saw was a Regina his own high spirits and his palace home had temporarily created. To the astonishment and secret fury of Rome society, Carlo declared that he was going to marry Regina. He loved her; he needed her. The fact that she was eight years older than he added to the attraction.

His relatives had all died, and there was no one in authority to stop the marriage on whatever trumped-up reasons a noble family might find as an excuse.

At the time neither Regina nor Carlo gave thought to exactly what this so-called love between them really was—in her case a world she had never dreamed she would enter; in his, a woman older than he, strong in character, attractive and elegant once he could dress her well, and someone he could lean on.

The truth hit Regina first. As the months went by she realized that Carlo was vain and weak and a spendthrift. She saw, too, that he was quite incapable of being faithful to her. She seemed to be forever guarding him against women and gambling, and two years after their marriage she discovered that the fortune his father had left him was fast being flung onto the gaming tables.

Regina's disillusion was as swift as her infatuation. When Carlo came to see her one night after a gambling session and admitted losses that shook her into fury, she saw that anger could not help the situation. He had come to her frightened and pleading for help.

"Regina, what am I going to do? I thought I was on a winning streak but nothing went right. And Teresa . . . " He stopped sharply. But he had said too much.

"Teresa?" Regina asked quietly. "She was with you?"

"Well, you know how she loves gambling, and neither of us wanted to go to the casino alone, and it doesn't interest you, and so—"

"You went together. And did Teresa lose, too?" Regina's voice was so soft that Carlo could only think of her strength, which he dared to pray would get him out of his dilemma.

It was exactly what Regina was intending to do.

"Teresa lost, yes. But it didn't matter to her. She has so much."

So much lovely money from two millionaire husbands, one of whom she had married when she was sixteen and who had died a month later and the other who had given her a fabulous sum in alimony . . . Little Teresa, so rich and so in love with Carlo . . . The two facts merged in Regina's mind. Any love she had felt for her husband was gone, and now her cold, shrewd streak came to her rescue, hidden behind the outwardly affectionate desire for his happiness.

"Just let's leave it for tonight. We'll work something out. Come to bed."

The next day she paid a visit to the pretty Argentine woman, Teresa. They had a long, intimate talk together. "Tell me, Teresa, are you in love with Carlo? No, don't be silly and scared to say if you are. For heaven's sake, we're women of the world. *Are you* in love with Carlo?"

Teresa was.

"Then," said Regina, "it is easy. You shall have him."

Her directness bewildered the young girl. She couldn't imagine any woman not lashing at her with words or even attacking her, and certainly not a woman like Regina who stood to lose so much by a divorce. Carlo had so little money left there would be no question of a huge alimony. Teresa decided that Regina must either have a lover or else be some sort of foolish saint.

Regina had no lover, nor was she a saint. She returned to the *palazzo* and told Carlo what she had done. "You can have your freedom from me and marry Teresa. She has enough money to sink a battleship."

"But you . . . Regina . . . what do you—?"

"Get out of it? I'll tell you." She had wandered round the room touching some of the lovely objects. "You explained your family's complicated will to me. That everything here belongs to you, your wife and your children. Nothing must be put on the market. But it didn't say that you couldn't make gifts to your wife."

"You mean—?" He looked from her around the room, at the paintings, the Chinese urns, the great gilded mirrors.

"I mean that I will free you if you will give me certain pieces from here, furniture, pictures, to take with me wherever I choose to go. After all," she pressed her point, "you are the last of your line until you have children—Teresa's, I suppose. There is no one who will miss a few of your possessions. I don't believe you even know all that you have here."

Carlo wept. Ostensibly because of this wonderful gesture from his wife and secretly because he was being freed from something that had grown stale, as everything did for him.

Regina had a mental note of the mass of rooms in the *palazzo* and while he wept she picked out in her mind, the things she would take with her. She could look after herself; all she needed was money to start her on her own career. She thought: *I don't need Carlo . . . I don't need anyone.* Only money. And money she was going to have.

She was delighted, now, that she had not been too hasty and sold Victor's chemical equipment when she married Carlo. It was going to be the foundation of her new life.

Carlo was pathetically reasonable. So she wanted to return to England? Very well then, he must make certain that she would have a home. He would buy her a little house in London and she must take with her whatever she needed from the *palazzo* to furnish it. His father's will had been hard, tying everything up so that he, Carlo, could not sell in order to keep himself and his wife in the only style he could be expected to live.

His father, Regina thought, had been only too aware that little would be left of the ancient treasures once Carlo got his hands on them.

Regina left Rome with Carlo's last warm kisses on her lips, a small fortune in Vivanesci treasures and a lump sum of money. Regina was still married to him when the plane for England rose over the Pontine marshes and Rome disappeared on the skyline; she was still married to him when she arrived in London. That had been the whole idea, the only way it could be worked, with the *palazzo* furniture and paintings merely removed by Carlo's wife from one house to another. There had been nothing to say that they could not be taken out of the country.

Regina had no knowledge of Italian law, nor was she particularly interested. She had a shrewd suspicion that a divorce had never gone through—maybe because Carlo had had second thoughts and was anxious about the gifts he had allowed Regina to take out of the country. No notification of a divorce came. Not that Regina cared. She would never marry again, and whatever she achieved in the matter of a career, she had a son who would continue it: Adrian.

She sold some of the pictures at Sotheby's, and was stunned at the amount of money they brought her. Although she sold some of the furniture, she kept a great deal and it formed the nucleus of the very beautiful collection that was housed at 500 Berkeley Square. She bought the house itself from the money Carlo had given her, supplemented by the huge extra check sent by Teresa as a "thank-you" gesture for Regina having sold her her husband. It was a practical and amicable arrangement all round.

Then, with some of the money realized by the paintings, Regina searched for a factory. She found it within seven miles of London; the staff she searched for diligently, wheedling and cajoling those she saw as good material as she made her rounds of all the beauty salons.

Thus, she laid the foundations of her empire. That had been twenty-five years ago, and although no longer a young woman, her energy was prodigious and her knowledge of chemistry was kept up-to-date with constant reading and discussions with Scott.

The family owned a house in the Cotswold country beyond Oxford. They usually went down for weekends, but these were merely a continuation of their London life, the house a meeting place for business associates from all over Europe and America. The house was, at the moment, undergoing extensive alterations and the family weekends were spent temporarily in London.

Unlike most of the very rich, Regina did not possess homes in various places abroad where she could stay during her rushed visits to her foreign branches.

"It's far too exhausting," she had once said to Eve, "to keep watch over places thousands of miles apart. When I travel I live in hotel suites where others can worry about looking after me and feeding me. I prefer my two lovely homes to be reasonably close to one another."

They were both very beautiful; the London house was a Georgian mansion, the Cotswold place an eighteenth-century stone manor with tall ornamental windows. Regina had come a long way since the small and cluttered laboratory of her Bucharest days.

And now, a girl she had brought into the business and her son had taken into their family was jeopardizing her authority and the unquestioning acceptance of her commands. Bitterness tore at her.

Regina lay on her back in her circular bed that night, her hair spread over the pillow, her fingers fidgeting and fretting on the silk sheet. A headache had started that morning soon after her brush with Eve and the demands of the day had made it worse. Before Regina had gone to bed, Solange had massaged her neck and the pain had eased. But she could not shake off the frustrating memory of her lovely daughter-in-law's cool defiance.

Lying there in the darkness, Regina was tormented by this one rebellious factor in her otherwise splendid life. She could neither tolerate nor understand it. After all, she only demanded from Eve what she demanded from herself and from Adrian—service to her beloved, overwhelming lover, Contessa Cosmetics.

She needed sleep desperately, for tomorrow was to be another heavy day. In the drawer of the little French Empire table next to her bed were sleeping pills. She so seldom took one and she was determined not to weaken now. She used all the relaxing methods she knew and at last, sensing that wonderful feeling of her body sinking into the bed, she slept. But her dreams became agitated, a wild series of incidents racing through her mind like a car whose brakes had failed.

Even in sleep, it was Eve who dominated. *My fatal error in letting Adrian marry her.* A raging regret at her own blindness in not seeing Eve's character as clearly as she saw her beauty tormented her. She kept waking from her restless sleep and thrashing about in the bed and then sleeping again. But Eve was there all the time, like a threat over her entire life.

Then, in her dreams, Regina became suddenly very calm; her mind steadied as if she knew what she had to do. She saw herself pushing back the bedclothes and rising, crossing the room to the door. She could even believe that she felt a silver light on her face and saw a patch of moonshine on the floor.

She dreamed that she walked along the passage from her suite up to the next floor of the penthouse where Eve and Adrian slept.

69

On a wide landing were *objets d'art* set out on a French ormolu table. In her dream she saw herself pick up something heavy and grip it so that the sharp edge dug into her palm. She even believed that she felt the pain. Then she drifted on toward Eve's bedroom, opened the door and went up to the bed. Moonlight shone on bright hair and a sudden tremendous emotion shook Regina as she lifted her hand.

The shock woke her. She flung up her arms and spread her hands, and seeing them empty, gave a sharp cry. She had picked up no blunt instrument, she had not opened Eve's door nor gone to her bedside. It had been a dream, but a dream far too terrible and real for comfort. Suppose it had all happened; suppose her dreadful subconscious wish had given her body impetus . . .

She dragged herself out of bed and, shaking, sat in a low chair by the window. Looking out into the blackness—even the moonlight had been only in her dream—she hugged her arms about her. She wanted to brush the dream away, but she could not. She had to face it because she knew that it had followed her waking thoughts so closely. If Adrian were free of his obsessive love for Eve, he could marry again and she, Regina, would make no mistake that second time. There would be beauty, of course, and conformity and children—her grandchildren—to carry on the dynasty. But it would have to be soon so that she would still be alert and vital enough to train them.

But Eve was living. She thought in terror and excitement *I dreamed of freeing my son* . . . And then catching hold of her wild mind, stilled her panic.

VIII

THE LETTER WAS ON THE TABLE in the small sitting room where all private correspondence for Eve and Adrian was delivered. It had arrived by the afternoon post three days after Eve's visit to the Curzon Street gallery.

Cassius More was "extremely sorry" and he hoped that Eve would forgive him his "shocking blunder." He had mistakenly thought that someone he had previously asked to work for him had turned the offer down, but apparently she had not. It was his fault entirely. He was, of course, morally obligated to take her because she had given notice at her previous job in order to work for him. He was sure Eve would understand. He hoped that she would call at the gallery soon, not only to prove her forgiveness but also because he had discovered a painter he thought quite magnificent whose work he would like Eve to see. She really *must* come—twice underlined—and prove that she understood that he must honor his obligation to the first applicant. He was, "with love," always her Cassius More.

The only two sentences Eve really believed were first that he regretted that she could not work for him and secondly that, whoever this new artist was, he must really be worth seeing if Cassius said so. But she was perfectly certain he hadn't made a mistake. Someone had heard of his offer to her and had intervened. And there was only one person who, although caring little for art, could make or break a professional's reputation merely by praising or damning his artistic experience and understanding to her clients. Regina. It might sound a ludicrous situation to those who did not understand the power of such women. Cassius did not dare risk arousing Regina's wrath.

Eve walked the room, trying to tell herself that her own personal disharmony with her mother-in-law was making her oversensitive. She had to have more than mere suspicion. She needed proof.

She picked up the receiver of the house telephone and asked if the Contessa had by any chance been in touch with the Cassius More gallery.

It would be more than the job was worth for an employee to listen in to a conversation between Regina and anyone to whom she spoke. But, quite unsuspecting and knowing Cassius to be a family acquaintance, Julia Marr, the chief telephone operator, assured Eve that the Contessa *had* been in touch with the gallery.

"On Friday, Mrs. Thayer."

"Thank you, Julia." She set the receiver on its cradle, and seething with disappointment and rage stormed out of the room and down to the executive floor.

Regina was not in the least surprised when she looked up and saw Eve sweep in. She was aware that her daughter-in-law would know who had engineered the loss of her gallery work. Sitting back in her chair, she watched Eve cross to the desk, but she gave her no chance to attack first. She seized the initiative.

"My dear Eve, you don't have to storm through my house showing your emotions quite so blatantly. Apart from the fact that I dislike signs of open warfare in my family in front of staff—and Marion is, I gather, in her office—nothing ages a face more quickly than anger and frustration. Now, sit down and let me talk to you."

"You have done all the talking that is necessary, Regina—"

"Then why come and disturb me when I'm busy?"

"I just want to hear from *you* that you have lost me the job I wanted at Cassius More's gallery."

"Oh yes." Regina nodded, unmoved. "I was quite certain you would guess. Cassius is too shrewd to make whatever silly mistake he probably told you was the reason he couldn't employ you—in a letter, I presume. And you are far too intelligent not to know that."

"I needed the job badly."

"It would have been inappropriate. You are no longer an ordinary young woman free to accept any work that takes your fancy."

Eve turned her face away from Regina's calm, triumphant expression. She was angry with herself. To have come face to face with her mother-in-law with the truth had been an impulse that could gain her nothing. She had not prepared her attack. And she admitted to herself now that it was too late, that even to have done so would not have helped her. She could never hope to win against Regina's determination and rigidity.

She went, without another word, to the door.

Regina asked, "What dress are you wearing tonight?"

"Dress? Tonight?" Eve glanced half over her shoulder.

"For my reception. I can't believe you have forgotten it my dear, so don't feign surprise."

"I'm afraid I've been too angry to give it a thought."

"Then forget your anger. It will do none of us any good. And now, for your dress . . . Max Remoir is coming and you know how these couturiers watch us. I think you should wear the Nina Ricci, the *eau de Nil* one. It's extremely becoming on you and it will vex Max that you aren't wearing one of his gowns. It will teach him a lesson after that last silk suit he made for me so disgracefully. Now, I'm expecting Scott here in a few minutes. Ah . . . " she broke off, listening.

A man's voice sounded in the outer office; the intercom buzzed. Regina answered, and nodded. "That's right, Marion, show him in."

Eve and Scott met at Regina's door. He tossed a light greeting to her. She managed to smile back and walked past him down the corridor, her own thoughts again rebuking her. She wanted only to get out, to escape from the house she felt was laying its own great weight on her.

And she knew where she was going. Friends had telephoned to tell her of a fête to be given that afternoon and evening in Chelsea. Charity fêtes and fairs were sometimes held in the leafy squares that dot London, and Eve's artist friends always attended this particular one in force, exhibiting their paintings and selling their small sculptures and pottery.

Eve had not planned to go, but now she went quickly up to the penthouse and changed into russet slacks and an emerald blouse. She slid into a coat, picked up her purse, and opening her door, came face to face with Shari.

"Where are you going?"

"To a garden fête."

"Can I come?"

"Would you like to?"

"Where is it?" Shari asked cautiously.

"At the far and unfashionable end of Chelsea," Eve said. "You won't find anyone dressed by *haute couture* people. But it's usually fun. They have lots of sideshows and music and stalls, and if they feel like it, they'll start dancing to the music."

Shari shrugged. "All right. I'll come." She glanced at Eve's clothes. "And no dressing up?"

"No. No dressing up. I'll wait for you by the conservatory."

Regina refused to allow casually dressed members of her family in her beautiful entrance hall while clients were around, and in that Eve agreed with her. She went down the back stairway and through heavy double doors to the enormous formal reception room, crossing the parquet floor to the conservatory door. She entered and sat in a seat by the fountain to wait for Shari.

On the floor below, Scott and Regina were discussing the new range of products to be launched that fall. The argument a few days earlier over Regina's wish to send Scott to America to deal with the staff difficulty there had ended in a stalemate Regina had chosen to forget. Scott had managed to convince her that the New York office was quite capable of dealing with the problem of Jeff Mackerson, and the meeting had ended with Regina convincing herself that she had made the decision not to send Scott flying over.

Regina had sent for him that afternoon to discuss whether a very successful moisturizer that had already been on the market for two years should be included in the new range. Scott wanted to keep to the same formula, which he said could not be bettered. Regina, however, had other ideas. "We are practically out of stock and I shall not repeat it. I want to put a new one on the market as soon as possible."

"You mean, you don't want to wait and add it to the new range?"

"No." When an idea flashed into Regina's mind it remained there, tight as a limpet on a rock. "I want to produce something unique . . . really unique. Scott, I want women to be able to use a moisturizer that will give their skin a radiance, not a mere shine as if they had oily skins. Nor, of course, do I want something that clogs the pores. And that is very important." She frowned into the distance. "There must be some ingredient—" She stopped frowning, aware of the furrow that was already forming between her brows.

Scott knew the look. It meant that her brain was racing through possibilities. He respected it, for he knew that where beauty products were concerned there was little he, or anyone, could teach her.

"Our moisturizer is excellent because it contains nothing occlusive," she said. "But I want much more than that—much more! Now that we have found a substance that doesn't clog the skin, we must do even better—we must find that extra constituent that will give the effect of radiance. You and I must think, Scott. I want something that will clear the dull outer layer most women have from the time they pass babyhood."

Scott laughed.

Regina regarded him coldly. "It wasn't meant to be amusing. I know exactly what I am looking for and I intend to find it. A luminosity that will make the skin come alive and yet be nonclogging and effective in sealing in moisture. It will have as its base, of course, the simple medical ingredient that we know can be bought over any drug counter. But it's the rest of the formula that must make it unique." She drew in her breath softly as though she saw her dream product and the radiance it would give to women.

"You want a miracle," Scott said.

"Perhaps. And perhaps it has a name."

Scott waited.

She said softly. "Cortisone . . . "

"What about it?"

"It has been used cosmetically. It can have a marvelous effect if—"

"Oh, no. I'm not touching that! Remember the warning in *The Lancet* that long use can cause thinning of the skin? In fact, I believe that even after a few uses it can damage certain skins." He saw Regina's mouth set in a hard, firm line and was alarmed. "For heaven's sake, you know only too well the legislation about cosmetics and damage to health!"

She made a familiar, impatient gesture of dismissal with her hand. "It's overscrupulous to legislate for women with allergies. They can always use the sensitivity test on themselves."

"Not every woman knows what it is. And, anyway, whether

they do or not, so far as cortisone and I am concerned, nothing doing! I'm not risking either my reputation or doing damage to women. A publication as important as *The Lancet* doesn't make alarmist statements. It's known—and *you* know it—that cortisone has serious effects on the dermal layers of the skin. So—"

"Wait, Scott," Regina interrupted him. "There is a way to find out if what I suggest could be marketed. *I* will be the guinea pig. The danger could be exaggerated. *I'll* find out. I'm certain that the use of cortisone in a small amount would give my new moisturizer the radiance I want."

"Regina, take care."

She laughed, her eyes shining. "I'm not afraid of ruining my skin. But I want you to work out a formula with petrolatum and cortisone—"

"*No!*" he shot at her.

"Just wait until I've finished speaking."

"I know what you are about to say. You want me to find a way of using cortisone that can be camouflaged, and even if I could, I wouldn't. It's all quite simple, Regina. Just 'N-O.' "

"Sooner or later someone is going to discover a way of using it cosmetically *and* safely—and it has to be us. *You*, Scott."

He went to the door. "Just remember, won't you, that I go on holiday next month—"

"It's practically May now."

"I know. And now I must get back. The traffic is bad this morning."

"Just keep one thing in your mind, Scott," she called to him. "I'm a fully trained chemist and if you refuse to cooperate *I* will work out a formula and use it on myself."

He paused in the doorway. "In *my* laboratory."

"Mine, I think," she said icily.

"But my responsibility should anything go wrong. I take the blame."

She was silent, shuffling some papers on her desk.

"Of course, the laboratory is yours to use always providing I am there," he said over his shoulder on his way out.

She raised slender eyebrows. "There's absolutely no necessity for that. And, anyway, I may decide to go one evening—one night, perhaps."

"Not while I'm responsible." He left her, without waiting for more argument.

He smiled at Marion as he went through the outer office, and walked away, whistling very softly to himself.

As he passed the tall window on the second floor he saw Eve and Shari crossing the garden to the garage, on their way to the fête. The wind was blowing Eve's hair. He paused, watching. Then he turned away. Lines read somewhere came into his mind.

> The while he saw her cataract of hair
> Flooding the cosmos, always, everywhere.

That was the hell of it. Seeing her everywhere.

IX

As Eve unlocked the large garage and they went through to the smaller one beyond, Shari said,

"What do they *do* at fêtes? Is it like those gorgeous festivals they have in South America? There was one on television the other night—and the people had super headdresses and everything was bright and lovely."

Eve laughed. "It's nothing like that. It's just a group of people getting together to sell things for charity. This one is for blind children. You'd better be prepared for something very simple—but fun. It's nothing like those grand social functions you've been taken to."

Shari was silent. Eve knew that, cocooned in her Mayfair

world, she had rarely seen the life of the streets through which they drove—the King's Road with its ghosts of Augustus John and his black-veiled model, Dolores; the artists who thronged the famous Pheasantry; then the Fulham Road with its mass of small secondhand shops selling everything from a brass Buddha to old English firearms.

Chestnut Square was down by the river. The tree-lined streets surrounding it were already crowded with cars when Eve and Shari arrived, but they eventually found a parking space outside a tall, shuttered house and made their way to the flag-decorated entrance to the gardens.

Shari said as they went under the bright, bunting-draped entrance, "It isn't a bit beautiful, is it?"

"No," Eve admitted cheerfully, "it isn't meant to be. But don't worry, if you don't like it we won't stay. I'll just look at the work friends of mine have donated, spend a little time with them and probably buy something."

They moved through the crowds, pausing at stalls selling homemade produce, books, assorted gifts. Eve heard music playing, and soon found her friends. They stood near their three stalls, laughing and talking, dressed for the occasion in bright clothes they hoped would draw the buyers—embroidered shirts and skirts in brilliant colors, gypsy-like and swinging as they moved, scarlet and turquoise pants on long slender limbs and a variety of makeup Regina would have deplored. Eve, who was their age, felt rather like an elder statesman because of her vastly different type of recent life experience. Some of them had babies, who were sprawled on the grass making faces at the paintings and gurgling or screaming until their mothers picked them up, hugged them and set them down again. It was all happy-go-lucky, a world completely alien to Shari, who gazed with cold dislike at the babies and answered a curt "Yes" or "No" when one of Eve's friends tried to bring her into the conversation.

Eve bought a picture. She gave only a passing thought to the fact that there would be no place for it in the suite she and Adrian called "home" at Berkeley Square. Nothing must be changed from the way Regina had furnished it, but she would find somewhere—perhaps propped on the small ebony table in the corner of her bedroom where she could enjoy it quietly and privately. It was a painting of a wild wind sweeping across a field—a picture of a freedom she no longer knew.

Jeremy Corn, who had painted it, said, "I might have known you'd go for a windy, rainy scene." He, and those gathered round him, laughed, and Eve laughed with them.

She left the painting to be picked up later and went looking for more friends. It was like the old days, when they would meet at one another's studios, apartments or at a fête, to catch up with the news and admire each other's work. Except that these days she had nothing of her own to show them, and no news. She was now just a questioner and a listener. "Where is Lena? Did she give up oil painting for poster designing?" . . . "Why did Marcus leave the Slade?" . . . "Did John really go to Africa to study and paint wild animals?"

Eve had her arm around Shari's shoulders as if to bring her into the group, but she was aware that the girl must feel very much an outsider in this utterly different world.

"Come on," she said briskly, "let's go and have a look round." She promised Jeremy to come and see his new studio, asked them all to keep in touch and led Shari across the lawn to a line of booths.

Shari caught sight of a fortunetelling tent. "Oh, can I have my hand read?"

"Of course."

"And you won't come and listen?"

"No," Eve promised and saw her disappear behind the bright curtain painted with signs of the zodiac.

Ten minutes later she came out looking happy. "She doesn't read hands, she looks into a crystal ball. She says I'm going to be married when I'm nineteen and I shall have a title. And I'm going to be very rich."

Eve thought with amusement that that couldn't have been a difficult prophecy for the fortuneteller when she saw Shari's clothes and expensive gold bracelet. But she said aloud, "Well, now you've got a marvelous future to look forward to. And whenever you feel bored you can just remember what Madame—" she glanced at the name over tent—"Lolita told you."

The church on the corner struck six. Every year when they heard it above the sound of the music in the garden square, the young artists began the dance that become one of the features of the Chestnut Square fête.

A girl with honey-blond hair started it all, her wide dress swirling round her. A young man followed, putting his hands on her hips from behind. It was the sign they wanted. In a rush they followed, making a long chain of dancers, snaking across the grass, winding in and out of the other visitors, laughing and singing to the music and being joined as they wound round the stalls by more and more people, so that from the air they must have looked like some brightly colored human ribbon weaving between the booths and the trees and the azalea bushes.

Eve drew Shari into the chain. "Come on, put your hands round Livvy's waist."

"I don't know her."

"Well, darling, this isn't the time for formal introductions. *Dance!*" Eve hissed, laughing.

The girl called Livvy turned, saw Shari's hesitation and pulled at her fingers. With Livvy in front of her and Eve behind, Shari joined in.

The long line of dancers collected crowds in the streets surrounding the Square, ducking under the low branches of trees, waving to friends who were remaining behind to man the stalls for any possible customer. The line doubled back, collecting the shy ones and the newcomers. The whole dance probably lasted only about ten minutes, and then the pace quickened and became so fast that the chain broke in hilarious disarray as they fell over one another and collapsed in laughing heaps on the grass.

Eve fell on top of Shari, picked herself up and said, brushing herself down, "I think we'd better call it a day now, don't you? But first, I want a word with Kelly."

"Who's Kelly?" Shari was neither laughing nor out of breath—she hadn't been singing.

"The girl over there with the yellow scarf over her head. She is studying eighteenth-century art at the Slade. I just want to know how she is getting on."

"It sounds a dull thing to study."

"But it means that she will one day be an expert and will probably end up at one of the great auctioneer houses—Christie's or Sotheby's. Or, if she's very lucky and very good, at a museum with an eighteenth-century collection."

Eve greeted Kelly and the other people with her, all of them collecting parcels of things they had brought from Kelly's corner, which had been the dumping ground they used while they chain-danced round the square.

The old adage about being wise after the event hit Eve with its unhappy truth not so very much later. She and her friends had been immersed in their gossip and hadn't noticed that Shari was missing. Only when glancing at her watch did Eve realize that they must hurry back to Berkeley Square and that Shari was no longer with them.

She wasn't worried. Nothing much could happen to a four-teen-year-old girl at a charity fête. Eve began searching the crowds, going from one practically emptied stall to another, wondering if Shari had decided to buy something. She even peered in at the fortuneteller's tent and startled the fat woman by dashing out again.

She found Shari at a booth where darts were thrown at discs for small prizes. A small pile of darts were set out in front of Shari and the tow-headed young man standing next to her.

Eve stood a short distance away watching them throw the darts, laughing together. She saw the boy put his arm round Shari's waist when she nearly hit a bull's-eye.

Eve moved nearer. "Shari," she called, "we must go now or we'll be late for dinner."

"I'm not ready." Shari lifted her hand, aimed and threw another dart at the disc. It fell wide with a clatter.

"Darling, we must go. Please come."

Shari swung round, her eyes blazing. "You've had your fun with your arty friends, now I'm having mine. You can go if you want to. I'm enjoying myself after being bored. You can tell Mama to send the car for me later."

"Don't be silly."

"That's right. If *I* want fun, I'm silly."

Eve said quietly, "I like to think of you having fun and I'm sorry if I'm spoiling it for you, but the fête is almost over anyway and we shall both get blamed if we are late for dinner tonight— it's a very special evening, as you know."

"I won't come!"

The boy, embarrassed by Shari's obvious anger, turned away, bought another lot of darts and began throwing them.

Shari, having finished her own pile of darts, picked up one of his. "Go away," she said to Eve. "Go on. Go and have fun with your own friends."

"Neither of us is going to have fun with anyone here any longer," Eve said sharply. "We have to get back."

Suddenly Shari's eyes became like hard brown stones. She lifted her right hand, the dart pointing at Eve, drew back her arm and aimed.

Eve swung sideways; the dart fell harmlessly onto the path.

A man's horrified voice came from behind the booth. "Good God Almighty!" A voice rich with the accent of London's East End cockney. Shari slunk against the wooden strut of the booth, staring at Eve. Her eyes were no longer stone cold, and her body was hunched as if she wanted to make herself invisible—a child afraid of a misdemeanor.

Eve picked up the dart and laid it on the ledge. The cockney in charge seized the darts and tossed money back at Shari. "Here, take that. I can't have any funny business!" The boy had disappeared.

Eve said in a tight, quiet voice, "That was a very dangerous thing to do. But you know it perfectly well. Now, come on home."

Shari made no further protest. She walked with Eve out of Chestnut Square and into the street. They made their way to the block where the car was parked and both got in without a word. Eve remembered the picture she had bought and had left at the artists' booth. Her friends would take care of the painting for her. All she wanted was to get home.

After a long silence during the drive back, Eve decided to break through the tension. "I can understand the fête wasn't your idea of fun and my friends weren't interesting to you. I'm sorry. Perhaps I shouldn't have suggested that you come. I thought it might amuse you."

Shari sat, hands folded in her lap, staring straight ahead of her at the crowded streets. "Nobody took any notice of me—"

"My friends tried to talk to you, but all you could say was 'Yes' and 'No.' That doesn't help conversation along much, does it?"

"—except that boy," Shari continued, as if Eve hadn't spoken. "He was teaching me to throw darts."

"I'm sorry, darling. I really am, if I spoiled your fun. But we don't dare be late for the party tonight."

"Mama would have forgiven me."

Eve thought: *But not me!* Aloud, she ventured, "Do you mind if I give you a word of advice?"

"What?" Shari asked cautiously.

"When you are with a group of people, try to talk to them, even if they aren't your kind. Just say something that will keep the conversation flowing, otherwise you'll always be left out. People don't mean to be unkind, but it's rather like tennis. If nobody hits your ball back, then there's no game."

To her surprise, Shari laughed. Then she said, "But I like listening."

"I know you do. And I doubt if there is anyone at— home,"— it was always a difficult word for Eve to say—"who overhears more staff gossip than you."

Shari said mysteriously, "And you've no idea how *much* I hear! You really haven't."

Eve knew that Shari was inviting her to ask questions. Instead, she changed the subject. "And just one final thing. Don't handle lethal weapons when you are in a temper."

Shari sat very still for the rest of the journey and didn't speak again. Then, when they reached Berkeley Square, she asked, "Are you still really mad at me?"

"In a way, yes. You did a very dangerous thing."

"But you don't understand. I never meant to hit you. I just threw the dart wild—Eve, I really did!"

"I believe you. But I could have ducked the wrong way when I saw what you were going to do and actually been hit."

"I didn't think . . . You won't tell Mama?"

"No."

Shari put out a hand and touched Eve's arm. "Thank you," she said simply.

But going to her room to change for the reception that night, Eve had a moment's guilty feeling that Shari's flash of violent temper at the fête could have been, in a way, her fault. The girl had been bored, then quite unexpectedly, she had found a companion, and a male at that. And she, Eve, had come infuriatingly between them, with her dreary call of "It's time to go home." She thought: *Somehow I'll make it up to her*. But how? There were the brothers of Shari's school companions, but none of them ever sought her out.

There had to be some way to help her develop and hold any friendships she might make. Had the tension between herself and Regina not been so strong, she could have tried to discuss with her Shari's curious isolation, her inability to make or keep friends. She knew Shari was considered spoiled and difficult, but Eve knew that this was largely Regina's fault. Shari was an adolescent in limbo, neither knowing who she was nor able to find suitable values in her life.

Once Eve had asked Adrian to help her change Shari's life style. He had merely said in surprise, "But darling, she goes to a marvelous school where she meets young people of her own social sphere; she plays tennis and swims with them. If she doesn't want to bring them home here, then that's her choice."

"I don't think it is altogether. I think she just doesn't know how to break through some barrier in herself. If we could help—"

Adrian had caught her close. "My sweet Eve, Shari wouldn't thank you for interfering. She's perfectly happy with her kind of life. Just leave well alone. If you want to help anyone, then look my way. Help me by pleasing my mother."

Eve remembered that conversation as she threw off her coat, undressed and ran her bath. When Regina heard that she had taken Shari to the fête she would not be pleased—in the early days of their marriage there had been firm hints that Eve must keep Shari well away from what Regina so unjustly called "those rakish artist friends of hers."

At every large gathering where Eve and Adrian were together she knew they would be watched for the first sign of a crack in their marriage. Was it an infatuation that was now fading? Separation? A divorce? Hope for someone's rich and pretty daughter—the second Mrs. Adrian Thayer . . .

Eve changed quickly for the reception, making up her face, sweeping her fine, obstinate hair into a smooth swirl—a style Lucien had set for her that morning. "It's beautiful on you. All you have to do is brush it round your hand—like this—you see?—and it will fall into the right shape. It is my cut that is important."

Lucien was right. It was sleek and sophisticated, although Eve was happier when she let it flow free, blowing wild.

Solange, Regina's maid, knocked on the door, entered and said, "I will help you dress, Madame."

"Thank you, Solange, but I can manage perfectly." She smiled kindly, but Solange met the smile with a faint scowl.

A lifetime of dressing the rich made her dislike this young woman who preferred to dress herself. Perhaps, of all those who came near to Regina in family or business, Solange knew her employer best and understood her most closely. And without having any love for her, she respected Regina. She had been witness to so much during the fifteen years she had served her—to hopes and despairs, furies and schemings.

"Very well, Madame, if you don't wish me to help you . . ." She turned and closed the door firmly behind her.

Eve was standing in the middle of the room, hugging her arms about her, staring at her reflection in the mirror when Adrian entered. Formal clothes only accentuated his natural elegance.

"You look so beautiful." He stood in front of her, his eyes burning with love. "The last thing I want is to go down there tonight."

Eve said, laughing, "But you enjoy these functions—"

"Only because they are important."

"To the business."

"Yes. Regina's receptions are the finest form of publicity."

"Then we'd better go down, hadn't we?"

He held out a small leather box. "Open this first." His voice held the impatience and excitement of a child.

Eve pressed the clasp and lifted the lid. A three-row necklace of golden chains looped together with medallions of amethysts lay on a bed of white velvet. The stones were a deep, rich violet and flawless, the small diamonds surrounding each one were fine blue-white. It was an obvious antique, very valuable and very heavy.

"The jeweler told me that it is rare to find such stones." He watched for Eve's approval.

She tried to be enthusiastic, saying, "The workmanship is beautiful." But she thought: *It's too large and heavy-looking for me. Regina could wear it splendidly, but she's a big woman.*

"You do like it?"

She smiled up at his anxious face. "It's lovely. But, darling—"

"But what?"

"You've given me so much already."

"And you," he said softly, touching her cheek with his lips, "have given *me* so much. You must get used to the fact that I want to shower things on you."

He took the necklace from her and slid it round her throat, securing the clasp. "It's wonderful on you."

"Wonderful . . . " Her voice, echoing the word, was scarcely audible. She knew that was what he wanted her to say and that her gratitude warmed him. Again, like a sculptor with his statue, an artist with his painting, he was perfecting what he saw as beautiful. But he didn't see that the stones were too large for her slender throat, the setting too antique for modern wear, the color too strong against her delicate skin. He saw what he chose to see, an enhancing of his possession. Just as all day long he worked obsessively to glorify Contessa Cosmetics, so at night he glorified Eve.

She leaned against him, watching their reflections in the mirror. Behind them, the room gave back its luxury of silks and rare objects—a headboard of embroidered silk, a Louis Quinze desk, the Savonnerie rug. Regina's riches . . .

Adrian leaned his face lightly against Eve's hair. "Do you realize that I'm as mad about you as I was on the day I married you?"

"I'm glad. Providing being mad about me makes you happy."

"Of course it does. Except—" he drew slightly away from her—"except when you and Regina—"

"Oh no, Adrian, please don't let's have that argument tonight. Darling, this is a party." *Not my kind, oh, not my kind at all, but a party all the same* . . . She touched the necklace. "You are very kind to me. Please never think I don't appreciate it."

He watched her reflection. "Odd, isn't it, how you can know hosts of people—women—and none of them touches you very deeply. Then suddenly there is one person among them all—as you were for me when I saw you in Regina's office that first day. I willed you so hard to take that job. If you hadn't, I'd have found a way to get to know you. Eve, darling Eve, you must be a witch." He put his lips to her throat. "And I like my bewitchment."

"Good!" She took his hand and held it against her cheek. "It really *is* love, isn't it?"

"Why ask?" Her voice was cautious, fearing one of the curious and often distressing outbursts of self-doubt that sometimes tore at him where their relationship was concerned.

"Sometimes," he said, "I'm so afraid that Regina might be right."

Regina again . . . Eve stiffened, drawing away from him.

"Don't," he said. "That's just it! We can never bring my mother into the conversation without tension."

She knew what she should have done. She should have passed it off easily, lightly, with sophisticated nonchalance. Instead, some small, resentful spark made her ask, "What did Regina say that could be right?"

He answered as if he were relieved that she had asked and he could tell her; as if he wanted reassurance from some anxiety. "She says that she has watched you and that you are bored and restless. She said that she feels we are failing one another and that we are failing her, too. She said that we weren't fulfilling our lives."

"I think that's for us to decide."

"You don't understand, do you? She cares. She cares so much for us as a family."

"Does she?" Eve walked to the door. The amethyst necklace weighed too heavily around her neck; the stones were cold to her skin. She turned and held out her hand to Adrian. "There's a party on. Let's enjoy it and forget differences."

She smiled at him as he joined her at the door, saying, "I want to forget everything except that, for me, there is really only you, Eve, in this whole damned world."

At that moment she knew he meant it. But his emotions were sometimes as wild as those ideas he would place before a meeting, only to have Regina cut them down to size and make of them something less brilliant but far more practical. Adrian lived on heights of emotion that touched every aspect of his life—his love, his work.

As they made their way to the ballroom, Eve's thoughts went back to a conversation she had had with her mother when she had come on a visit to England just before Eve's marriage. "I'm so afraid you are going into a life too alien for your nature and too far away from your own world. Your art studies and your friends have given you no preparation for the kind of existence Adrian is offering you. You've had a life of immense freedom. Stop and think, darling, what it will be like once you live behind the doors of that Berkeley Square house."

"I *have* thought and it's exciting. Mother, I like a challenge. And if you love someone, the different kind of life and its demands can't matter. When you're young and happy, you enjoy the chances you decide to take."

"But life isn't made up of being young. When you are older, I wonder if the challenge will be as sweet?"

"You *are* putting a damper on my marriage, aren't you?"

"Darling, that's the last thing I'd do. All I want is that you be certain before you take such a huge step."

"Oh, I'm certain."

"Then that's fine." Her mother had slid an arm round her and had never mentioned her doubts again.

Eve knew, with the wisdom of hindsight, that her mother had seen more clearly into the future than she had. She had tried to warn her without spoiling what seemed to be a profound love affair. And now it was all too late, and there was nothing to be done.

If her stepfather hadn't suffered a heart attack, Eve might have gone to her mother in Paris and asked her advice. "I love Adrian and he loves and needs me. Yet I'm living a life which is suffocating me. I believe my mother-in-law is beginning to hate me and I don't know how to cope."

But with a husband who never gave up, who, if not watched, would remain at the embassy all hours and exhaust himself, her mother had enough to worry about, and Eve could not add to her burden.

Then ask advice of friends. To say what? "I love Adrian, but I have a constant fight not to be swallowed up by the house. And the only way to achieve any sort of harmony with Regina is to *be* swallowed up. And I won't! I can't!"

Friends would probably tell Eve that everything is compromise and that she was fortunate to be able to compromise in luxury.

Someone called to Adrian and Eve went on alone.

Shari was lurking in the shadows near the elevator. She gave her small, cautious smile as Eve approached. "I'm sorry . . . I mean about what happened . . . "

"Let's forget it, shall we?" Eve touched her hand lightly. "Only don't ever again throw lethal weapons at people. I like your dress. I've never seen you wear it before."

"Mama bought it last time we went to Max Remoir's."

"Then come along, let's go and show it off to Regina's guests."

They went together into the glittering ballroom.

X

THE HOUSE WAS FILLING RAPIDLY as the guests climbed the Grand Staircase to the ballroom. The huge, ornate doors closed off the salons so that from the columned hall only the flower-laden gallery where Regina received her guests and the illuminated room to the left were visible.

Nearly a hundred people poured into the room. Regina was always catholic in her mixing of guests, though she never offended. Although she had few friends, she knew a host of people and they came for the entertainment value of her receptions and the hope that some columnist might mention them in the next day's newspaper or a monthly glossy magazine. Titles abounded, couturiers wooed customers with charm and social talk. Nothing, of course, as vulgar as business was mentioned, although that was always at the back of their minds.

The women's clothes competed for notice like the colored advertisements in *Vogue* and *Harper's;* hair styles ranged from the perfect taste of expensive stylists to a few that were giddily *outré.*

Eve watched from her safe corner as the women greeted one another, cheek to cheek, careful not to disturb their makeup. Eve thought with amusement, "While Regina lives, glamour will never be entirely lost in England."

She knew she must emerge from her half-hidden position behind a column and walk into the crowds under the chandeliers; chat and laugh and make light conversation.

She looked away across the room and saw Adrian watching her. Tall, longsighted, he missed little that Eve did at any function, as though an invisible thread joined them and she could never be free of his vigilance. Beyond him, pausing in the doorway, she saw, to her amazement, Scott Somerset. Regina must have invited him, and the reason would be important to her since he was not socially minded and this was not a reception that included any of her staff.

She wondered what great new idea must have been nagging at Regina that required his presence on such an occasion. Scott moved into the room and Regina left her receiving place at the Grand Staircase and joined her guests. For a moment their eyes met and Eve interpreted that hard, determined stare. "Play your part . . . mix with my guests . . . charm them . . ." Obediently, Eve moved toward a group of people who were accepting their champagne glasses from Benson, Regina's butler, and the men hired to help him.

Time passed pleasantly enough. Eve moved among the guests, making certain no one was left out, drawing people together with a smile and an introduction, answering questions, and skillfully avoiding the columnists to whom she was still "news."

Later, needing a break from the effort of talking against the background of laughter and conversation, she went to stand by the dais where the musicians played—Regina would have no canned music at her receptions.

"Isn't it odd how a lot of jewelry makes a woman seem much too fat or much too thin?"

Startled, Eve turned. Scott stood beside her.

"You know," she said with amusement, "I've never thought about it!"

"Well, look round the room and see."

"I suppose you're right," she said thoughtfully. Then she added, in a changed tone, "But what are you doing here? I didn't know it was your kind of party."

"It isn't. But Regina wanted to see me. I came. So far I don't even think she has noticed me except when I was in the queue to be greeted at the top of the Staircase. But I'm not staying. I'll give her another ten minutes."

"If she really wants to see you, it must be important. Please wait."

"But not here. The jewels dazzle me. I look at them and look away and see stars. I've been to parties in my time—you'd probably think them dull—but the conversation was interesting and the people had powerful aims in their lives. Parties of academics," he looked at her, "and they weren't long-faced affairs, either. We laughed and we joked a lot . . . I'm sorry, it's boring listening to talk about other people's parties."

"No, it isn't."

"And bad manners talking like that to one of the family giving the party. My only excuse," he added lightly, "is that I didn't come here for the social pleasure of it. I came because I was sent for, which is very different."

"The parties I went to before I married were very different, too. We danced in studios to cassette music and sat on floor cushions and talked painting and painters. We would suddenly leave a studio in a group and go on to another place just to see some new artist's work. We talked art as you must have talked science. This isn't my real world, Scott." She stopped suddenly, thinking: *Why should I mind whether he thinks it is or not?*

"There's a woman over there with lemon hair and hawk eyes and I think she is going to make a beeline for you as soon as she can shake off the people she's with. Do you want to talk to her?"

Eve recognized her. "Last time we met, she looked me up and down and said: 'It must be an extraordinary feeling, Mrs. Thayer, to be taken out of your . . . er . . . environment into all this. Like one of those fairy tales come true. And you cope so well!' As if," Eve laughed, "I ate peas with a knife or bought my clothes at rummage sales in the days before I was married. Whenever I see her, I run the other way."

"Then come on, run." Scott grabbed her arm. "Let's make for our escape route."

They wove through the crowds to the conservatory, Eve saying as they went, "I'm supposed to be sharing hostess duties."

"Good. You are—to me. Everyone needs a breather."

The conservatory was a riot of green and the air was heavy with the damp scent of outsize ferns and tropical plants. A small fountain sprayed diamond darts of water into a green-tiled basin, and scattered between the urns and pots of azaleas and orchids, was Regina's collection of gem rocks—large, rough pieces of semiprecious stones and brightly colored minerals—citrine, a chunk of green chrysoprase, onyx and agate. They ranged from the glittering purple of the uncut, concave amethyst, to the soft opaque beauty of rose quartz.

Scott blew out a sharp breath. "This isn't exactly my idea of breathing fresh air, but at least it's quiet. I've been cornered by people I've never met before and am never likely to meet again—not because they like my face or my conversation, but because they want to talk shop." He laughed. "There's an art in bringing the conversation round to the question you intend to have answered without being brash about it. Regina's guests are far too well-bred to ask outright for some magic formula I might concoct just for them—something safe to brighten their eyes or destroy wrinkles, but the questions are there, politely clothed in nonchalance." He laughed, drank from the champagne glass he held and brushed his free hand along the fronds of a dark-green plant with crimson undersides.

Eve said, "There should be some kind of little gadget you can hang on to a chain that connects by remote control with your host, so that if you find yourself cornered for too long you can sound the alarm which only she can hear and can come and rescue you."

"That's a very good idea. Perhaps you could make a fortune patenting it. I'll be your first customer."

As they laughed together, she felt her necklace slide from her throat. It fell with a gentle rustle of golden chain and gems to thud on the ground.

Scott picked it up and held it curled like a small purple snake in the palm of his hand. "Amethysts." He looked from the necklace to Eve's throat and then said curtly, "Here, take it. And you'd better be careful to secure the clasp next time you put it on, unless subconsciously you want to lose it—and I wouldn't blame you."

"Why do you say that?"

"I'm sorry. It's not my affair what jewels you choose. They're very beautiful stones," he added politely.

"But you don't like them."

"It's not for me—"

"Oh Scott, stop talking in that 'best behavior' way!" she protested. "It's out of character. You always say what you think."

"Very well, then. No, I don't like that necklace on you. It's a dowager duchess's choice on a rather beautiful young neck."

"Adrian chose it."

Scott just looked at her and she knew he was thinking: *Then Adrian should have had more taste* . . . But he changed the subject, saying conversationally, "I really must leave now. This isn't my place, and patience was never one of my virtues. I'm off."

"*I'd* like you to stay." Without realizing it, Eve caught his arm.

He disengaged himself so gently that she scarcely realized that he was free from her touch until, in a few movements, he was at the door leading down to the garden.

"I'm going this way to avoid Regina's eye. I need my sleep and I'm very afraid if I stay for that talk she wants with me, I shall have to remain until the party is over. There's always tomorrow to talk business."

"But Scott—"

His eyes were bright with amusement. "If she asks where I am, just say I've gone to the North Pole because I have a sudden yen for icebergs." He closed the conservatory door behind him and she heard his footsteps descend down the outside stairway to the garden and the staff door to the side street.

Alone and quiet, Eve felt the stimulus that had lifted her spirits fall away.

"So here you are, hiding! I've been looking everywhere for you." Regina bore down on her, both voice and expression heavy with subdued anger. "What *do* you think you are doing? My dear Eve, get out and play your part. Francis James, the columnist for *The World and Its Ways* magazine is asking to meet you."

"Poor man, I shall disappoint him. I'm not news."

"Oh, but you are. He wants information about you as the new Contessa Girl. He won't vulgarize any information you give him and he has promised to be brief."

"Regina, I can't! I've explained and gone on explaining. If Francis James interviews me, I shall have to tell him that he has made a mistake."

"Oh, no, my dear, you won't—"

"I'm sorry, but—"

" . . . for Adrian's sake," she said and walked back to the door, waiting.

Eve followed, aware that this was something she was helpless to avoid.

Francis James was waiting for her in a small anteroom off the hall. He promised to be brief, but he slanted his questions toward Eve as the Contessa Girl.

"I'm afraid I can't discuss it with you. Nothing is settled yet," she told him.

"But the Contessa told me—"

"That it was suggested that I model again? Yes, it was. But there are a lot of factors to be considered and I can't talk about it. I would like to tell you, though, about the proposed charity ball in aid of the homeless. I'm on the committee and—"

James was polite, asking the right questions about it but obviously not planning to use the information in his column. He was disappointed, but far too well-mannered to show it. After all, he had little difficulty in finding material. The rich and famous were all anxious for paragraphs about themselves.

Returning to the ballroom, Eve saw that the guests were already preparing to leave, crowding round Regina, complimenting her; some fawning, some genuinely admiring.

Eve stood near Regina at the top of the Grand Staircase, knowing that she, like Adrian, must be there, standing a little apart from Regina, but ready to receive their share of compliments and thanks. Max Remoir was one who came, took Eve's hand and kissed it with a cavalier flourish everyone, except his cronies, mocked behind his back.

"Eve, I have just *the* most marvelous gown for you. You *must* come and see it. Rosina is putting the finishing touches to the skirt. It's cut on Grecian lines and is pure white. You would look magnificent in it, and I'm sure Regina would just adore you to wear it when you are photographed as the new Contessa Girl."

"Thank you, Max. I'd love to see the dress, although I have far too many clothes as it is. Goodnight . . . Yes . . . Yes, I'll call you."

Max went over to speak to a middle-aged couple whose patronage he was seeking, not only because they were rich, but because their title went back for seven generations. Eve watched him, amused at the spate of false, bright charm. Then, as the last stragglers took their leave, she moved away.

The party was over; the guests had gone. Her duties were finished and she was free. She went back into the ballroom where Benson was supervising the clearing of the champagne glasses and the silver dishes.

She had developed an after-party routine. She would seek the quiet and freshness of the walled garden—even in winter she seldom failed to escape for just a few minutes to its isolation.

Adrian had once teased her. "I have a feeling, Eve darling, that that is the best part of the whole evening for you. Is it? Just going off by yourself."

Eve had just laughed and kissed him and admitted nothing.

At the far end of the ballroom the conservatory door stood invitingly ajar. She entered and crossed the tiled floor between the banks of giant ferns and the orchids to the door leading to the outside staircase. But when she opened it she shivered as a waft of chill air caught her bare arms and throat. She went back and into a small private cloakroom where she kept a thick blue tweed coat. She flung it round her shoulders and passing Benson, said with a laugh, "I'm just going to look at the moon. Don't lock me out, will you?"

"We always know that you like a breath of air after a party, Madame. It's a beautiful night, too."

It was. Eve went onto the little platform and looked at the bright three-quarter moon, whose silver beams mixed with the yellow lights flowing out from the house. She walked down the staircase. Great twisted trunks of wisteria flung shadows across the steps, and Eve rested a hand on the iron railing as she went.

On the fourth step down her foot slipped—or rather she felt in that flash of a second before she fell, the step itself seemed to move. It was as if it disintegrated beneath her. She cried out, clutching more tightly at the rail to check her fall. But the steps were steep and whatever had been there had moved as she put her foot on it and had slid from under her weight. The heel of her shoe became caught in the iron grillwork and as her weight pulled her down, the heel was torn off. She crumpled, unable to find her balance, and hurtled the rest of the long flight to the ground.

She fell on to the lawn, and lay for a moment shaken and stunned by the unexpectedness of a fall down a staircase she knew so well. Almost simultaneously with her own fall, she heard the thud of whatever loose object had been lying on that step. It landed somewhere near her.

She felt a sharp pain in her leg, but as she put out her hands to raise herself she realized that the pain was only superficial and she had not broken any bones. She stood upright, picked up her coat and wrapped it round her. Her dress was torn and her hands were grimed with earth and grass that she had gripped as she landed on the lawn.

Her first thought was that the iron step itself had given way. But when she peered up at the staircase she saw that every step was intact. She had trodden on something hard lying loose on the step. Searching for it, round the base of the wisteria and on the lawn, she could not find anything that could have caused her to fall. The lawn was smooth, the narrow pathway between it and the house swept clean. There was no broken ironwork or fallen masonry. But there had been *something* . . . She parted the thick wisteria branches and still found nothing.

She returned to pick up her ruined shoe from the lawn and as she did so, she saw, by the lights streaming from the house, small gleaming chips of mauve stone. She picked some up, holding them in the palm of her hand. They were unmistakably pieces of amethyst, and there was only one place where they could have come from—the large, concave gem rock that stood by the azalea plant just inside the conservatory door.

She sat down weakly on the iron steps. By some unknown means that amethyst rock had been on the staircase and had rolled and given way as she stepped on it. She tossed the tiny chips to the ground and began searching again for the rock, plunging her hand among the flowering bushes against the side of the house. But it was too dark to see clearly. As she looked she realized that Scott had left earlier by that staircase, and the rock could not have been there then.

The search in the dark of the shadowy bushes was hopeless. She went up the staircase and into the conservatory. It didn't surprise her that the amethyst rock was gone. She stared at the empty place near the azalea, facing the fact that had she not clung quickly to the stair rail she could have broken her neck in the fall.

The ballroom was empty, and only a distant light illuminated the splendid room. It was all so normal and quiet. No one had heard her fall and cry out, but that was probably because the rattle of dishes and the moving of chairs at the time of her fall would have drowned out the sounds.

She looked for Benson, but couldn't find him. He was probably in the kitchen supervising the final clearing up of the party. It would be useless to storm in and demand to know if anyone had taken the gem rock from its place in the conservatory. None of the servants would touch anything there. Thomson was the gardener, and only he was allowed to touch the plants and to clean the gem rocks.

She limped to the penthouse and found Adrian in his room, wrapped in his dark-red dressing gown. He turned as she entered. "For God's sake, what's happened?"

Eve tossed her shoes on to the floor, slid out of her coat and told him.

"But I don't understand. How could that great chunk of amethyst find its way to the outside staircase?"

"It did. I can show you the chips that were broken off it as it fell."

"You're hurt." He went to her and lifted the ruined folds of her dress. "Your leg is bleeding. Eve, sit down and let me clean it. There's some antiseptic cream in the bathroom. I'll get it."

"No, I'll go. I need to wash." She longed for a bath but was too tired and too shaken to bother.

Adrian called to her. "I'll ring the doctor."

"Oh Adrian, no! Not for a slightly bloody leg. I'm fine, except for being rather shocked."

"I'm going down to look for whatever it was that threw you. Someone is going to have to explain it tomorrow."

"Adrian, don't go now. It'll still be there in the morning because I doubt if anyone passing through the garden will see it, it's too well hidden, where it fell."

He bent and kissed her. "But I'm going. I won't be more than a few minutes. Love, you look exhausted. Get into bed. I'll make a bet with you that one of our guests—or maybe one of the staff, taking sips of drinks from various discarded glasses—thought it a fine joke for someone to trip over on that stairway."

Eve bathed her leg and put a dressing on it. Then she slid into a robe and cleaned the makeup from her face.

Someone thinking it a joke to cause what could have been a bad accident on that iron stairway did not seem in the least likely. Yet Adrian could be right—unlikely things happened, idiotic drunks did idiotic things . . . One of the staff, for certainly no guest of Regina's would think of so dangerous and inane a joke.

She heard Adrian returning. He entered and closed the door carefully behind him. She watched him. "Well?"

"Darling, I'm afraid the amethyst was where it always is—by that azalea plant."

"*But it wasn't . . .* " She heard the note of hysteria in her voice. "Adrian, it wasn't there when I looked only . . . oh, ten minutes ago. Don't you see? Someone took it from the conservatory and set it on that step and . . . must have seen me fall and then seen, also, where the amethyst fell and put it back after I'd come up here."

"But why?"

"Yes," she said in a frozen voice. "*Why?*"

He was lying beside her, holding her in his arms. "Sweet, listen." His voice was gentle and conciliatory. "I'm not doubting that you stumbled over something on that step. All I'm saying is, it wasn't the amethyst. It was probably a piece of the scrollwork running along the top of the house—we must get the builders in to check."

"If it was that, why did I find amethyst chips?"

"Thomson probably knocked the piece when he took it with the rest of the gem rocks to be polished. You know how he piles up that basket of his when he takes them to his workshed to clean. He probably knocked the stone against the iron rail as he carried the basket from the conservatory."

The explanation was so simple and so obvious—but she didn't believe a word of it. Adrian seemed convinced and she, who had experienced the whole scaring episode, had no proof that he was wrong.

She didn't want Adrian's love that night; she wanted only to be alone, to try to think. Yet she knew that thinking would not help her.

For the first time ever, she let Adrian make love to her without feeling anything more than a vague pleasure in his passion—too vague; too detached . . . She was relieved when he held her in a long kiss and then left her. She heard the doors close between their rooms and lay with her eyes shut.

It could be that Adrian was being reasonable and more logical than she, and that the amethyst chips meant nothing; it could be that something had fallen on to the step by accident . . . It could be nothing more than the old cliché—"just one of those things." Her tired, frightened mind wanted to believe it.

Only later, when she was half asleep, she thought: *Suppose what had happened had really been deliberate—a warning to her? Suppose the gem rock had been put there quite deliberately by someone who knew that she always went for that cool nightly stroll after the heat and noise of a party. Someone who had seen her fall, then waited, and when she was safely out of the way, had picked up the amethyst from a spot where it had fallen, and replaced it.* She roused herself sufficiently to push the semiconscious thought from her and it slid out of her mind as she turned over, tucked her face into the soft pillow and slept.

XI

ON THE TOP FLOOR of the house was a short flight of steps that led down to the west wing. Here were two rooms, one empty and the second furnished with odd pieces Regina had discarded. This room had been given over to Shari and contained her piano. Regina, who had no liking at all for any kind of music, refused to have the piano anywhere where she could hear Shari's frantic, rather inept rendering of the martial music she loved.

The two rooms were just past Eve and Adrian's private suite, and when Eve returned from collecting the painting she had bought at the fête, she heard Shari's playing as she came down the passage. She had just met Adrian coming out of the Accounts

Office and he had told her he had spoken to Thomson that morning. He was insistent that, on the previous morning when he had taken the gem rocks to his worksheed for polishing, he had piled them as usual in his basket and had not accidentally damaged the amethyst. He was completely puzzled at Eve's report that there were chips of the rock on the ground the previous night. He and Adrian had searched, but had found none.

"I'm not surprised," Eve had said. "It rained hard in the night and the pieces I saw would have been washed deep in the grass."

His secretary had been coming along the corridor and he had said hastily, "We can't talk now. Later . . ."

But Eve knew that so far as Adrian was concerned, the presence of the amethyst had been her fantasy. All that had happened was that she had tripped and fallen.

Regina was standing at the end of the passage. She turned as Eve approached. "What have you done to your leg?"

"I fell last night on the outside staircase."

"If you *will* go down to the garden that way in high heels then you ask for trouble on the open ironwork."

"I tripped over something that was lying on one of the steps." She could have left it at that but she didn't. She added, "I believe it was the amethyst rock from the conservatory."

"My dear, rocks don't walk!"

"Someone must have dropped it there."

The sound Regina made was the nearest she ever got to laughter. "Why? And who? I can't imagine one of my guests or one of the servants trying to run off with a comparatively inexpensive piece of gem rock when I have a houseful of valuable art objects. I'm afraid, my dear, it was just a case of slightly too much champagne."

"You know I drink very little!" Eve protested. Then she gave up the argument. There was no proof now, anywhere. Only her word—and no one was going to believe that.

"Shari seems very bored these days," Regina said. "It's so tiresome! Now that the Easter holidays are here she won't even go and play tennis. She just moons around here listening to all the gossip she can. I think I shall have to insist that she take extra courses at school—*that* will occupy her. More dancing lessons, and deportment—although she should have learned enough about that from watching my clients who come here. Singing? No, I don't want her squealing on high notes all over the house. Cordon Bleu cookery? No, I think not or she might hang around the kitchen and that would annoy Cook."

They stood together, watching through the open door as Shari's skinny little body wove backward and forward with the music. Regina's determination that her family should be right there with her had prevented her from sending Shari to boarding school. Instead, she went to an expensive girl's academy near Kensington Palace.

It was unusual for Regina to remain chatting in this confidential manner to Eve and Eve started to move away, sensing that Regina might be wanting to speak to Shari. But Regina broke the silence. "You know, Eve, I'm afraid Shari will be very upset at the thought of giving this room up."

"But why does she have to?"

Her mother-in-law turned her head very slowly and looked at Eve, her purple eyes holding a curious, almost hypnotic power. "Because obviously this room and the next will need to be yours and Adrian's."

"But we scarcely ever use our sitting room, anyway. We certainly don't need more space."

Shari stopped playing. The three powerful chords with which Shari always ended her sessions at the piano came now, almost drowning Regina's voice. But not quite.

"You and Adrian will need those two rooms as a day and night nursery."

There was a curious silence. Shari had swung round on the piano seat and was watching them.

Eve said quietly, "But Regina, as I've told you, we are not planning a family yet."

"My dear." Her mother-in-law turned so that her back was to Shari and the room. "Let us get everything quite straight once and for all. It is all perfectly clear how our lives here must be planned. For a year you will be the Contessa Girl again and, by the time that is over, I pray—to put it quite bluntly—that you will be pregnant with my first grandson."

"*You* are planning *my* life."

"We are a family. We plan together."

"Not on this subject we don't!" Eve said angrily. "In fact *we* don't discuss it at all. It is, as I told you, between Adrian and me—"

"Shari!" Regina's voice cut in. "How many times have I told you not to walk like that? Stand straight."

"But, Mama, I *am* standing straight. It's how the models walk."

"You aren't a model."

"I like walking this way," Shari said sulkily.

"Models are trained to show off clothes, but it's bad for the spine to slouch. If you start doing it at your age while you are still growing—yes, darling, you *are* still growing—then you will have pain and trouble when you are middle-aged."

"I don't ever want to be middle-aged."

"That's silly. And don't let me see you walk like that again. A woman's back looks best slightly curved, but even models don't go through their lives walking that way. Now, come here, darling. I don't like the way your hair has been shaped."

"Mama, what do you mean about Eve having this room?"

"Don't worry, darling. You shall have a much nicer one, that huge room next to Martha's sitting room."

"That's the servants' quarters."

"You'll love it once it's furnished—and you can choose everything yourself. It's a beautiful sunny room."

"But Mama . . ."

"We'll get Carl to make your drapes and cushions and there is some lovely modern furniture that I'm sure you would enjoy having. I know," Regina managed a bright smile. "I'll have your piano lacquered to match whatever furniture you choose."

"I don't *want* the room next to Cook's. I want this one. It's mine and—"

"This room must be turned into a day nursery. The one next to it will be the night nursery."

Shari swung round on Eve. "You haven't *got* any children yet!"

"No," Eve said very steadily. "No, I haven't."

"But plans have to be made well in advance for these things," Regina said. "You see, Shari, we aren't ordinary people. Everything in these two rooms for my grandchildren will have to be carefully chosen and very beautiful. I plan to have hand-made furniture and the walls painted with frescoes—all that takes a long time—a year at least." She turned her eyes on Eve. "And that year will be a very busy one for you, my dear, before you settle down."

"It's always Eve." Shari flashed her a look of resentment. "It's isn't fair. Just because she's supposed to be beautiful—"

Eve turned and walked away. She went into her sitting room and closed the door and leaned against it. She was tense with humiliation that Regina had chosen to discuss her very private life with a child, and particularly in a way that banished Eve herself from the conversation.

She went to her desk and collected the letters she had written earlier. Then, hearing Regina and Shari still talking in the corridor, she put the letters down, prepared to wait until they had gone. Then she crossed to the telephone and dialed Margaret and Scott's house.

Mrs. Mack, the housekeeper, answered. Yes, Miss Somerset had arrived home the previous night. She was out, but she had said she would not be long.

"Would you please tell her I called?" Eve asked. "And just say 'Welcome' from me?"

"Of course, Mrs. Thayer."

Eve replaced the receiver. A sense of warmth surrounded her now that Margaret was home again. Her affectionate, vital personality seemed to touch and reassure her. When they first met

Eve knew she could talk to her, and that Margaret, highly experienced, would listen and understand. But she felt too restless to wait in her sitting room hoping that Margaret might call. She put on her coat again, collected the letters and, opening the door, glanced into the corridor.

Regina had disappeared and Shari was coming up the stairs from her room in the wing.

Eve said, on impulse, "I thought I'd go and look at a new collection of paintings at the Biedermeier Galleries. I'm not sure you would enjoy it, but why not come along with me if you've nothing to do?"

Shari's small, forlorn face took on a faint light of interest. "All right. I'll come."

"Fine! Then go and fetch your coat. It's not a very warm day."

Eve waited for her by the elevator and when she returned, a coat slung over her shoulders, Eve asked, "Would you like to study painting?"

Shari shook her head.

"Or music?"

"I study that already at school."

"Oh, I mean seriously, with a fine master. Perhaps if I suggested it to Regina—"

"No, don't," Shari said quickly. "I don't want to study anything seriously except"—she swept her arm in an arc—"all this. Eve, this is *me*; I know it is."

"Then one day," Eve said lightly, "perhaps you'll be a second Contessa."

"I'd have to marry a title to do that, wouldn't I?" She giggled, the child in her sliding uppermost again. But when they reached the hall, she said sadly, "It hasn't been a nice day. Mama wants to take my room away from me and give it to you and Adrian because you're going to have a family."

"That," said Eve firmly, "could be in quite a distant future. So just forget it, and for the time being enjoy playing your piano there."

"Margaret came home last night, didn't she?"

110

The abrupt change in the conversation made Eve stop for a moment. "How do you know?"

"I was just going to telephone Janetta—you know, the girl whose mother married that Dutch baron. And when I picked up the receiver, I heard Mrs. Mack tell you Margaret was back. I think she's rather mean not to telephone me."

"Telephone *you*? Why?"

"Well, she sent that postcard from Peru and said she was bringing me back a present, and she hasn't."

"My dear girl, she has only just returned!" Eve heard the impatience in her voice. "You and I are not her first consideration. She was on a sponsored expedition; she has work to do and people to see."

"But she lives so near, she could have —"

"If Margaret had telephoned anyone in this house," Eve said firmly, "it would have been me. And *I'm* not offended because she hasn't. In fact, what you and I are going to do is go to Constance Spry's and send her flowers. Come on."

They were three-quarters of the way round Berkeley Square. The flower shop on the corner was lit by sunshine as yet too gentle to damage the lovely blooms. Eve ordered tulips and iris and hothouse roses and wrote a card with their love. Then they turned back through Berkeley Square to Bruton Street where the Biedermeier Galleries were showing sculpture.

The owner of the galleries, a Mr. Tolly, always managed to draw crowds to his exhibitions and although it was only four o'clock and cocktail time some two hours away, there were a number of people wandering round, consulting catalogs and commenting on the bronzes and the fiberglass sculptures.

Eve was fascinated. The works in the exhibition came very near to some she might have designed herself, had she not married Adrian. She loved three-dimensional art even more than painting.

Shari gave an occasional glance at the catalog Eve held, but she could not quite hide her boredom. She showed enthusiasm for just one exhibit, an exquisite figure of a girl fashioned in fiberglass entitled, for reasons known only to the artist, "Leonora."

"I would like that. I think I'll buy it."

"You're too late," Eve said. "There's a red sticker on it. What a pity we didn't come earlier."

Shari accepted it philosophically. "Oh, well, I don't know that I like it *that* much." She began edging toward the door. "We've seen everything, haven't we? And if we hurry we can get to Dior's before it closes. It's only just across Bond Street and I want a scarf."

"You've got dozens."

"I *like* dozens."

She had the money; she had the freedom to buy any small things she wanted and she had, after all, allowed herself to be taken round an exhibition in which she really hadn't been very interested. Eve said, "Then we'll look for a scarf."

There were times when she could see what Regina meant when she had once said, "Shari is too young to be groomed—neither her features nor her figure is formed yet. But when she is older I will take her in hand. She will never be beautiful or even pretty, so she shall be a *belle laide,* and I'll find some way of making her stand out among the pretty ones of her age."

Eve saw the possibilities. Choosing the scarf brought an animation to Shari's face. Her dark eyes sparkled, the lines of her mouth softened. She picked up a silk square of mink brown and coral, charged it to Regina's account and bore her parcel home, walking by Eve's side like an overexcited seven year old. It was touching the way her mood could change with the spending of money, and it was a pity that she was here, walking the sophisticated streets of Mayfair, instead of being with her friends.

Back at Berkeley Square, they went straight to the penthouse. Solange was passing and Shari undid the wrapper and waved the scarf at her.

Solange said, "It is a Dior . . . I know. You are too lucky, Shari," and walked past them.

"She doesn't like me. She never has. As if I care!" Shari laughed.

It was five o'clock, and on the salon floors below the staff was leaving. Eve went to her room, slid out of her coat and was just slipping off her shoes when Adrian entered.

"I was looking everywhere for you," he said, crossing the room and glancing in her triple mirror, smoothing his hair. "You were supposed to be making the appointments for the publicity photographs."

"I went out and took Shari with me."

"Eve, you know—"

"About the publicity discussions? Yes. I'm sorry. I should have called and told them I wasn't coming. Adrian, please—" she stopped his protest. "Perhaps I'm being difficult. But you know how I feel about the new Contessa promotion. There are so many beautiful girls for Regina to choose from; she doesn't need me."

"But she does. That's just it."

"I'm not a model. Adrian, make it easy for me to say 'No' to Regina . . . please do!"

"Perhaps I could ask *you* to make it easy for *her*."

From his point of view it was, she supposed, a fair comment. But she remembered his promise on the day of their engagement. "You'll soon finish with all that razzmatazz; you're going to leave the limelight and be my wife. Darling, I promise you—"

Had he ever meant it? Hadn't he known, even then, that Regina would never let her be out of the limelight? People promised so much to get what they wanted . . .

Adrian was saying, "And you are making it difficult for me, too. I have two loyalties—to the business and to you."

She made no comment on the fact that he put the business first. Instead, she changed the subject, knowing that they were doing what so many did, arguing their differing cases to deaf ears. "Do you know that Regina is planning to take Shari's little room in the wing from her, the one where she has her piano? It is wanted, Regina says, for a night nursery and Shari must give it up."

"I think that's a good idea, don't you? Having a nursery very near you—that is, when we want it."

"It shouldn't have been discussed in front of Shari. Or at all! Regina has everything planned. To be the Contessa Girl for a year and then start a family."

"Well, at least it shows she wants grandchildren—and for *you* to be their mother," he said lightly.

"I don't see it like that. And I wish you didn't." She heard the new sharp note in her voice and regretted it, but there seemed no way she could get through to him.

"What in heaven's name am I to do with the two of you?" Adrian burst out. "Both of you pulling different ways. Just tell me. What the devil do I do?"

She said sadly, "It's an impasse, isn't it, Adrian?"

He pulled her close to him, laying his cheek against her hair. "It mustn't be. Neither of us want a family yet, so let's leave argument. Nothing must be insoluble between us because I can't exist without you."

She thought: *Nor could you exist without Contessa Cosmetics* . . . But she moved in his arms, saying lightly, "Darling, I'm *here!* And I think it's time we changed for dinner."

"I want to make love to you." His eyes had that blue blaze of urgency she knew so well. The intense stirring of her blood and the quickening of her heartbeat drew her back. Holding herself closely against him, she murmured, "Adrian . . ."

A clock struck.

The fire went out of Adrian's face. He lost the look of blazing desire that had made him tremble and became suddenly alert and controlled. "Good heavens, you're right! We must hurry." He pulled away from her. "Wear your green chiffon tonight. I love you in that."

A clock had struck; they must hurry. There was no time for loving.

Adrian went quickly to his room. Alone, Eve slid out of her dress and sat down at the mirror.

114

Sudden longing to have Adrian to herself, in her bed, had left her trembling. She put her elbows on her dressing table and stared at herself. There were slight mauve shadows under her eyes. She supposed they were caused by stress. The shadows didn't matter to her, the reason did. She loved Adrian and yet she was making him unhappy. On the other side of the coin was the fact that if she made him happy it would be at the expense of her own individuality. Did it matter? Didn't love for Adrian come first? She found, to her dismay, that she could not honestly answer that. Yet surely, if the love was real, she could have done so?

She took her hands from her face and her right arm brushed against the small cut-glass cat that Tamarisk Glassworks had given her the previous Christmas. It flew to the floor, breaking into three pieces that glittered in the last golden flash of sunset shafting through the west window.

Eve bent down and touched the broken crystal. She had loved the little cat, and felt a rush of dismay. Then, as her fingers closed round the largest of the pieces a curious sensation swept over her. The diamond brightness of the broken glass in the sunlight excited her and became suddenly linked in her mind with the sculptures in their sapphire velvet cases in the salons. Here, caught in the sunlight, as Regina's crystal treasures were caught in the special lighting fixed in the cases, were pieces of pure radiance and almost unearthly beauty.

Regina's clients were always fascinated by the sculptures, and as Eve turned to find something with which to scoop up the broken glass, the thought became linked with another. Margaret Somerset's collection of perfume bottles.

Eve sat back, making no attempt to clear up the glittering debris. An idea shot through her mind, bringing with it an excitement that tensed her.

For those rich clients whose dressing tables were loaded with cosmetics and who coveted Regina's valuable collection of sculptures, cosmetic containers of cut crystal—each one individually created and signed—would surely be popular. She could visualize them glittering in the sun—cut crystal for creams and powders and lotions . . .

Eve opened a drawer and pulled out a handful of tissues. Then she reached for a small yellow bowl and swept the broken pieces of crystal into it.

She walked around the room, expanding the idea to herself. Even lipsticks could be held in a crystal stand, and to pack the ingredients into the containers at the factory would mean that nothing of the quality of the products would be lost. Tamarisk designers were great craftsmen. If they worked on her idea, between them they could create rare pieces of crystal that would one day become collectors' items.

It was the clock striking the half hour that once again roused her to the fact that she should already be down in the drawing room. There were guests that night—Regina had called to London her chief marketing director from the French office, Philippe Gros, and Georg Audo, his counterpart in Holland.

She moved swiftly, coaxing her hair into the sophisticated swirl that gave the clear line to her profile that was required of her, and that Adrian loved so much. She slid into the green chiffon gown and chose a thin gold chain with a single diamond in the center, gave herself a quick glance in the mirror and was ready to join those already in the drawing room. All the way down the delicate ironwork staircase, a word rang in her brain like the theme of a song. "Crystal . . ."

She had one swift thought before she opened the door of the drawing room: *If only I could walk in and hear them all laughing!* It would have been good to know that there might sometimes be a release from seriousness over the beauty business, a flash of spontaneous amusement. But the only joyful ghosts were those of past kings and princes, lords and ladies who had once walked through that vast house—and they could no longer be heard.

XII

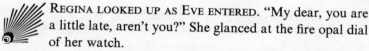REGINA LOOKED UP AS EVE ENTERED. "My dear, you are a little late, aren't you?" She glanced at the fire opal dial of her watch.

"I'm sorry. I'm afraid I had an accident. I broke the beautiful little cat Tamarisk gave me for Christmas."

Regina shook her head. "Never mind. I'm sure they will replace it for you." She turned, and spoke to the room in general. "Eve really has the most beautiful composure, hasn't she? It's one of the things that makes her the perfect Contessa Girl." Her smile was charming. "Adrian, I think we need our second martini." She lifted her glass and then continued her conversation where she had broken it off on Eve's entry. "About the Dutch market. I think we could improve the sales if we opened another office there—perhaps in Rotterdam."

Eve sat a little apart from the rest and listened and watched. The Frenchman and the Dutchman had been on Regina's payroll for years, and they were ready for any questions or challenges flung at them. Georg Audo disagreed about a second office, arguing against dividing managerial staff, which would make the whole Dutch side of the business unwieldly. He knew perfectly well, as did everyone else in the room, that Regina was flashing out her ideas merely to keep her executives on their toes.

They were still considering the point when they went in to dinner. Regina settled the argument by announcing that she would go to Holland herself and look into the matter from there. Then she swung the conversation to other matters. How was the translucent eye shadow selling on the Continent? Philippe was her senior executive outside Britain, he must keep a watch on sales in all the European countries. And the pineapple face mask?

Regina sat at the head of her table in the crimson-hung dining room and questioned and listened. Adrian supplied figures—his memory for them was remarkable. But then he knew what kind of questions she would ask and so he would come prepared.

"I want a complete revision of the advertisements and press releases for the new range I'm bringing out." She was addressing Georg. "From what I've seen, the quality of promotion in Holland has fallen. Pep it up. We're not a firm selling tinned vegetables, so don't give the public basic facts. They're dull and ponderous and they attract no one. We sell glamour and this is tending to be rather weak in your advertising at the moment. I don't want any more pedestrian publicity. 'We have the perfect answer for greasy hair.' . . . 'Do you have wrinkles? ' " She gave a heavy, irritable sigh. "My God, man, every woman over forty has wrinkles. You don't need to ask them—that advertisement was a disgrace. Excite women into believing that we can improve their looks, however plain they might be. Let your publicity efforts glitter with *hope,* not with dreary questions. Adrian,"—she turned to him—"after dinner take Georg into the study and show him our publicity files, although I'm sure copies were sent to Holland. And Philippe"—she glanced across at her French guest—"I think we will have to redecorate the Paris salon and regroup the departments. The house is too tall, but we have never properly used its potential."

Attack . . . demand . . . question . . . Regina enjoyed every moment of it—she believed in stirring up her executives to great effort, even if, as was often the case, her criticism of them was unjust. Suddenly, breaking off in the middle of a sentence, she looked at Shari.

"Darling child, how often have I told you to stop propping up your chin with your hands? It's bad manners while you are at table and it breaks the delicate tissues of the face. Sit up. You don't want a sagging chin by the time you are thirty, do you?" She swung her attention back to her guests.

"And by the way, I want all the files on registered names for products manufactured in your country and perhaps not available over here in England. I have a name I want for my new range of cosmetics, but I must know if it has been used or is likely to be used in the near future."

Adrian said, "I can quite easily have that done from here. There's no need—"

"Then they can double check." Regina smiled at him.

All through dinner she had scarcely looked at her daughter-in-law, yet Eve was quite certain that she was more than usually aware of her. She felt that the question of herself as the new Contessa Girl would be brought into the conversation at some time or other during the evening and dreaded it happening, with the resultant argument, in front of Philippe and Georg. She tried to plan how she could avoid it and hoped to attempt a quick getaway as soon as they rose from the table.

Toward the end of dinner there was a momentary lull while Philippe and Georg mulled over Regina's idea of taking the tints of makeup a stage further. Gold and silver in minute particles were now accepted. Regina wanted to know if there was any way in which tiny chips from cut stones—rubies, sapphires, topaz—could be used by some intricate crushing process to give a rich glimmer to lipstick and rouge and eye shadow.

She flung the idea at the men and watched Shari. "If you wish to eat those peaches, then eat them. Don't play with them on your plate."

"They're in brandy, and I don't like brandy. Mama, are you all going into the library for coffee? Can I come? Just this once. You never let me . . ."

"We shall be discussing business."

"But that's why I want to come. I love listening to what you say."

"There is plenty of time for you to learn about the business. You need to prepare for school, for one thing. It will start again in a few days. Run along." She made a move to rise and Benson drew her chair back for her.

Regina glanced round the table as she turned to the door then, with a rustle of silk, she went out of the room.

Eve rose, too, but instead of following Regina she went to the telephone in her small sitting room and dialed Margaret's number. She felt a desperate need for contact outside, and if Margaret was out, then she would telephone other friends.

Margaret's voice came richly and warmly over the wires. "Eve. Dear Eve . . . I was just waiting to return your call. Knowing the glamour-place in which you live I guessed it was useless to try to reach you until later in the evening because you'd probably be guzzling caviar and peaches."

"You guess right about the peaches." The light voice on the telephone had lifted Eve's spirits. "But no caviar! And now"—she listened for a moment and heard Shari's door close—"I'm on my own."

"Then I can thank you for those gorgeous flowers. They're beautifully sophisticated after my wild months in South America."

"Were they tough?"

"Not for me. But then I thrive on scraping soil from bits of hidden civilization." Her laughter was always infectious. "The only thing was, we didn't find our second Eldorado. But everyone at Cuzco was kind. And now you. How is life?"

"On the surface I'm a wife steeped in luxury."

Margaret caught the inference swiftly. "It can't have been easy for Cinderella, either. From a broom in the kitchen to a glass slipper."

"That's odd. I seem to remember saying that to Adrian!"

Margaret said, "If you're free, why don't we meet—now? Telephone conversations are never quite the same, are they? Scott has some Oxford friends in but—"

"Then we'll meet out somewhere." Eve named a small club to which a few artist friends of hers belonged and in which she had kept up her membership. "Suppose I pick you up in, say, ten minutes?"

"Fine."

Eve replaced the receiver, slid out of her chiffon dress into sweater and slacks, flung a coat over her shoulders and picked up her purse.

Shari had heard Eve open her door. She flew to hers, flung it wide and looked at Eve's changed clothes.

"You're going out."

"Yes. I decided I wouldn't be needed in the business talk so I'm going to see Margaret."

"Can I come?"

"Not tonight, Shari dear."

"Why not? She wrote to me, too. And she *said* she had a present for me."

"So I'm sure that she has. But—"

"But I'm not wanted!"

"Not tonight you aren't," Eve said firmly. Then, more gently, "You mustn't mind when two adults want to have a get-together. I'm sure you'll be seeing Margaret very soon, and anyway you have homework to do for school on Monday."

"Thank you for nothing!" Shari snapped, and backed into her room and slammed the door.

Eve went out by the garden, crossed to the garage, then drove through the Square to Margaret and Scott's small house. It was in a fascinating street—a cul-de-sac off Shepherd's Market. Here, set between tiny ancient shops, were a few houses with delicate wrought-iron grilles and rounded first-floor windows. The houses were small, enchanting and very old.

It was quiet in the street except for the rustle of leaves from a giant plane tree. Margaret was waiting for her at the door. She got into the car, hugged Eve and then said, "Someone rang just as I was coming out. Scott answered it and whoever it was put the receiver down without speaking. This sort of thing doesn't worry Scott, but it's odd—in spite of roasting in arid places and getting my lungs full of dust, it's the silent caller at the other end of the telephone that scares me most. Silly, isn't it, the unimportant things that upset us?"

They slowed up at the ancient arched entrance to the club, parked the car in a tight space behind a battered sports Panther and went into the room where drinks and coffee were served.

There was a quiet corner table and they fetched their coffee and sat down. Margaret's life was bounded by her archaeological travels in Latin America. Whenever she returned from her searches for ancient cities, lost temples or even humble shards, she was in great demand for lectures. Tall and red haired, with a charming, vivid face and a lovely speaking voice, she could delight any audience, from those at a university to a women's luncheon club.

Now, after their second coffee, she said, "Enough about my work. Tell me what you are doing."

Eve said, "Trying to fight off being the Contessa Girl of the Year again."

"Is that what they want?"

"Yes . . ." She stared at the group of people, recognizing many she knew and hoping that they wouldn't have seen her in her shadowy corner. She wanted to talk to Margaret; she needed an outsider's point of view.

Margaret answered honestly and directly. "You have said 'No,' and that should be that. It's your life, and marriage to Adrian doesn't make you a slave to the business. But I think you've got to have something to offer Regina in place of that, some way in which you can satisfy her and justify your own existence. Just living in the scented cocoon you call Contessa Cosmetics is no way to experience real life."

Eve said, "I've thought it all out. No, that's wrong. I didn't think it out at all. It happened after I had an accident with a piece of Tamarisk crystal." She paused, looked at Margaret's tawny lifted brows and added, "Perfume bottles. Your scent bottle collection."

"What do you want to do? Borrow them for some charity exhibition or—?"

"Draw them . . . copy some of them. You see"—she launched into her idea for the crystal holders for cosmetics and then added, "If you would let me come and sketch some of them I would get Tamarisk Glassworks to think out ways we could adapt the shapes to hold creams and lotions. Lovely signed pieces of crystal . . . "

"And you say Regina doesn't know?"

"She would veto the idea straight away. No, I have to work the whole thing out—design, costing, the probable markets—everything—before I can put it to her."

"I think it's an excellent idea, and of course you can come when you like. Unfortunately I have to go to the University of Essex to talk to a professor there and after that to Cambridge to meet the rest of our team and discuss our not very interesting 'finds.' But Mrs. Mack will let you in."

"I'd always find out first if Scott were home because I wouldn't want to disturb him and I could only come in the early evenings. Regina and Adrian shut themselves in the office from half past five until about seven o'clock discussing the day's business and that's the only time when I wouldn't be missed. But if Scott were around—"

"Oh, you wouldn't worry him. I'll unlock the cabinet for you tonight so that it will be ready whenever you can get away."

"I'm a quick worker when I sketch, so I may only need three visits."

"Take a dozen if you want to. I think it's a marvelous idea, providing you can find enough people with the money for buying unique pieces of crystal. I suppose, though, in years to come these pieces would be collectors' items."

Eve said, with her fingers crossed, "You'd better wish me luck in keeping it all from Regina until I have everything needed to convince her the scheme is moneymaking. Once that's done, I hope I can persuade her to let me run the whole thing."

They sat for another hour, talking. Then Eve drove Margaret back to her house. The rounded windows were full of soft light.

"Come in and meet Scott's friends. They're scientists, but they aren't stuffy," Margaret urged.

Eve said laughing, "Scott sees enough of the Contessa crowd without having to meet me after working hours. Thanks, Margaret, but I must go home."

XIII

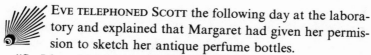Eve telephoned Scott the following day at the laboratory and explained that Margaret had given her permission to sketch her antique perfume bottles.

"So I heard last night. Fine. Come whenever you like."

"I'd try to work before you arrived home in the evening. I'd hate to disturb you."

"Would you, now?" His voice held laughter. "But maybe I'd like to be disturbed."

"So you wouldn't mind if I came after five o'clock? It's the time when I wouldn't be missed here."

"In other words, as I gathered from Margaret, you want to keep your plan as secret as possible. Don't worry, I won't be telling what's none of my business. Go ahead and sketch all you want. Maybe I'll make an extra effort to get home in time to see what you're doing. I've never seen any of your work."

"They'll only be pencil sketches."

"That'll do me fine," he told her lightly.

When Eve arrived late that afternoon, Mrs. Mack let her in, but as she entered the sitting room Scott held up a glass.

"You see? I've timed it so perfectly that your martini is awaiting you." His eyes were full of amusement. "All right, I'm not psychic, but I happened to go to the window to straighten a curtain and I saw your car turning into the street." He handed her the ice-cold martini glass. "So, Eve, you and I have a charming secret which only Margaret shares."

"For the moment, yes." She looked across at the large cabinet. "Margaret really has the most marvelous collection."

"For which dealers have offered her a magnificent price! But she won't sell; nor would I. It's a very personal thing—most of the bottles hold memories of particular journeys she has made." He wandered over to the open cabinet. "Lapis lazuli, coral and jade—I remember how she brought them home in triumph from the Far East. She would return without a penny, and with bottles she knew she couldn't really afford. But she always used to say that they were siren voices, and that she couldn't resist them."

Eve said, "Every time I see them I find them more lovely." She took out an exquisite silver-gilt bottle set with turquoise, her fingers stroking the cool metal. She knew that Scott himself had paid for a number of the bottles, indulging Margaret without criticism, perhaps the unawakened artist in him enjoying their beauty as much as did his sister.

Scott moved away from her, took his whiskey and sat in a chair at the far side of the room. "Go ahead. Don't mind me. I'll catch up on the day's news." He opened a newspaper as Eve picked up her small sketchpad, sat in the chair pulled up for her and began to draw.

She started with a rare eighteenth-century opaque emerald glass bottle with painted panels which the Tamarisk craftsmen

126

would probably engrave in intaglio, etching the panels below the surface so that they appeared concave. She moved from that to a heart-shaped bottle in silver, then a porcelain one modeled like a shepherdess. Some of the bottles were of rose quartz, some of jasper, some jeweled, others hand-painted.

Eve forgot time, she forgot Scott, she didn't even hear the Beethoven symphony playing softly in the background. Completely absorbed, she sketched and turned the pages and sketched again, reveling in the wealth of ideas and shapes she could use with certain practical changes. She sketched cameo insets that could be turned into beautiful and delicate engraving on the glass; she knew that the orifices would often need to be entirely changed—made wider so that any cream the bottle contained could be easily scooped out. When it came to the actual adaptation she would have to be very careful that the opening would be in keeping artistically with the rest of the design. She sketched in detail the gold mounts of some of the bottles, the elaborate panels, the wheel-engraved sea horses and the Victorian bows. Nothing must be left out, nor must anything be added, for almost every bottle Margaret had collected was perfect in line and shape—from the seventeenth-century Chinese ones with their blue underglazing to those of ruby glass and others with enameled flower decorations of the English nineteenth century.

Scott's voice broke her absorption. "I think it's about time you went home. It's nearly seven o'clock."

She started and glanced at him as if she had come out of a dream. "Oh, Scott, I'm sorry. I've been here too long." She picked up her forgotten drink. "It's odd, though. I've seen these scent bottles so many times and yet I never really *saw* them."

"I think we all do that, with people as well as things. We look without seeing and then one day we see—and—"

"And what?" She closed her sketchpad.

"Well, we're either shaken with pleasure or dismay. But don't let's go into that too deeply." His warm gray eyes rested on her face. "But if you don't hurry back, you'll have some explaining to do, and then your beautiful secret will be out."

"Can I come again?"

"You know you can. Whenever you like. Margaret told you, I think, that she'll be away for some time. You've no idea how archaeologists talk shop. I know. I've listened. Far into the night, they're still hard at it," He added, almost casually, "I shall miss Margaret's friends when I go away."

"Scott, you're *leaving*? Is that what you mean?"

"I never intended to spend my life at Contessa Cosmetics."

"Does Regina know?"

"Not yet, but she must have a pretty good idea. When I renewed my contract four years ago I warned her that I would leave after that."

"Oh, Scott!"

He said lightly, "It won't affect you. You'll go on being beautiful even if the whole cosmetic world ceases."

She glanced back at the sitting room Margaret had made so charming. "You'd leave here?"

"I'd have to, wouldn't I, if I got a job somewhere out of London. As a matter of fact I take my holiday in a few weeks' time and I'm heading for Canada. There's a big opportunity out there in Ontario—the kind I've always wanted—in medical research."

"Then I must hurry with my sketches."

"Well, don't sound so forlorn about it. You can come here as often as you like. You know that."

"Yes. But—"

"But what?"

"I hate the thought of you going."

He propelled her toward the door. "And you, a well-married, beautiful woman? What in the name of goodness does it matter to you that some outsider chooses to change his life style?"

"You're not an outsider."

Scott opened the front door. The light from the hall lamps shone onto the narrow street. It was deserted except for a man standing in the shadows outside an antique furniture shop opposite. He glanced their way and sauntered off. He was just a face and a raincoat in a little side street.

"Then I can come—perhaps the day after tomorrow? It does depend, of course, on whether Regina has dinner guests."

"Don't bother to telephone, just arrive. Mrs. Mack will be here if I'm not."

"You're a very kind man, Scott!"

He laughed. "Don't say it with such surprise, and I'm not certain it's kindness. Maybe I like to see you decorating my sitting room while I sit with my newspaper and a drink. Now go—"

She thought, as she turned her back, that she felt his lips touch her neck, but told herself it might only have been his fingers. She went down the two steps into the street. A couple was coming toward her, arms around one another; a car passed and stopped at a house a little way down; somewhere a dog barked. It was all so normal, so everyday.

Eve returned to Berkeley Square, garaged her car and entered the house by the garden door. No one saw her cross the hall and her footsteps echoed softly on the marble floor. She took the elevator to the executive floor and then climbed the twisting stairway to the penthouse.

Halfway up she raised her head, sensing someone there.

Regina was standing at the top. Her black dress hung in silk folds to the floor. Diamonds glittered in her ears. For a moment their eyes met. Then Regina turned and walked away without a word. But in that flash of time, one shattering realization tore like a knife-thrust through Eve. Regina hated her.

XIV

When Eve went again to the little house in Quintin Street, Scott was not in. She found the door to the cabinet unlocked and a chair set for her.

She went to the window to draw a curtain against the half-light of the cloudy evening—the detail she needed to sketch would be far easier to see by artificial light.

A man who had apparently been looking in the window of the shop opposite, raised his left hand and glanced at his watch. Then he looked up at the house where Eve stood and sauntered to the end of the street. She didn't know why she noticed him particularly, since there were other people passing, except that he had seemed to link the house with the time by his watch.

She turned away from the window wondering, with a touch of amusement, whether Mrs. Mack had a date that night. But there was a faint and lovely smell of boeuf bourguignon coming from the kitchen, and Scott's housekeeper would never leave her cooking for any night out.

The drink tray was standing on a table, but Eve sat down at once and sketched. While she did so, she thought over the rest of her plan. She would have to go carefully, trying not to miss anything over which Regina could catch her out. The most delicate part of it all would be when the designs were perfected, the costing down on paper to the last detail, the possible countries of sale and the time factor. After all that, there would be the daunting task of winning Regina's approval. If she succeeded, Eve felt she would be able to argue that she would be far too busy putting the scheme through all its phases to have the time needed for the publicity of the Contessa Girl again.

She knew that it was a gamble, but she was fully prepared to take it. She had reached a stage where she was afraid of her own frustrations and a possible explosion that she would regret later.

She wasn't sorry for herself. The life she had walked into had been her choice. Thousands of women would sit back and enjoy the luxury and find it easy to be what Regina wanted. Eve could not, because she was a doer. Adrenaline flowed through her like a flame at the thought of action. When a woman married a man already three-quarters married to a business, then the only solution was to have an interest of her own. And it was here, in her sketchpad and her pencil and the exquisite designs offered for her to copy.

Scott arrived before she had finished; glancing at her sketchbook, he said, "If you can draw like that, you'll never be out of work, even if Contessa Cosmetics falls into ruins round you. The detail is really fine."

"Thank you, but so it should be. I had enough tuition, heaven knows. And if you love something you usually end by being good at it, don't you?"

"Do you?" He lifted his eyebrows, amused and doubtful. "I love music, but I can't tell B flat from A minor on the piano. Never mind, have a drink before you go. It seems that whenever you are here I end by pushing you out. But if you're going to keep this job a secret then you'd better not be late back at Berkeley Square." He had mixed her a martini. "Do you think we had better drink to your success, or are we tempting fate by doing so? You don't wish theatrical people 'Good luck' at the first night of a new play, so let's just say 'Hi' and drink."

"Regina still doesn't know?"

"Know what?"

"About your plan to leave us?"

"No."

"You could change your mind."

"Now why should I?" He was challenging her, his face full of laughter.

"Don't ask me." She turned slightly, putting down her empty glass on a low table. *No, don't ask me because I could say again, "I don't want you to go . . . "* She said, giving a slight and obvious sniff, "You're going to have the most delicious casserole tonight."

"That's the worst of small houses, kitchen smells permeate."

"Well, maybe, wherever you go from here, you'll live in a mansion and the kitchen will be half a mile away!" She left him and went to the door, picked up her coat and slung it capewise over her shoulders. "Thank you, Scott, for the drink and for letting me come. Goodnight."

He held her back, took the coat and said, "That was a very high-hat remark, but let it pass. Put your coat on properly, it's a cool night. Come on." He took one of her arms. "Into the sleeve it goes. Now the other." He adjusted her collar and then bent and kissed her cheek. "When I get my mansion, wherever it is, I'll invite you to champagne and caviar. Or no, that won't be much of a change for you, will it? Then a hamburger and a Coke. Okay?"

She laughed as she went out. "That's an invitation I'll accept."

*   *   *

On her third visit to Scott's house she asked, as she was leaving, "I have a feeling that you still haven't told Regina that you won't be renewing your contract. If you had Adrian would have heard about it and told me."

"I warned her some time ago."

"But she didn't really believe you?"

"She told me she would be very surprised to see a letter of resignation from me on her desk."

"And you've been hesitating. You're still hesitating."

He blew a smoke ring from one of the cigarettes he rarely smoked. "Either I'm a very transparent man or you read my thoughts. Yes, I'm hesitating. Oh, not about leaving the cosmetic industry. That I intend to do, anyway. But I don't know that I want to leave England. I'm very British, I suppose. Silly, really, when I'm all for the whole earth belonging to everyone." He swirled his whiskey gently round his glass and chuckled. "I, the least sentimental of men, am probably sentimental after all. I want to do research work at one of the universities in England, but if a tremendous opportunity is offered me in some other country, I'd be mad not to grasp it, wouldn't I? And Canada may offer what I want."

"Regina will be terribly upset."

He smiled. "It's salutary for my ego to imagine that I'm expendable and I'm afraid almost everyone is. Only geniuses should be chained to their own countries and, dear Eve, no one could call me that!"

"But it must be satisfying to know that you've achieved so much in your life."

"Good God, girl, I'm not an infant prodigy! I'm a man of thirty-four and I've thought out a few formulas to enhance pretty women's faces and that's about all."

"Regina doesn't think of your achievements that way. But never mind," she laughed, went into the hall and to the front door.

As she stepped out of the house, Scott said in a voice that had lost its lightness, "Take care, Eve. Always find time to be yourself." He made the gesture she was now used to from him, and touched her cheek gently. "Don't let anyone swamp you and drain your vitality. And now, after that homily, good night!"

Unseen by either of them, someone on the other side of the street turned from looking in a shop window and walked away, whistling softly to himself.

The following morning Adrian flew to Edinburgh for a conference with the Scottish marketing staff of Contessa Cosmetics.

Eve shut herself in their small sitting room and spread her designs over the table by the window. Her head was bent so that her hair fell like a soft curtain at either side of her face. She sat looking with delight at the intricate drawings she had carefully detached from her sketchpad, aware of the great deal of work needed to enlarge each of them to a size necessary for the Tamarisk experts to utilize.

The house telephone rang. Marion was calling. The Contessa wished to see her immediately.

Eve locked the sketches away, checked her makeup and went down to the executive floor.

Regina was standing by the window. No one could better fill a room with the impact of her own mood than she. And Eve felt it, like an ice-cold wind, blowing toward her. Regina was in an intense, rigid rage.

She didn't speak, but held out a newspaper folded to an inside page and marked with an emerald green cross. The paragraph was part of a newspaper popular among readers who liked their news to be spiced with as much scandal as the law of libel permitted.

Eve read: "We are intrigued by the comings and goings of a certain much-photographed beauty. What—or rather who— lures her so repeatedly to a house not so very far away from her own splendid home while her husband is busy working at the demanding task of making women beautiful?"

Eve read the paragraph through twice. Then she laid the newspaper on Regina's desk. "That's just the kind of scandalmongering this newspaper is famous for. I remember that last year someone brought a case against the columnist. But I didn't know we ever had the paper delivered here."

"We don't. This was sent to me."

"Why?"

"Surely you don't need to question? My dear Eve, don't pretend to be so obtuse."

"I'm not pretending. I am."

"That brief paragraph is obviously directed at you."

Of course. "A much photographed beauty . . . "

"Did you hear what I said, Eve?"

"Yes."

"Then what have you to say?"

"If this columnist—" she leaned across the desk to make certain of his name as she remembered it, "Merlin Saturn—good heavens, could anything be more phony!—if he thinks he can make a scandal out of nothing, then the answer is clear. Action for libel."

"After the one you mentioned happened last year for which this paper had to pay heavy damages, I doubt if he would again risk writing anything that was blatantly libelous."

"If the paragraph refers to me, then it is just that! Libelous," Eve said angrily. "And so far as newspaper gossip is concerned, I read not so long ago that the Press Council has threatened to check all press freedom if society columnists don't stop prying into people's private lives."

There was such a long silence that Eve wasn't certain if Regina had even been listening. Then, through the quiet, came her firm, hard voice. "Who is he, Eve?"

"Who is—who?"

"Please don't play for time. I'm very busy." Regina swung round and looked at Eve across the great room. Below them car tires hissed on a wet road.

"Please, Regina, I am asking you to contact David Tindall. This is a matter for him."

Although her back was to the light, Regina's eyes glittered as if incandescent with anger. "I will consult my lawyer when I choose. And I repeat, this man with the ridiculous name wouldn't dare print what he knows would be libelous because he is perfectly aware of what I could do to him."

"Then in that case, I'm not the one referred to."

"Can you think who else?" Regina asked. "No, you can't. So let's not waste time trying to think of a way to bluff the matter out."

"If I had been meeting someone in secrecy, then it would be Adrian's concern and it's for him to question me." Eve's anger was as much with Regina as with the columnist. The wave of faintness that rushed over her had nothing to do with weakness. It was blind fury that Regina should be standing over her like an inquisitor—and from the look of triumph on her face, perversely enjoying it.

Eve took a deep breath and steadied herself. "I don't know why I should try to justify myself to you—I'm not on oath to swear the truth, but this *is* the truth. *I have no lover.* I see my friends outside this house on occasion because I enjoy being with them. I don't bring them here because art talk bores Adrian and he's not interested in music, either. But I've no intention of giving them up—I'd be very lonely if I did, because everyone has to find people who talk their own language. And, on the subject of loneliness, Regina, you might try to think of having parties of young people here for Shari. Ask her to make a list of friends she would like round."

"I have suggested it many times," Regina said impatiently, "but Shari doesn't want parties of her school acquaintances. It's this house and the people I bring here that she enjoys. She's not a typical schoolgirl, you should know that. And she is not, at the moment, under discussion. *You* and your life style is what happens to be paramount in my mind." Regina's tone was icily formal. "I am extremely surprised, now that you are one of the family, that you choose to mix with people you know perfectly well would never fit in here. But we will leave that for the moment—"

"Oh, no we won't!" Eve said quickly. "I want you to understand one thing. My friends are not the unemployed idlers you seem to think they are. They've had good educations, they are gifted and they have their own aims in life. I've known most of them since my college days. We've worked together and played together. Some of them are highly successful, some aren't—but that doesn't affect our friendship. Our ties are not made of matters of success and failure, but of liking each other, finding things to be serious about and to laugh about." She was tense with the effort of defending her gifted, colorful companions.

Regina had been looking at her watch while Eve spoke. She said, "I haven't got all day to spend over this discussion and I refuse to be sidetracked by your eulogy of your friends."

"I'm trying to make you understand me a little."

"Oh, I understand you, my dear."

"Then trust me and let Adrian question me—*if* there is still anything to question. And then contact David Tindall and sue the newspaper. Because, whatever friend some snooper has seen me talking to, I intend to continue talking to him if I happen to meet him in the street. I'm an individual, Regina, not a commodity to be manipulated."

"We are all caught up in something that controls us," Regina retorted. "You, like myself and Adrian, in the cosmetic world. Rubinstein and Arden in an earlier generation built up their success, as I have done, by single-mindedness."

Eve heard herself asking a question that surprised even herself. She hadn't planned to ask it, but the words came from some compulsion. "Did you ever love anyone, Regina? A person. Or was it always—this?" She made a sweeping gesture with her hand toward the richly furnished room where only the carved and gilded desk was allowed to be untidy.

Regina reached out, her back to Eve, and closed the inner panel of the storm window. The traffic outside became muted and for a few moments Regina neither heard the change in the volume of sound nor saw the moving cars she appeared to be staring at. Even Eve, confronting her with her young defiance, was somewhere behind and invisible.

Did you ever love anyone?

Yes, oh yes . . . in my way. The fair Victor in his beloved laboratory; the black-haired charmer in his Roman palace, sweeping me away from that sober, dedicated scientific life into a gaiety I had never known and a richness and a sensuousness . . . Love. Oh yes, in my way. And Shari, that plain child—and Adrian, my son . . . In my way . . .

She heard movement behind her and pulled herself together to find Eve's lovely eyes fixed on her. She'd be damned if she would show her feelings to that too-independent—independent what? Enemy? Yes, enemy. Regina's mouth tightened. "You are impertinent to ask me such a question."

Eve thought: *But you took too long to answer.* She said, more gently, "I'm sorry. I'm so very sorry for all our sakes because this is an impasse."

"It doesn't need to be. Youth no longer understands duty."

Eve shook her head. "No, I don't think we do—not as people used to understand it; not as something to be done because people say we *ought* to do it. Perhaps we reason more; when we do the things people say we should, I think that we do them more positively, without resentment."

"You twist words."

"No. I'm just trying to tell you how I honestly feel. I am—"

"*I* will tell you what you are." Her strong face was expressionless. "You are a beautiful woman who has infatuated my son."

"And loves him. But I promise you one thing. If Adrian ever loses his love for me, I'll leave him without bitterness."

"Ah, but you know, don't you, Eve, that that will never happen. His is an infatuation that enslaves him. Just as—" She stopped speaking and momentarily closed her eyes.

"Just as?"—Eve urged.

"Just as Victor loved me," Regina said in a flat voice.

Eve thought: *But that wasn't what you meant to say . . .* and waited.

But Regina suddenly seemed to lose all composure. Words came, torn out of her with such a helpless sincerity that they became free of histrionics. "Adrian will never stop loving you . . . heaven help him—and us! I know my son. You are his obsession."

"That's a word that has no love in it!"

"Love! Love!" She hit her desk with her fist. "The mistake was all mine. Mine! *I* chose you for my daughter-in-law."

"Oh no, Regina, you aren't God. You can dictate to a business, but not to people's hearts."

"Adrian came to me and told me he loved you. I could have stopped the whole affair. But I didn't. I saw you, Eve, as part of my family; I saw you as a magnificent asset."

This in monstrous! Eve went cold. *Regina imagines herself as a puppet mistress who, for once, has pulled the wrong string.* And yet, in her way, Eve saw that Regina was suffering, too. She said, "We are caught up in an argument we can never resolve. Shall we get back to that wretched little paragraph? You must do what you think wisest, but you know that it can't hurt you or the business."

The intercom buzzed. Regina flicked the switch. "Oh, that tiresome woman! Very well, put her through. Eve, don't go. Sit down."

Eve remained, but she stood, leaning against the side table where magazines lay in neat rows.

Regina was saying, "No, of course the yellowing of your skin has nothing to do with my cream. Really, Esther, you've used it long enough to know that if that had been the reason you would have noticed the symptoms long ago. And I really can't go into it all now on the telephone, but I don't need to be a doctor to tell you what is the matter with you. You are obviously one of those people who can't assimilate Vitamin A properly, and the result is a yellowing of the skin because you are eating too many yellow vegetables . . . Of course I've studied diet; you know that perfectly well. And I've known you for—what is it?—ten years. You are always on some fad diet or other and this particular one sounds crazy. Get off it and eat sensibly. Meat, my dear, and green vegetables and fruit and fish—everything in moderation. And now, Esther, I'm very busy. Shall I see you at the Maddison's party next week? Good. And you'd better have a session with Amanda, my dietician here. You are so good about looking after your face and hair, but these fads of yours are ridiculous. Make an appointment with Amanda tomorrow."

Eve listened with only half her mind. The shock of seeing the gossip writer's malicious paragraph had partly paralyzed her. The break in their conversation gave her time to think. As she watched, waiting for the long tirade to finish, Eve's mind cleared.

Of course. Scott . . .

She recalled the small, seemingly unimportant incident when she had twice seen the same man standing opposite Scott's house in Quintin Street. But because she had no sense of guilt, no alarm had sounded a warning. Whether she had, or had not, been watched by the man standing so nonchalantly by the antique shop was not important. What was of a more immediate significance was the feeling Eve had that Regina's apparent anger was triumph. It was as if she saw the incident of the gossip paragraph as the first crack in the relationship between her son and her daughter-in-law.

The question was, who had her watched? She could not believe it was Adrian, except that obsessive love sometimes carries with it obsessive suspicion. She shook the thought from her mind.

Regina? The anger at Saturn's paragraph could have been feigned. Regina would be quite capable of having her watched, perhaps ever since her resistance to being used again as the Contessa Girl. She could even have had one of her telephone operators listening in and reporting her calls, or even taping them. That would mean that Regina would have known about her call to Scott, which would account for someone being paid to watch her arrival at Quintin Street. And perhaps, for extra cash in his pocket, the man had leaked the knowledge into Saturn's scurrilous ears. That could be the reason for Regina's anger.

Eve watched the smooth, elegant head tilted slightly to the telephone receiver.

"Barbados?" she heard Regina saying, "Well, just be careful this time. You are taking Thiazide for your high blood pressure so just don't sit in the sun. Your doctor must have warned you. And now, Esther, go and take that poodle of yours for a walk or buy yourself something from Aspreys, but leave me to get on with my work. Goodbye, you maddening woman."

The telephone receiver was replaced. Regina sat back and looked at Eve.

"While you were on the telephone," Eve said, "I remembered."

"*Ah!*"

"I went to Scott and Margaret's house three times during the past week."

"Now we're getting to the truth. What a good thing Esther rang and gave you a chance to think again!"

"I'm not confessing because I have nothing to confess. Going to Quintin Street was so innocent that it didn't occur to me to connect it with Saturn's rubbish."

Regina's face was expressionless. She rustled some papers on her desk. "I shall have to think what to do. For the moment, I have too many other important matters on my mind. But before you go, Felicity Montclair wants you on her charity committee for the ball at the Dorchester in aid of deaf children. I have told her you will be at the preliminary meeting next Tuesday at her house, so make a note of it in your diary."

"If I can help, of course. But Regina—"

There was a pause.

Eve said, "I shall have to tell Adrian about *that*." She glanced at the newspaper still on Regina's desk.

"Leave it to me." Regina spoke quickly. "And I mean that, Eve. It's quite possible that you would only make things worse by being emotional. I can deal with Adrian."

"Don't you think I can, too? After all, he *is* my husband and it seems that this is my concern."

The door opened suddenly, jerking Eve's shoulder. Marion entered and gave a little start of embarrassment which wasn't quite genuine. "Oh, Contessa, I'm so sorry—I didn't know you were engaged."

"It's all right. Eve was just leaving."

Eve knew that Regina had pressed the hidden bell under her desk which secretly summoned Marion whenever she felt an interview had gone on long enough.

Walking down the corridor past the offices, one thing reassured Eve. Regina knew nothing about the crystal cosmetic containers.

XV

IT WAS NEARLY SEVEN O'CLOCK and the sky was the color of aquamarine. The trees in Hyde Park were vivid with new green and the water of the Serpentine glittered. In Rotten Row a few soldiers from the barracks were exercising their horses and the dome of the Royal Albert Hall loomed ahead of them.

As Adrian drove the car, with Eve beside him, along the twisting road that divided Hyde Park from Kensington Gardens, she said, "I love it in the mornings if I come this way and see the guards in their uniforms riding down to take up position at the palace. Do you remember Cicero, that marvelous drum horse?"

She turned to Adrian and realized that he was not even listening to her.

Ever since they had left Berkeley Square for a dinner party at Diana and Frederick Eversleigh's house in Prince Consort Road, Adrian had been silent. He drove a few yards further on, then drew into the side of the road, switched off the engine and said, "I think it's time for an explanation, don't you?"

"Here? Now? Adrian, we're on our way to a dinner party and—"

"And damn the dinner party." Refusing to look at her, he glanced up at the trees that hung branches over them like a green canopy. "I thought I could hold out until we got back home tonight, but I can't. That newspaper column—"

"Regina told you, of course. I'm sorry. I wanted to tell you myself, but you came up late to change for tonight and there wasn't time. I wanted you to be relaxed while you dressed."

"Regina didn't tell me. She was going out to dinner."

"I thought she had probably told you before she went. So how did you hear about that newspaper gossip?"

"Regina left it for me to see. It was on my desk when I got back from a meeting. There was note with it suggesting I ask you for an explanation."

"And I can give it. Margaret Somerset is home. She is a close friend, you know that."

"Am I to believe that that is supposed to make everything simple?" He lit a cigarette, took two deep puffs and rammed it in the ashtray. "I would have thought I might be important enough to have a more detailed explanation."

She thought: *Oh darling, don't be so pompous.* But she knew that it was the only way he could react when he was hurt.

And because she couldn't bear that hurt, she said, "I went to see Margaret, yes. But we only met once. She had to go to Essex University and then on to Cambridge with the rest of the Peru team. There was another reason why I went to Scott's house."

"And that is?" His voice was tight with tension.

144

"If I tell you, it's in confidence. Please, Adrian, give me a promise you won't pass on what I say to Regina."

"Just tell me."

She sat hesitating, knowing that the tension would be unbearable unless she took him into her confidence. Adrian spoke again.

"All right, I promise." His voice was cold and uncompromising. "I'll say nothing; I'll keep your secret—whatever it is."

Staring away from him across the long stretch of the waters of the lake turned to liquid gold by the sun, Eve told him of her scheme for engraved and individual crystal cosmetic holders.

"And you imagine Regina will agree to that?"

"If the whole thing is presented to her in every detail, then I hope so."

"And the cost? Each piece engraved by master artists, each piece signed? Good God, couldn't you have thought out some less ambitious excuse for—" he stopped.

Eve silently finished his sentence for him. *For going to see Scott?* But she said nothing until, after a too-long pause, she explained, "I just sketched some of Margaret's scent bottles; Scott was scarcely aware of me, I'm sure of that. He sat and read the newspaper and had his drink. I had a drink with him but that's all there was to it. Someone had been sent to watch me and that unspeakable paragraph is the result. Adrian, I want Regina to take the newspaper to court, to sue for libel."

"And then God knows what would come out!"

"The truth," she said. "Now please let's get to this dinner party."

While Eve and Adrian drove in a tense and unhappy silence, Regina was seated in her private sitting room, gowned in purple and pink silk heavily embroidered with gold. She wore Cartier rubies in her ears. Scott Somerset had announced himself to Benson and sat easily in the chair opposite Regina. He reminded her that he had warned her some time ago that he was taking his holiday in May.

Everything was working smoothly at the factory; Robert Chase was a good man and could be trusted to carry on for the month Scott would be away—in fact he could be trusted to carry on for good if need be.

"*For—good?*" Regina sat up very straight in her chair. Her fingers made their familiar drumming on the carved arms—always a sign of approaching anger. Scott, though aware of the pattern, said calmly, "Well, no man is indispensable. I'm not. And Contessa Cosmetics won't grind to a halt because I've left."

"Left? What are you talking about?"

"I've always made it clear to you that I had my sights set eventually on medical research."

"I don't think you've read your contract very carefully." Regina spoke with icy calm. "You are reckoning without my refusal to let you go."

"I'm nobody's prisoner. You can't stop me."

"You overestimate your own will, my dear Scott, and underestimate mine. There is no 'mutual consent' about this decision of yours to leave me."

"I've stayed longer than I intended—or you expected me to." He gave her a slow smile. "My first contract was for four years. I stayed because you gave me a magnificent laboratory. My second contract was for a further four years. That time is up a month after I return from my holiday—as you well know."

"If you propose to use that holiday in an attempt to look for something you might mistakenly think would further your career, then you can forget it. And now I must ask you to leave. I am due at a reception and any further argument would only be a waste of time."

Scott didn't stir from his chair. "Then it's only fair to tell you that I shall be going to Canada, to Ontario. There's an opening in a large research center there. I shall be flying the day I leave for my holiday—that's next Friday."

"Apart from any other considerations," Regina said acidly, "your contract forbids you to work for another cosmetic company within at least three years of leaving here."

"I keep to that. This is a medical research center."

"But you won't get there, so you may as well accept the fact and take your holiday somewhere pleasant nearer home."

Scott had risen and was at the door. "I've given you the facts. Try to face them."

Regina rose also. She came and stood with her back to her desk, leaning slightly against it. "There's a stipulation you seem to have overlooked." Her pause was deliberate in order to give her words greater effect. "If a new project is in the process of being tested in the laboratory, then you are tied until it is finalized and ready for production."

"Your new unnamed range has been passed by the authorities and that is where my responsibility for it ends."

"But it isn't marketed yet. It won't be until late fall. You know that."

"Of course I know that, but it's not my province. Mine is the completion of the laboratory tests. Everything for the new range is ready and has the national safety code approval. The only outstanding product is the moisturizer and we have agreed to put on the market again the one that has been successful for the past two years."

"I think you are brushing off your responsibility far too lightly."

"Oh no. You know that, apart from my month's holiday, I shall be giving you, according to my contract, another four weeks of work on my return. That will mean everything will be cleared up and no loose ends left before I go. Good night, Regina." He gave her a brief smile and closed the door behind him.

For a long time after he had gone, Regina sat quite still. Then she lifted the house telephone and told Solange to bring her wrap to the car.

Ever since Carlo had revealed a weakness for every pretty woman who came his way and had destroyed any love Regina was capable of, she had grown to despise men. She used the clever ones for the success of Contessa Cosmetics; she admired a few others for their importance in business. But she believed with absolute conviction that, given the opportunity, she could manipulate every one of them if she chose.

She wished that Adrian had been there to discuss the interview with Scott. She felt frustrated that there was no one around to vent her anger on, and she also wished, uncharacteristically, that she was not going out that night. She wanted to think over the interview with Scott at once. Such was her temperament that she preferred to plunge straight into crises and cope with them finally and without delay.

XVI

AT THE BEAUTIFUL EVERSLEIGH HOUSE, Adrian and Eve had little opportunity to be together, so that the abortive argument in the car hung unhappily in their minds as they played their parts socially.

Each of them, in their way, was enormously popular at functions. Eve was a good conversationalist and there were usually people at these gatherings who knew something about art and enjoyed hearing her opinion on modern painters. If there was nobody, it made little difference. That quite unconscious radiance and beauty that had so attracted Regina was like an aura round her. She was neither witty nor highly intellectual, but she was interested in people and she let them know she was interested in them.

Adrian, for his part, was always the magnet for lovely and sophisticated women. Men also liked him because he understood the intricacies of big business.

The Eversleighs' large drawing room looked out across the wide steps that swept in a straight line to the Albert Hall. Eve, standing near a window talking, saw crowds of young people pour out from a concert of modern music, saw them run laughing and talking down the steps to the street, their bright clothes swinging, their hair blowing in the wind.

Half listening to the conversation around her, she watched crowds swirling round the huge, unbeautiful building with its ghost echoes of marvelous music. She remembered the wild and wonderful last nights of the Promenade Concerts where crowds of young people, who had queued all night to get in, waved and shouted and flung streamers and yet who were, at the lift of the conductor's baton, as still and quiet as statues. Only three years ago she had been there, joining in the singing of "Jerusalem," laughing and applauding and seeing life as not very affluent but lots of fun. And now . . .

"I'm sorry." She turned quickly, finding a small, rather fat man next to her, "You were saying—?"

He, too, was staring out of the window. "It's such a pity that this wonderful and dignified area of London is so often spoiled by that mob of young people swarming around."

"Do you think so? I like it. The whole scene seems to me so gorgeously full of life and enthusiasm."

"Of course," the man said, "but then you are young and very beautiful." He moved a little closer, lowering his voice. "Shall we go and find a place where we can talk?"

"About—?" Her clear eyes met his.

"Ourselves." His eyes narrowed slightly.

Eve knew that look. She didn't bother to answer him but turned away from the hot eyes and the sensual curve of the mouth.

150

The dinner party broke up at about half past eleven and when they arrived home, Eve and Adrian found Regina awaiting them. She had just returned but, unlike Eve who was tired, she seemed to be burning to talk. She called them into her sitting room and immediately spoke to Adrian.

"Did you know that Scott is planning to leave me?"

"He mentioned it some months ago."

"Why didn't you come and discuss it with me?"

"I thought you and he had talked it over."

"As we discuss the matters of the day together, you must have known that this was something we would have to talk about. So, why didn't you? Why let it get to this stage?"

Adrian said with a flash of spirit, "Why didn't *you* bring the subject up, Mother?"

"I can't be expected to think of everything. You—"

"All right, so I should have thought about it! But I didn't. As it happens, does it matter? Scott is leaving and it's just as well." He didn't look at Eve, but she knew that she was linked with that remark. In Adrian's mind, at least, this midnight conversation was linked with Saturn's gossip paragraph.

Eve sat quietly, folding a rose-colored taffeta wrap.

Adrian was saying, "Robert can take his place as head chemist and you can find a promising man straight from university to train under him."

"Adrian dear, I am just telling you what has happened, not asking for advice. Now, pour me a whiskey, will you? A small one."

He gave her a slightly stunned look. Regina only demanded whiskey when there was something that threatened or agitated her.

She took the drink, sipped it and said, "If Scott tries to take this post he is after in Canada, then I shall sue him and I am a great deal more powerful than he. *I'll break him.*"

It was histrionic, but that was one of her characteristics—she could be theatrically melodramatic when the occasion suited her. She continued, "No commercial house will employ him after I have finished with him. Now, what I want you to do, Adrian, is to find out the name of the university or research station in Canada which is giving him this interview."

"But—"

"Dear God, no 'buts'!" she cried. "Just do what I ask you."

From her chair a little in the shadows, Eve said, "Perhaps Scott has a very small chance of getting this post in Canada. The rules of the university or the research station or whatever it is, could probably state that the post *has* to be thrown open to everyone, but that might be a mere formality. The post could already be filled. There must be a great many good chemists in Canada without looking elsewhere."

In the momentary silence which followed, she had a feeling that both Regina and Adrian were interpreting her intervention into their discussion in different ways. She knew how Adrian's mind would work. *Eve is willing the post to be filled. She wants Scott here, near her—if she dare, now that there are suspicions . . .*

And Regina? It could be that she couldn't bear to lose a brilliant chemist—or it could be a far more deeply laid scheme. Eve felt uneasy. She said, "I don't think there is much use in discussing Scott, do you? Because he'll do exactly what he wants. He belongs to no one."

"You know him so well, then!" There was sarcasm in Regina's voice. Her steady stare was more sinister than words.

Eve said quietly, "What Scott *is,* is there in his face. He is the most free man I have ever met."

"And that's another thing," Adrian burst out. "That gossip paragraph . . . those meetings of yours—" His eyes blazed.

"We're not discussing the paragraph."

"I'm quite sure you understand to what Adrian is inferring," Regina began stiffly. "In discussing Scott, we have to involve you and—"

"No!" Eve said feeling suddenly strong, strangely in control of herself, "we won't discuss it tonight. You can talk over Scott and his contract, but that has nothing to do with me. I'm very tired.

Good night, Regina. And, Adrian, I really *am* going to bed and to sleep."

She hoped, as she closed the door, that he would have got her message that she didn't want to be disturbed; that she wanted to sleep without first enduring recriminations and questions, and then the demanding, excessive proof of her love. It was becoming more frequent, this shattering fact that she did not want Adrian in her bed.

When the door had closed Regina picked up her whiskey glass and said, "Do you really believe that Eve's visits to Scott's house are entirely to see his sister? Three times in one week on her own admission?"

"I must believe it!"

"Why—*must*?"

He turned away, hiding his face and his expression from her.

Regina watched him, then said, "It's because you can't face the knowledge of her unfaithfulness. That's it, isn't it?"

He swung round, his eyes blazing. "I have no such knowledge. And neither do you. Just some bloody newspaper—" he broke off, his hands working, tensing and clawing at one another, his eyes lit with a strange red blaze. "That gossip is all to boost sales for their cheap—for their . . . " He was shaking so badly that he was fighting for words.

Regina said in a suddenly changed voice, "Adrian, no!" She leaned forward and laid a hand over his fretting ones. Her voice was soft, placating. "Those kind of reactions are not for you. You'll never be like that again. Dear, you know that! The doctors told you. When you have to face something that challenges all you've set your heart on, you'll face possible defeat calmly. *Calmly* . . . You will . . . you must . . . " She felt him relax slightly. "That's better."

"I'm sorry." He brushed the palm of his hand over his hair; there was sweat on his forehead. "I almost let myself down then, didn't I? It's all right, Mother. Really, it's all right. We can discuss whatever has to be discussed without my losing my control."

153

Brought back by her powerful will from the dangerous brink, she was "Mother" to him. And in that quiet, early morning hour, she knew that it was safe to say what she wanted to.

"Adrian dear, you are intelligent enough, in spite of your obsessiveness, to face the fact that beautiful women have many temptations."

"Do you think I haven't watched the men cluster round Eve?" he demanded. "God knows, I have! She is always charming though a little aloof with them, yet I still panic in case one day a man will be there and it will all be different." He paused and again seemed to pull himself out of growing agitation. "But Scott won't be the man. I keep telling myself that. He's not her type. He's too uncompromising, for one thing."

"And that's just what intrigues women—the man who plays at being unknowable. It's the hunting instinct in a woman, my dear, which is as strong as that in a man. Adrian, listen to me, please. Face the truth about Eve. You must see that she'll eventually break you if you let yourself be so obsessed."

"Eve is kind. I keep telling myself until I say the words in my sleep—she'd never destroy our love for one another."

Regina said impatiently, "You won't understand, will you? It's not a matter of whether she is kind or not. It's a matter of temperament, of character. She is too independent. And no man or woman can say, 'What I have is forever.' That's a lesson you have to learn, Adrian."

"I'll keep her!"

"Will you?" Regina shook her head, "That scurrilous newspaper would not print that paragraph about Eve unless they were sure of their facts."

"Eve has explained why she went to Scott's house."

"Has she?" Regina's eyes darkened.

Adrian got up and began to pace the room. Not so many hours ago Eve had extracted that promise from him not to reveal the real reason she went to the house in Quintin Street. Crystal . . . rare crystal bottles for cosmetics . . . Eve's secret, which he dare not reveal. The shadow of doubt snaked through his mind. Had

154

it been the truth, or merely an excuse that she had hoped would placate him? But he believed her. As he had told his mother, he *had* to. He wished to heaven he could tell her about that conversation in the car, but he wasn't at all certain that Regina would believe the story—he could even imagine her scorn. "A few sketched scent bottles? A cover for some sordid little affair!" Was it . . . *was* that it?

Regina sensed his returning agitation. *Go gently . . . go gently, or you will smash the slender force that holds him together.* But how could she, knowing as she did, that the house and the people in it must be free of Eve—somehow, and soon?

She changed her tactics, watching Adrian pour himself another drink. "You aren't happy, and I can't bear to know that. Eve has let us all down. If you could accept that, I think you would lose this obsesssion for her."

"But she hasn't let us down. After all, her life before she joined us was easygoing; she still finds it hard to accept that she has a position here with us that restricts her freedom. Mother, there's nothing—I'm sure there's nothing—between Eve and Scott. Apart from Eve's reaction to him, he shows no interest whatsoever in her when he comes here."

"Of course he doesn't! What do you expect him to do? Make love to her in my house?"

"You go too far!" He raised his voice, hammering out the words. "You don't understand. In some ways Eve *is* me. I can't explain it. But nor, it seems, can I convince you that I will never lose her." He paused and then said in a voice that was almost a whisper, "And *you* should know what I mean by that!"

Regina turned her face away, saying steadily, "We'll take things one at a time, Adrian dear. But everything *has* to be talked out. We can't go on warring—"

"Take things as you wish," he interrupted her, his voice thick as if the words hurt him to say. "But remember: I am master of my personal life and I will never let Eve go. Not to any man—I'd rather see her dead." He spoke from the wildness which was beginning to rage again inside him. He strode to the door.

"What's more, I won't believe Eve cares a damn for Scott Somerset." He leaned against the doorpost. "I mind her talking to him, but then I mind her talking to any bloody man. It's not the man's fault, whoever he might be, and it's not Eve's. She can't help that magnetism of hers any more than she can help breathing. Any man who is human would feel excitement talking to her." He walked through the door muttering, "Good night."

Left alone, Regina wandered to the window. Adrian had the same almost blinding tenacity as she—what he wanted he would have and keep. His tragedy now was, as it had been all those years ago, that he wanted what Regina had decided must not remain his. Eve . . .

I'd rather see her dead. That had been a meaningless outburst—or so she told herself standing now in her quiet room. She put her hands to her face and remembered other words spoken at a fashionable Hanover Square church wedding.

"Till death us do part."

Shutting her mind swiftly to the memory, she crossed the room and switched off the lights. Then she went to bed and lay staring up at the beautiful ceiling just visible in the streak of moonlight through a chink in the curtains. But she didn't see the painted Eros and the gods and goddesses in blue and crimson and gold cavorting across her ceiling. She was thrashing her tired mind, trying to keep awake in order to think . . . to think . . .

XVII

WHEN SHE LEFT ADRIAN and Regina, Eve went to her room, undressed and put on a robe of turquoise velvet. Then, against all her hopes of a night of immediate sleep, she sat in a low chair and waited for Adrian. She thought, helplessly: *This is what happens so often. It is I who walk out on them. They are complete in some strange, psychological way that will always exclude me.*

She wasn't aware of time. She just sat quietly and presently heard the sound of footsteps and the opening of Adrian's bedroom door. Listening, she heard the little click the first door to the anteroom made as the handle was turned, then the second door opened. A draft of cool air from Adrian's open, uncurtained windows blew in on her.

"I want to talk to you," he said.

"I was almost afraid you'd come!" she said. "Does it have to be now?"

"Yes. Now." He walked back to the door that led to the small anteroom from which he had just come. "I have something to show you."

She went and sat on the fauteuil. It was upholstered in coral silk and was stiff and uncomfortable and she hated it, but she chose it now deliberately because it was impossible to relax on it. Comfortable chairs put people at a disadvantage and she sat up straight, watching Adrian go to his private safe above the group of bronze horses. She heard the click as the combination numbers fell into place and saw him take out a large ornate box. She frowned, recognizing the box with its pearls and turquoise insets, and watched Adrian set it by her side on the fauteuil.

He said in a cold, flat voice, "In this box is the reason for my enormous debts."

She looked up at him and heard her own swift laughter. "Oh, darling, what *have* you been doing? Gambling? Wagering Contessa Cosmetics on the turn of a card? Or do you keep a harem?"

"I'm not joking," he shouted at her.

She hunched her shoulders against the harsh voice. "That," she said, "was almost loud enough to wake Shari down the passage." She glanced at the ornate casket. "I thought that was always kept on the Louis Quinze table in the hall outside your study." Then, sensing that he was scarcely listening, she said gently, "Not that it's important. But, darling, how can you be in debt? Your salary—"

"Damn my salary! My debt is due to you and the bloody impermanence of marriage these days. I've grown up surrounded by women who play married for a couple of years and then, like some child's game, change partners. That's what I couldn't bear to think about. Changing partners—losing you. And so I'm up to my ears in debt."

"You are blaming me for the fact that most marriages among your set—*your* set, Adrian—are temporary affairs? If I may say so, I think that is unutterably unfair and even more unutterably silly."

"Have it your way! If you read the lives of even the greatest men, they've done idiot things, they've made fools of themselves. Well, I have. And I'm no great man."

She watched him stroke the lid of the box. "Shall we get down to the facts, instead of generalizing?" Her voice was cold.

Adrian was sitting very upright next to her, the box on his knees. The tiny golden hairs on the back of his hand glistened in the lamplight.

" 'Win her with gifts, if she respect not words;/Dumb jewels often in their silent kind/More than quick words do move a woman's mind.' You see? Shakespeare understood."

"Which is more than I do. And I'd like the facts, please."

"I'm playing for time," he said, "because I'm scared. Grown men can be scared, you know, without having to face anything as drastic as the firing line or a rogue elephant. Oh God, there I go again, expatiating because I don't want to get to the truth."

"If you can't tell *me* quite simply—"

"Then I'm not much of a husband. Maybe I'm not, at that!" He had a tiny gold key in his hand. He turned it in the lock of the casket and lifted the lid. "Jewels! They drew me—every damned jeweler's shop I passed just pulled me inside as if they were devilish, invisible hands." He laid the box, lid open, in her lap.

Eve looked down upon a blaze of jewels. They lay entwined in the soft purple velvet of the box—diamonds and rubies, a single emerald in a ring; a necklace of peridots as green and gleaming as wet Irish grassland; an elaborate coral and diamond bracelet.

Adrian leaned forward and put his hand into the box. She watched his fingers move with a slow, almost sensual delicacy among the glittering hoard. Her main thought was that every piece should be in a carefully padded box and not lying loose, sapphire on emerald, ruby on turquoise.

159

She thought, with a kind of incredulous bewilderment, *It's like walking into* Faust *and looking at Marguerite's treasure chest. A devil's bribery* . . .

But of course, it wasn't. This dazzling mound of jewels had nothing to do with her. She reached out and touched a marquise-cut diamond ring lying in a little velvet niche in the lid of the casket. "If this is some kind of investment—"

Adrian took the ring and put it on her second finger. It was too small to go over her knuckle. He slid it onto the third finger of her right hand. "You see how it fits," he said with delight.

The stone was flawless. She dragged it off and put it back in its small velvet cup. "Just tell me, what is the idea of all this? Security against inflation?"

"Security. That's right. Payment for my possession of you."

She said slowly, "I hope I don't understand. I don't like to be classed as a commodity."

He gave her a strange, long look. "Oh yes, Eve, you understand well enough! All women would. They know their worth."

"You aren't making sense."

He was still touching the jewels, his short, delicate fingers loving them. "It's a gamble for a purpose—a terrifyingly expensive gamble. But it's *got* to work, because no man can be absolutely certain of holding a beautiful woman forever. And I can't, I won't, let you go to anyone else. I live in fear that at some damned social event there'll be a man with more than I can give you—I may be rich, but for all the millions we make, Regina holds onto them. I have no freedom of access, *you* know that."

"Because you have been apt to take risks and Regina dreads a gambler. Your stepfather was one."

"So, I live in fear of losing you to someone who can give you more than I as much as I fear your arguments with Regina. I ask myself time after time, 'Will Eve find she can't take the strain of their disagreements and leave me?' And then, in a panic, I go and buy another piece of jewelry and store it against the time when you and I have our next argument—or you have yours with Regina."

"To hold me! To win back my love? As if I could stop loving you because of some argument with your mother and *you* could win me back with diamonds? Adrian, that's crazy!"

She picked up the box and handed it to him. "Take the thing away. It makes no sense to me. If you thought you could win me by jewels why not one at a time? Why collect them like people collect stamps? I'm sorry, but I just don't believe you bought them solely to hold me. I'm the excuse . . . but I'm not the complete reason. It's in *you*, Adrian, that craze to possess—" she stopped speaking because she saw that he wasn't listening.

He held the casket with fingers that showed strained muscles. "All the Mayfair jewelers know me and they gave me credit because of who I was. It was fascinating, the ease with which I could spend thousands at a time. But now there is no more credit. When I saw a pair of ruby earrings in Bruton Street, I went in to buy them. Do you know what the manager said to me—to *me*? He was obviously embarrassed, but he said it. 'I'm sorry, Mr. Thayer, but I'm afraid we must ask you to pay in cash.' I went back the next day and I paid him in cash. It was 'borrowed' from Contessa Cosmetics and then—well, damn it, it was all too easy for me, I borrowed for this"—he picked up the emerald ring—"and this,"—he let the necklace of peridots slide through his fingers—"and this—the diamonds are small, but they're perfect in color and—"

"I don't want to hear."

"For God's sake," he burst out, "the business will be mine one day. It's worth millions—and yet I'm in debt for a few paltry thousands!" His voice went flat, and then he said, staring into space, "I may as well tell you, I did something similar once before, when I bought the yacht. I 'borrowed,' but that time I convinced Regina that I was justified (although I shouldn't have done what I did that way) because it was a good investment— good for our image, although I hate that overworked word. I explained that we could entertain royally on the yacht, but in fact we use it very seldom because Regina discovered, when we began to entertain on the ship, that she hated the sea. But you and I will use it one day . . . Eve, you and I—"

"Suppose we stop talking about the yacht and discuss that— that *hoard?*" She could not help the anger in her voice.

He seemed not to hear her, speaking as though to himself. "She never forgot . . . Mother never forgave me for what I still think of as merely 'borrowing' from what was mine, after all. Before that I had freedom—but from then on, all I am allowed is the salary she pays me—a huge one, but not enough, God help me, to cover all this."

"Then," Eve said steadily, "you must take the lot back. And *tomorrow.*"

Once again, he seemed not to hear her but talked, as if in a trance. "I fooled the accounting department, because manipulating money is my concern. But I can't deceive the auditors and they'll be coming soon. Eve"—he put the box on the low coffee table and turned to her—"I've done what is called 'cooking the books.' And I'm scared to death." He was no longer in a frightened trance, but a man very much aware of the moment and of Eve. His eyes held stark despair. "I did it for you—out of love. Understand, damn it, *understand* . . . "

A wave of shock and anger swept over her. She put her hands to her face to shut out the sight of Adrian, the room, the jeweled casket. What tainted Regina was lust for power. In Adrian it was—what? Not love for her, but acquisitiveness, frantic and undisciplined. And excused by being called love.

She said, taking her hands from her face but unable to look at him, "The solution is perfectly clear. Do what I say. Take the whole lot back and get yourself out of this mad debt."

He turned, reaching for her. She shot up from her seat and faced him. She felt no pity, no harrowing heartbreak that he had done this for her. He hadn't. And the fact that he believed he had was pure fantasizing on his part.

"Adrian, just listen, please, listen! Even had you not loved"— she hesitated and then repeated the word,"—loved me, you would still have spent a fortune on something—maybe not jewelry, but on *something*. You're making me the excuse and I refuse to be. Can't you see for yourself—oh, but you must. You *had* to spend and spend and acquire. Well, now you must recoup, mustn't you? Because when the auditors come and Regina finds out—"

"Stop reminding me!"

"That's childish! You've been reminding yourself. But you need a bad shock from outside to make you give up what you've acquired. You don't surrender your possessions, do you, Adrian?"

"They were for you—everything I've done since our marriage has been for you." His eyes wavered before Eve's steady gaze.

"You have made yourself believe that, haven't you? And nothing would shake that belief except the shock you're now going to receive. It's a kind of reckoning, Adrian, and it's a tough one." She got up and went to her own small jewel case and took out the heavy amethyst necklace she had worn just once. She laid it in the casket. "That, too," she said. "I don't ever want to see it again. And now—that reckoning."

His face changed; the skin blanched and his eyes took on a queer, glazed look. "Don't threaten me, Eve!"

"I'm afraid I'm going to do just that. If you don't return all that jewelry immediately, not only will you have to face Regina and the auditors, but I shall leave you."

He shot toward her and as she backed away from him, he seized her. His fingers gripped her arms, pinning her to the wall, then a hand caught her throat. He held her imprisoned and gasping for breath. She lashed out and her thrust was so unexpected that he stumbled against the low coffee table which tilted, sliding the casket to the floor and spilling the jewels.

Adrian spun round and stared for a moment at the glitter. Then he fell to his knees and began shoveling the hundreds of thousands of pounds' worth of stones back into the casket. There was a sound of sobbing, but it didn't come from Eve. She was standing, feeling only the pain from the grip of Adrian's fingers on her arms and throat. She stood and watched him close the casket and get to his feet. She didn't move as he turned, still holding the box, and looked at her.

Then, without a word, he walked out of the room. He closed the door between them and she thought she heard him at the safe.

She got into bed and hid her face in the pillow. It was useless to tell herself that intelligent people didn't behave as Adrian had done. They did. Compulsive spending was as much a psychological illness as drink. The wrong, the worst evil of it, was to blame someone else . . . to give, as its reason, the name of love.

"Eve, oh, Eve, don't ever look at me as you did just now!"

She hadn't heard Adrian enter her room, but he was there, the mattress swinging slightly as he got into bed beside her. He took her in her arms and buried his face against her. "Love me, Eve . . . Love me . . . "

She felt devoid of any feeling—of resentment or pity or love. The tension under which she had been living since her marriage had taken its toll of her energy.

Adrian was touching her gently, his breath soft on her face. "I will do what you want—whatever *you* want, Eve . . . My beautiful love, I can't lose you."

She thought, but could not say again, "You possess me and you can't face losing a possession." She was too relieved that she had frightened him sufficiently, by threatening to leave him, for a streak of sense to cut through his blind obsession. Oh, Adrian . . . It was compassion, not love, that made her reach for him.

Immediately he was fired and forgot his natural tenderness, his wonderful sensitivity in making love. He was a man seized with a violent need for her, a stranger seizing her soft body, hurting her so that occasionally she cried out. In those minutes they were like antagonists who, when their flesh touched, could not tear themselves from one another, yet knew, in that contact, a fiery despair.

XVIII

IT WAS ONLY HALF PAST TEN. Regina consulted her diary and saw that she would be wrestling all day with business problems. Usually they stimulated her, but as she sat in her chair, scribbling a few quick notes on a pad, she felt a wave of unfamiliar exhaustion sweep over her. She closed her eyes.

In a week's time she would be sixty-five, although none of her staff dared remember it. It was no age, she argued, not these days. But years of ceaseless devotion to her business, the constant pouring out of both physical and nervous energy, the infrequency with which she carried out the relaxing exercises she insisted upon her executives practicing, were taking their toll. Nature had her rules and you obeyed, or you eventually paid the price. She refused to admit that, for her, payment was due.

There was so much she had to do. At the top of the list was the need for action which would give both Adrian and herself freedom from Eve.

Eve must go. The method was the dilemma, for she had to cope not only with the strong, dogged character behind Eve's lovely face, but also with Adrian's obsession. She knew she must take great care to move with caution or she could destroy the very thing she wanted to protect.

She pushed the thought of Eve from her mind and again considered herself. She was physically fit, the doctors had told her so. But they warned her of overstretching her still considerable physical resources.

Ease up! For no man, no woman, is indispensable. *But I am. Without me, what would happen to Contessa Cosmetics? And when I am dead?*

It *had* to continue. Adrian might be able to carry on with the help of a brilliant group of executives, but she had little doubt that the business would have to become a public company. That would mean that eventually the founder would be forgotten, the power would go out of the family grasp.

The business must have blood connections. And she knew now, with absolute certainty, *that she did not want Eve's children to inherit.* For Eve would never allow her to have the control she would need over them. So, the tie between her son and daughter-in-law must be broken.

After a few minutes she stirred, collected a sheaf of papers on her desk, checked the time and went out of her office to the meeting she had called.

There were ten people seated round the polished table. A portrait of Regina, wearing olive-green silk and with rubies on her tapering fingers, dominated the room.

The staff was gathered to discuss the further development of the new range of products planned for the late fall. Eve had been summoned, wearing the gold-flecked nail varnish for them all to see and approve.

Dates and marketing were discussed. Suggestions were made and Regina's flashing mind dismissed or improved on each. The points on the agenda were marked off one by one.

"And now," Regina said, "to the repeated question, What to name the general range? I finally have a solution, a perfect choice: 'Radiance'! Find out if it has been used."

There were murmurs of praise and approval around the table. As Eve watched the proceedings she realized that no one there would dare raise any objections even if the name was terrible. But, she admitted to herself, it was not. Regina's great talent had again proved itself. The new product name was, as she had said, perfect, if only it was still available.

Regina consulted the agenda before her and went on to the next matter to be discussed. Eve moved her chair back, wanting to escape.

At the same moment Regina was called out of the room for a transatlantic call. Eve waited until Regina had disappeared and then rose, crossed to where Adrian sat at his mother's right hand, and said, "I'm leaving now."

"You can't. Eve, please go back to your place."

She laughed. "The escape of the guinea pig will never be noticed among the lions. I've served my purpose here." She waved the colorful fingernails of her right hand at him and left.

When Regina returned her sharp eyes noticed the empty seat. "Where is Eve?"

Adrian answered, "She didn't think you wanted her any longer and so she has gone. She's not really concerned with the business matters we're now dealing with."

Regina's expression was impassive. She made no comment. "Now, for this matter of our camomile cream. I have decided to discontinue this line. It's a slow seller—"

Adrian sat back, not listening with his usual keen attention. He was wondering where Eve had gone.

*　　　*　　　*

She was, in fact, in the last place he would have expected to find her, driving along the Great West Road and out of London at speed. She had an appointment with the head of the Tamarisk Glassworks.

For the past week she had been working hard, and without Adrian's knowledge, at adapting designs of Margaret's collection to suit the purposes of various cosmetics. When she had completed a number of designs she had telephoned Peter Lerner, head of the factory and grandson of the founder, and took him into her confidence, explaining that she was not ready to discuss her idea with Regina and giving an assurance that, if the plan fell through, she would bear all the expenses. She knew that they would be heavy, but Adrian was generous with his allowances to her and she was not extravagant.

The traffic leaving London was heavy, but despite the snarled-up lines she arrived only ten minutes late.

The Tamarisk factory was a modern building erected on the site of the founder's rambling collection of sheds and outhouses. A number of the company's lovely sculptures were on exhibit and the place was set in woodland bought in order that nothing ugly should spoil the views from any factory window. Peter Lerner cared for the artists, technicians and workers he employed.

He was a little apprehensive about the suggestion Eve had put to him over the telephone. He knew Regina only too well and he was not overanxious to face her wrath if this scheme was revealed to her as a *fait accompli* without her involvement. On the other hand, he liked and admired Eve and was prepared, at least, to listen.

When she arrived, she lost no time in putting her project to him in more detail. Peter Lerner was both enthusiastic and cautious. "The idea is excellent and it's one we would enjoy working on here. However, it's an extremely expensive undertaking, and I wonder, are there enough rich customers to make the scheme commercially successful?"

"That's a chance I'm prepared to take. It's possible that Regina will veto the whole thing, but she likes challenges and this would be one."

"She still knows nothing about it?"

"No. Everything must be worked out in detail first—costing, advertising, publicity."

Peter looked through the detailed sketches again. "All these, of course, are opaque?"

"No. I want the bottles for perfume to be of beautiful, clear crystal. The bottles for creams and lotions, though, will be of opaque glass. It wouldn't pose any problems, would it?"

"None, since any designs these days can be translated into glass. But let's call in Vivian Mote—I told him to stand by in case we wanted him." Peter reached to the intercom.

Vivian was Tamarisk's chief designer; it was he who had produced the masterpiece of Eve's sculptured head at Berkeley Square.

He entered the room, bearded, tall and gentle, and was immediately enthusiastic about Eve's scheme. He was in his late thirties and in all his working years he had never given cost a thought. He dreamed elaborate dreams that became glorious realities in glass. His latest masterpiece had only recently been bought for the Musée des Arts Décoratifs in Paris.

Vivian studied the designs Eve had made, approved of some and decided that a few were too heavy in decoration, in spite of her adaptation, for the result she wanted.

She saw immediately how right he was, saying happily, "This is what I like—to be pulled up when I get too ambitious."

Vivian said, with apparent sincerity, "There's little here to pull you up about, Eve. But look, this wouldn't give back the light as you want it—it's too fussy in design. And this . . . You've colored it mauve, but it isn't really, you know, it's *verre de soie,* and if I'm right, the scent bottle has an iridescent sheen to it."

"Yes, it has. But I couldn't reproduce that in my sketch."

They talked for nearly an hour, going through each drawing in detail. Eve made certain that no one involved with the plan, from Vivian who would be helping her with the final adaptation, to the craftsmen and polishers, would break the secrecy. Until the first bottle was ready to be shown to Regina, she must know nothing.

Eve left the Tamarisk Glassworks with high hopes, thrilled that she had been taken seriously both as an artist and as someone with a good idea to sell.

Her car was in the drive. Those of the Tamarisk staff were in their own parking lot. Just behind her Volvo stood a Mercedes. Eve knew it. For no reason she could explain, she felt her heart turn over as if the gray car had a significance that both excited and frightened her.

There was no reason why the occupant should have been waiting for her—in fact there was no reason why he should even be there, miles from where he worked. But he was, and he was leaning against the car watching her. The door of the passenger side of the Mercedes was invitingly open.

"Hullo," said Scott. "Get in."

She stopped still in front of him, laughing. "I didn't send out a call for help. My car is in perfect running order so—"

"So why am I here? It's no coincidence, I promise you. I went to Berkeley Square this morning and saw you go out to your garage and drive off. Regina had sent for me, but while you were getting your car out, I saw Marion coming down the steps. She told me that Regina would be at a meeting for at least the next hour and a half and I never enjoy sitting around like an out-of-work actor waiting for the big boss to say 'Yes' or 'No' in his own time—particularly when Regina won't be my boss for much longer. So, as I refused to wait and left, I saw you drive off and I followed you—that's like a cliché situation in a movie, isn't it?"

"Why?"

"Why what? Follow you? Because I wanted to say goodbye to you before I fly to Canada tomorrow and I didn't want Regina breathing down my neck while I gave you the farewell kiss."

"Are you going to do that?"

"Yes, but not here." He reached out and caught her arm. "It's no use resisting because I'm stronger than you and I didn't come all this way to say my farewells in front of office staff at those huge windows, watching us."

"All right, I'll go quietly." A little shaken, she got in the passenger seat and watched Scott settle himself behind the wheel. Then she couldn't resist asking, "What makes you want to say goodbye to me especially?"

He switched on the engine and the car moved forward. "The fact that you and I understand one another."

"Oh, no, we don't." She watched the line of the road race toward them as the high-powered car reached speed. "You and I have *known* one another for some years, but knowing and understanding are vastly different."

"Then let's use it as a one-way thing. *I* understand *you.*"

"I doubt that, too."

"Women usually like to be thought difficult to understand. It flatters their instinct for playing at mystery. But not you, Eve; you are too direct. Isn't that right?"

"In that, yes. I'm not devious."

"Then I do understand you."

Eve said in faint alarm, "Scott, this is crazy! We could have got into the car and said goodbye and . . . well, left it at that. What are we doing careering across the countryside? And when Peter sees my car still parked in the drive he'll think I've been kidnapped."

"Or doing a tour of the Glassworks, more likely. And we aren't going far. There . . . " he nodded toward a hawthorn lane, turned left and drove some way down it. Then, just where the bushes opened out and they could see across the fields to the far-off towers and turrets of London, he stopped.

"Shall we see if it's too cold to sit out?"

"It won't be, but I can't stay." She glanced at her watch. "It's nearly twelve o'clock now and—"

"And there'll be salmon for lunch and white wine and hot-house strawberries and cream."

"There'll probably be cutlets and *crème brûlée,*" she replied lightly. And then, seriously. "But Regina will be asking where I am and what do I tell her when I actually arrive?"

"The truth, I hope. That I took you for a nice country run and kissed you goodbye because I doubt if we shall ever meet again and the sun should go down on a charming memory."

He was in a mood she knew so well—half mocking, defiant of the world and what it thought, ready to walk out on all he had known for so long. Like Margaret, when they had met in the Chelsea club for coffee the other night, hinting that she might be leaving England for good. Both of them going without regret, wanting no fuss, no farewell parties, no "drinks with the boys." And yet, she thought, as they got out of the car and flung themselves down on the soft warm grass under an oak tree, he would be missed. Adrian had once said of him, "Scott has an easy way with everyone. He's brilliant, but he never bothers to impress; he's the sort of man who makes no awkward efforts to please and yet pleases. And if he doesn't, I doubt if he ever loses any sleep over it."

The only sound as they rested against the great tree was that of distant traffic, so faint that it isolated them in a world of their own.

Eve asked, "What is going to happen to your house?"

"Oh, an agent will sell it, if and when Margaret really decides to leave England. I may send for some of my furniture—I don't know. My books and my music I must have. I'll have to arrange for them to be sent out." He looked her way and ruffled her hair lightly. "People make such chores of ridding themselves of possessions."

"The people at the laboratory will miss you."

"I'll miss them. But if liking is sincere, then whenever I return on a visit, we shall catch up on friendship again. I hope I'll never be a stranger to those who are my friends."

"Why did you really follow me all that way to the factory?"

"I wanted to talk to you. I detest people who interfere in other people's lives, but that is just what I have brought you here for."

"Oh . . . then . . . "

"Then to kiss you goodbye was just an excuse? Don't you believe it! That was important, too. But to be serious—you can listen to what I want to say or we can go back to my car and drive to the Tamarisk Glassworks without any serious talk at all."

"What's the proposed lecture about?"

"Heaven forbid that I should lecture anyone! But you seem to have no good, solidly practical parents or relations in this country to watch over you." He picked up a fallen leaf and smoothed it in his palm. "You've entered a world which is both public and yet closed to everyone except the few who are acceptable to it— the kind of people who would drop you tomorrow if you were not Adrian's wife and Regina's daughter-in-law, and you know it."

"I see my old friends."

"Oh, maybe, but how often?"

"It's difficult because our social life is mostly concerned with business."

"That's exactly what I'm telling you. And you, dear Eve, are losing your will to say 'enough is enough.' "

She bridled at that. "You're quite wrong. Don't you know—I thought everyone did—that I had refused to be the new Contessa Girl. That's a start in the direction of being myself and not what others want me to be, surely."

"I suppose so," he admitted, "but it's a drop in the ocean."

"And short of brainwashing me, which they can't do, there's no way I can be forced to do what I would hate. I'll never let anyone change me."

She saw the doubt on his face. "You're very young, aren't you?"

"*No.*" She met his eyes almost angrily, feeling that he was condescending. "I hope I'm adult."

"I don't mean that. I mean 'young' in the ways of big business. Where ruthless determination and subtle machinations are concerned you are a baby, my dear. Regina will win, you know."

173

"Then what must I do?" She heard the small cry of despair in her voice.

Scott said, "Surrender—or break away."

"I can't do either. I won't give up my whole life to service for a business. And I happen to love Adrian, and breaking away from the business would mean breaking from him. I can't, Scott, I can't!" She sat looking ahead of her at the piled black clouds over the hill. She was surprised at the ease with which she could talk to Scott.

He was also staring ahead of him, hugging his knees. "I know how difficult it must be for you, and it isn't for me to give you advice. Your life is entirely your own business and you can tell me so in good strong 'go-to-hell' terms. And then, just forgive me, will you, and forget me."

It could have seemed that Scott was both hesitant and embarrassed by what he was saying. But Eve, sensitive to atmosphere, knew that he wasn't in the least regretting his impulse to bring her to this quiet green place and talk seriously. Yet she had a strong feeling that his real reason for talking to her was still obscure and it troubled her.

A sudden impulse made her ask, "Why are you afraid for me?"

"I don't know. That's the devil of it, I just don't know. I'm not being alarmist or frantic for your physical safety. But people can be destroyed in less melodramatic ways."

"I won't be destroyed. I value my freedom too much. Because you do mean, don't you, that Contessa Cosmetics could destroy me?"

"I'm not even certain I mean that! Something is nagging at me without my knowing what the hell it is, except that it concerns you. I don't for a moment pretend I'm psychic or that I 'hear things'—I'm not that way inclined and yet, damn it . . . oh, come on, let's get back. There's a cloud over there that's full of rain. I know you are as in love with getting wet as a mermaid, but I'm not."

He put out a hand and drew her to her feet. For a moment they stood close together, their eyes steadily on one another.

174

Then Scott moved away from her, saying almost coldly, "And don't go thinking I have second sight. I haven't. I'm probably talking out of the back of my head. Forget my 'gypsy's warning.'"

Still holding his hand, Eve said, without taking her eyes from his face, "Why do you mind so much what happens to me?"

He snatched his hand away and turned on her furiously, his eyes darkened with angry emotion. "Because, damn it to hell, I'm in love with you!"

Without waiting for her or turning to see if she was following him, he stormed away, crossing the lane to his car. Shaken, Eve followed.

She got in beside him and sat watching the approaching clouds. Scott swung the Mercedes round in an arc, mounting a low bank and then, with only one more turn, maneuvered it to face the way back. They drove down the lane under the archway of trees and for a few minutes they might have been strangers sitting side by side.

Eve spoke first. "Scott . . . I don't know what to say—"

"It's best to say nothing."

"But—"

"Don't." He cut her short. "Don't try to make conversation, it will only spoil it. I want what I said to be my last very private words with you. Leave it like that."

The rest of the drive was in complete silence. Yet Eve was more aware of Scott than she had ever been before. She could feel his strength, his uncompromising attitude and, as never before, his sheer masculine attraction.

When he stopped the car outside the factory, Eve leaned toward him and kissed him. "Dear Scott, good luck with your Canadian interview." Then she opened the car door and fled.

Scott drove off fast, passing her as she was unlocking the door of the Volvo without giving her a sign or a glance.

She got in, started the car and looked up at the sky. It was beginning to rain and the great slate-gray cloud seemed to enter into her and she could have wept.

More than once, in traffic jams, men in cars drew up at her side to await the green lights and glanced at her with long, interested looks. Eve was used to it. Glances and superficial interest and even heady assurances of love were things she accepted and forgot. Only now, driving away from the quiet place where Scott had said he loved her, she felt as if, for a brief time, she had re-entered her old world of ease and stimulus and unspoken warmth. Yet, behind all her jumbled emotions, was a deeper disturbance.

Without making a statement which he could not—or dare not—prove, Scott had been warning her of some danger to herself. She turned her own thoughts into an argument. *He should have given me some hint; helped me by pointing to where my danger might lie. But he had admitted he didn't know.* Whatever had been in his mind, he could not help her now. He had gone out of her life, choosing to leave England with so little fuss, handing her as a kind of parting gesture the cool, angry gift of his love.

I shall never see Scott again . . . All right. So he was gone, and soon his love for her would be just a memory passing through his mind in some quiet moment of the Canadian day. Nothing more.

And she?

The traffic lights changed and the cars crawled forward. Eve didn't answer her own question.

XIX

IT WAS NOTHING NEW for Regina to make a sudden decision to appear unheralded at the factory, to walk around, her eyes missing nothing, questioning and testing the vast flow of beauty products there. She was usually accompanied by one or two of her staff. But this time she had gone alone.

The general assumption was that, because Scott was away on holiday, she wanted to assume, in his absence, the responsibility for the working of her laboratory. But that innocent reason was farthest from her mind. Regina was a bad enemy and the thought of a possible revenge gave her a violent energy so that she could scarcely bear the inactivity of even the briefest traffic delay on her drive to the factory.

Her arrival caused undercover consternation; she swept through every department—critical, appraising. She demanded spotless overalls and hair coverings; dust-free work benches; fresh-air-filled rooms. Light and as much quiet as possible were her essentials—what she called the "basic integrity" of her factories all over the world. Strangers should be able to walk through any of them unannounced and find the conditions perfect.

Emulsifiers, oils, fats—the ingredients for skin moisturizers, alcohol and refined clay for face masks; eau de Cologne, rosemary and basil for herb baths—Regina inspected them all and then, satisfied with what she saw and heard, went to the laboratory.

She talked to Robert Chase, Scott's deputy, in the small room that was the chief chemist's office, for over an hour.

The first thing was to be certain that he understood the absolute secrecy of their discussion. Assured of that, she told him of her scheme for a moisturizer that would, she believed, sweep the beauty world. They discussed the fact that it had been suggested they should use the same moisture formula for another year, and she told Robert that she had decided to manufacture one containing most of the basic ingredients they already marketed, but with one single important difference—nothing, she explained, that the authorities governing the manufacture of cosmetics could object to.

She said, reassuringly, "It will be perfectly all right, Robert. What I propose to introduce into the formula is only a very small amount of another ingredient."

She had no intention of telling him what it was. If he asked, she would make up a name to give him. Now that Scott was away, she could explain to Robert that she had discussed the matter with her chief chemist and that he had been in complete agreement. In the meantime, Robert was receiving the vaguest of facts concerning the moisturizer.

"But if there is the slightest change in the product we must advise the authorities and have it analyzed," he said cautiously.

She fixed him with her violet stare. "With Scott away *I* will take over all responsibility. All you have to do is to leave this matter entirely with me. The stock of our present moisturizer is finished, and this new one must be rushed through. It can be, too, because there will only be one small additive and it is nothing that will hold up production at the factory. But one thing I ask you, Robert! You must regard this conversation as confidential."

Robert understood and he had perfect confidence in his employer. The Contessa was a qualified chemist and she had never been known to produce any product that was in any way suspect. When Scott finally left, a month after his return from holiday, Robert saw himself in the place of chief chemist. He had a wife and a too-large family. He saw in his mind's eye all the little luxuries they would be able to have.

Regina left the factory in a state of elation. What she had described to him as "a small amount of another ingredient" was a byproduct of cortisone. She knew where she could get a supply; where, in fact, she had already received a minute amount for her experiment.

While the Rolls sped back to Berkeley Square, she told herself she had handled a tricky situation the right way. After his holiday, Scott would not be leaving for another four weeks, when his contract ended. That would mean, since he had just over three weeks to go on his holiday, that she had ample time in which to work out the formula that was teasing her mind. She would rush it into production while he was away. When he returned he would still be, for a month, head of the laboratory and thus responsible for anything that had been manufactured there up to the very day of his departure. She smiled at her thoughts and stared out at the rows of small houses as the car sped past them.

It would be easy to manipulate matters, should the need arise. If the moisturizer she planned to create proved to be, in the long-term use, dangerous to women's skins it would, officially, be Scott's fault. Wherever he was then working, she would find him and the blame would be his, *and* the disgrace once the authorities were informed.

On the other hand, if she should use so little of the cortisone that it would be relatively safe, the new moisturizer could be a world-beater; a wonderful, luminous lotion that would overshadow those of all her rivals. All she had to do now was to find the formula.

She sat chuckling to herself, losing sight—in an utterly uncharacteristic way—of her own carefully guarded integrity.

The first evening that Regina arrived after half past nine at the laboratory the night watchman neither felt nor showed surprise. He had patrolled the building with his guard dog for twelve years, and in the past, had known the Contessa to come unbidden long after the staff had gone. He knew that she liked to wander around her beloved factory without her staff eyeing her covertly while they worked.

But his curiosity was aroused when she began coming on consecutive nights, remaining shut up in the laboratory for three or four hours at a time. He had disturbed her on her first visit by knocking on the door and asking her if she would like a cup of tea or coffee. She had called out that she wanted nothing and would he please not disturb her.

No one except the night watchman at the factory knew of these evening visits, for she drove herself instead of sending for her chauffeur, Sanderson. Although it was unusual for her not to see Adrian sometime after dinner if she was home, it was quite easy merely to say that she herself was going out without having to tell him where.

So, on her own and undisturbed, Regina worked in her laboratory. She mixed and tested and experimented.

By working with the product that had, for the past two years, been so successful she hoped to avoid another testing by the national cosmetic safety experts. Legislation had recently made it a criminal offense to market any cosmetic liable to damage health. But Regina refused to consider that what she had in mind was going to affect adversely anyone using it, except perhaps a few women who were allergic—and she told herself with absolute conviction that no one could legislate for those.

She was quite certain that the old moisturizer formula only needed a carefully worked-out quantity of a byproduct of cortisone and the risk of the dangerous thinning of the skin would be negligible. She knew what she was doing.

She worked with excited absorption, mixing and testing, and using herself as guinea pig, studying effects in the long glass wall at one side of the laboratory, fully aware that the few hours she could give to her own skin-testing was insufficient time, but unable to resist trying her tests herself. She forgot time, forgot frustrations; she was a chemist and her excitement at being in a laboratory and working swept away all other thought.

It took Regina many days of hard research to find the exact proportions she wanted. At last, with an almost delirious delight, she succeeded. She filled a small test flask with the moisturizer and took it home with her, driving the Rolls as if every street belonged to her and there was no speed limit.

The fact that she was not stopped by the police was, to her, a good omen. She was going to be lucky; she had created a magic formula; she had beaten her rivals . . .

Before it went on the market, she knew that the moisturizer had to be tested by someone other than herself. Eve was, as usual, to be her guinea pig, though because Eve's delicate skin already possessed a certain luminosity, she was not the ideal woman for the test. Nevertheless, for a two-week period, Eve must use the moisturizer. And then, while Scott was still away, Regina would rush it into production.

Something alien had entered into her; she had cast caution aside, she had developed an unusual excitability so that she felt she was walking on air. She felt herself indestructible.

When she arrived home she sent Solange to find Eve, who was watching a television drama with Adrian. It was nearly midnight, but when Eve entered Regina's private sitting room she was amazed at the almost fanatical light on Regina's face.

She was holding out a small flask. "I have found my wonder moisturizer," she said. "It's a very special formula I've been working on and I want you to try it."

Eve took the flask, saying in surprise, "Adrian told me you wanted to change the formula, but I thought it was very successful. I had no idea you were going to change it completely."

"I haven't, I haven't," Regina said impatiently. "It's practically the old one with a mere suspicion of an additive. I've tried it and it's wonderful. I want to find out how it suits you. Use it for a fortnight and then come and let me see the result. It may or may not be immediate. These things depend a great deal on the type of skin."

The following morning Regina was so tired that she did not go to her office until nearly ten o'clock. On her way, she came upon a bored and aimless Shari. Shari was going to tea that afternoon with two sisters, neither of whom she particularly liked but whose parents had a villa in Greece for which Shari was maneuvering a summer invitation.

Regina found her hovering round an elaborate makeup display stand, and learning that it was a one-day school holiday, suggested she run an errand for her. There were many people to do this kind of job but Regina knew no other way to divert the girl from drifting round the salons. Shari was not yet an ornament to Contessa Cosmetics.

Because she knew Shari loved shopping, Regina sent her to Aspreys with a package containing a rare eighteenth-century gilt-and-enamel snuffbox which had a broken hinge. She was not allowed to use the Rolls, but a taxi was always called when Regina sent her on such errands.

Shari arrived at Aspreys and dismissed the taxi. Two little silver bracelets Margaret had brought her back from Peru jangled on her wrist. She delivered the parcel, gave the doorman what she believed was her social smile and walked out.

She took her time walking down Bond Street, peering in shop windows, coveting furs, clothes, jewels. Then, having reached the

Piccadilly end of the street, she turned and crossed to the other side, pausing in front of a small and very expensive jeweler's window.

In pride of place, on white velvet, was a necklace of three gold chains linked to one another by enormous purple amethysts, each one in a frame of small diamonds. A card beneath it described it as a unique nineteenth-century Russian piece. Unlike a small parure of pink topaz, which had a card attached describing it as having been among the jewel collection of the Empress Eugenie, no mention was made even vaguely of the name of the last owner of the amethyst necklace. But Shari knew. It was unique. It was valuable and it had last graced the neck of Regina Vivanesci's daughter-in-law.

Shari stared at it, wanting to go into the shop and ask who had sold it to them, but knowing that they would never tell her. Eve must have sold the necklace very soon after Adrian had given it to her. Shari's eyes were avid with curiosity.

Her life was Contessa Cosmetics and all who worked there; she adored gossip; she was stimulated by signs of trouble; she listened and probed into every small explosion of temperament among the staff. She badly wanted someone to know that she had seen Adrian's gift to Eve in a Bond Street window.

It was nearly lunch time and the crowds passed her, many impatiently jogging the sauntering girl. She thought: *When I am old, I shall write my autobiography, and it will be exciting. I'll have known everyone who is important—just as Mama does. And I shall have wonderful jewels and all the beauty treatments in the world so that I'll never look old.* She was suddenly a child again. She began to hurry, skipping between the crowds.

There was no one in the entrance hall of the house, but when she reached the penthouse she saw Eve going into her bedroom. She called to her, "I've just seen something. Guess what?"

Eve answered lightly, "The Queen's coach? A Scotsman doing the highland fling? That palomino horse we sometimes see in the park?"

"A necklace in a shop in Bond Street. Harkness & Rogers . . . you know it?"

"Yes."

Shari followed Eve into the bedroom and went straight to the dressing table, fingering the bottles.

"Well," Eve said, "what was it you saw? Something you'd love to have?"

"Oh, no. I think it's hideous, but it's just like the one Adrian gave you the other week—that amethyst necklace. You *did* say it was very rare, didn't you? And that was what the card in the window said, too. It was in a case with a white velvet lining."

The case that had lain on her dressing table when Adrian had slid the necklace round her throat had a lining of white velvet. Eve was folding a cyclamen scarf; Shari was opening bottles, sniffing at scent.

"*Is* it your necklace, Eve?"

Dissembling would be useless. Shari was secretive only where it suited her and that such a recent and valuable gift should have been displayed for resale in a Bond Street window was too intriguing for the inquisitive child to keep to herself. Eve said, "Yes, I think it probably is the necklace Adrian gave me."

"You *sold* it?" The clear young voice held disbelief. "You mean you actually *sold* it?"

Eve opened a drawer and put the scarf inside. She felt an enormous sense of relief that Adrian was obviously keeping his promise to her and ridding himself of the glittering hoard that, if discovered by Regina, would probably cause unimagined trouble between them all.

Shari was perched on the dressing stool, looking at herself in the triple mirror. Eve caught sight of the test flask of Regina's moisturizer, realizing with a pang of conscience that, in her absorption and worry about Adrian, her own project with the crystal bottles and—she checked her thoughts and admitted—yes, and her distraction over Scott's departure, she had forgotten to continue to use the moisturizer. It surprised her that Regina hadn't been watching and checking. But then, although she had used it faithfully for the first few days, Eve hadn't noticed that it made much difference to her skin. Regina had told her that there was enough in the flask for a fortnight's use and she would begin the process again that night, explaining her lapse to Regina if it became necessary.

Shari was watching Eve's reflection in the mirror. "Wasn't Adrian furious?"

"About—? Oh, you mean because I no longer had the necklace?" She met the small, sharp mirrored eyes coolly. "Sometimes the presents husbands give wives aren't quite up to their liking. They don't suit them. And when that happens, if you love someone, then the truth that you dislike what has been given you—if it's something very expensive—can be explained away quite kindly. I think it would be all wrong to keep something very valuable locked away. The necklace was too heavy for me and I'm not really the type to wear antique jewelry."

Shari's dark eyes narrowed. "*I'd* never get rid of anything valuable—not unless I was offered twice as much money as I paid for it. Did they give you a lot for that necklace?"

"You'd better ask Adrian," Eve said. "That will prove to you that he knows. And it will be lunch time soon. Tidy your hair before Regina sees you."

Shari switched the conversation. She opened her left hand which she had been hiding as she got up from the dressing table stool. "This is Mama's test flask, isn't it? Is it the new moisturizer I heard her talking to Adrian about?"

"It is. But Regina doesn't want it discussed yet. Do you understand?"

"Can I have some? I won't talk about it, but I want to try it."
"No."

Shari's eyes danced. She opened the flask and poured a little in her palm. Then she turned to the mirror and smoothed the liquid over her cheeks. "Look, Eve, look. It's lovely. It's got a sort of— not shine exactly, but it makes my cheeks look as if they were lit up—nicely lit up."

"You're imagining it! However good it proves to be it doesn't show any result after only one usage. Shari, please put that flask down. The shine on your face is merely because the moisturizer dampens your skin when you first put it on—it's nothing more marvelous than that."

"Then let me have some more for tonight."

"Go and get ready for lunch."

Shari put the flask back on the dressing table. The telephone rang and Eve turned to answer it. When she glanced behind her, the receiver in her hand, Shari had gone.

A friend was calling to ask if she would come to a celebration for the sale of a number of his paintings. She was delighted with his success, promised to come—and forgot all about the trial flask.

Replacing the receiver, her thoughts went back to Shari's news. If Adrian had been successful and sold most or all of the jewels, then he would probably be solvent and all her anger and harsh protests would have done good.

She was quite certain that Shari would tell Regina, if only to hope that she might witness some possible acrimonious argument.

Eve was about to go down to the dining room when Adrian entered. He looked agitated and slightly angry.

"Is my bag packed?"

"Yes. It's in there." She nodded toward the anteroom.

He said, "Why I have to fly to Brussels to collect those damned papers, I can't think. They could easily be picked up by air courier."

"That's the way it's usually done. Why *do* you have to go this time?"

"There's friction, apparently, between Van der Aben and Pieter and Regina wants me to sort it out. She detests small niggling quarrels between staff and she's right, of course. It breeds bad workmanship."

"What time are you leaving?"

"About half past four. Sanderson can take me to the airport. Are you ready to come down to lunch?"

"Adrian—" she hung back.

He turned, looked at her and said softly, "I'll probably only be away a day, I'm not quite certain. But"—he kissed her and put his arms round her—"this is what I'll miss."

When he drew away from her, she said, "Adrian, the jewels—"

"What about them?" His expression changed. "Well, what about them?"

"You've sold them?" She hadn't meant to ask; she had wanted to keep silent about them in order to prove to herself that she trusted the promise he had made to her.

"I've got rid of one piece, yes. The rest—"

"The rest—*what*?"

"Oh, I'll get rid of them—" he repeated.

The way he said it roused her suspicion. "But you still have them—in—there," she looked toward the anteroom. "Adrian, *have* you still got them in that safe?"

He answered with a weak effort at joking, "Well, darling, I can't very well drape them over the furniture, can I?"

"I want them all gone."

"I'll sell them." he assured her impatiently. "I've told you."

"I want them gone from that safe. If you don't sell them at once, then that is your responsibility if Regina finds out. But I won't have them there, right next to my room."

"You're being unreasonable."

"Yes, perhaps I am. But please take them away—put them in the safe in your office—but get them away from me."

"You don't expect me to carry that casket down to my study at this moment, surely! With Regina and our inquisitive little Shari hovering around? 'What have you got in that box?' from Shari. 'Why have you moved that casket from where I put it?' from Regina. And having to explain—and the whole damned business brought to light just when I'm keyed up to cope with trouble in the Brussels set-up."

She saw his point. "Then will you promise me to take it down to your office the first night you're back?"

"All right. I promise." His irritation left him. "And now let's kiss on it."

He held her close, needing her, smoothing back the soft, fine hair. "Dear God, love isn't an easy thing, is it? It's a fire and a fight."

She didn't answer him. There was no time for arguments or discussions. Regina would be waiting for her prelunch martini.

But Regina was not at lunch. Marion met them in the circular hall of the penthouse.

"Oh." She gave them her swift birdlike look. "The Contessa has asked me to tell you she will be out for lunch but she wants to see you and Mrs. Thayer at tea in her study at three o'clock. It's to be an early tea because of your Brussels flight, Mr. Thayer."

They drank a martini, talking trivialities. Adrian said as they entered the dining room, "We will have some time together before I go . . . I have no intention of returning to my office between lunch and three o'clock!" His right hand slid round her, pressing her to him, then dropped swiftly as they saw Shari already seated at the table, chin propped on her hands in the way Regina so disliked.

"Hullo, Adrian. I saw that necklace you gave Eve this morning in a jeweler's shop. Did you know she had sold it?"

Adrian took his seat at table. "I knew it was sold because I was the one who sold it."

Shari said, "You didn't need the money, did you? So *I* think if Eve didn't want it you should have given it to me."

"My dear girl, you could never wear it."

"But it's valuable and I could keep it."

Adrian said tersely, "Don't be silly! And get on with that melon."

Shari subsided.

XX

ADRIAN HAD COME TO EVE in her bedroom after lunch
and they had lain together and made love. But the mood
and the heat of passion was missing.

As she lay quietly by Adrian's side Eve thought that it was
perhaps her fault. She had let him love her, but she knew, and
she felt that he must know also, that although physical desire was
there, her heart was not involved. The pressures of this close
family world, she told herself, were responsible. If she and
Adrian could have a place of their own, so much that frustrated
them would vanish. But, as she felt Adrian's arm drawing her to
him again, she knew that that would not be the solution.

The early May sunlight streamed on their bodies and she

wanted to cry to Adrian, "Not again . . . please, not again . . . "
But she knew she couldn't, just as she knew that once again, when he made love to her, her heart would be in some limbo, unable to find the link between herself and Adrian.

Later, when they dressed, neither of them spoke of it, both making a pretense that all was well, smiling at one another, laughing together because Adrian's strong corn-gold hair would not lie flat.

At three o'clock they entered Regina's study together.

Adrian said, "I won't be able to stay long. Is it important?"

"I wouldn't be sending for you now if it wasn't," she retorted. She was seated in a chair before a book-lined wall. Tea was already set on the low table and Regina poured it out. Eve shot an amused sideways glance at Adrian, who liked strong Ceylon tea in his office every afternoon. Regina's choice was the delicately flavored Earl Grey.

Lifting the red-and-gold Crown Derby cup, Regina regarded the half slice of lemon floating on the top and said, "Clothes. We must start discussing clothes for the new Contessa promotion. Don't look so dismayed, Adrian. You may not be a couturier but you know what suits Eve and it's really a matter of finding out what will be the fashion look for late fall and winter. And also, of course, for next year."

He said, protesting, "Really, that isn't a matter for me, is it? It must be discussed with experts."

"I know. But the family must all be in on this. It's very important because this is going to be the biggest campaign I have ever embarked upon."

Sitting quietly, letting the conversation flow over her, Eve was quite aware of what this "family" talk really was.

Regina loved to have what might be called small "rehearsals" prior to meetings about every creative side of her business. She would talk to Eve and Adrian and then, once the matter was clear in her mind, go to the appropriate meeting knowing exactly what she wanted to say.

190

She leaned back in her chair, tea ignored. "We've had the gamine look and the unisex and heaven knows what else. This time, in spite of all that political claptrap about still watching the budget and being careful with the pounds, I shall go for luxury. Whether those who flip through the glossies and see my advertisements or stop at my Contessa show counters in the stores can afford the kind of luxury I shall dress Eve in is beside the point. Give people a sight of glamour, of riches, and their imagination will clothe them in that way and"—she snapped her ringed fingers—"your product is sold. I think she should go to Marie Farencian—she's the top couturier here at the moment. I'm tired of Max's clothes. And, anyway, he is becoming far too sure of himself. Or I may send Eve to Paris."

Send Eve to Paris . . . Everything addressed to Adrian *as if,* Eve thought, *I were a piece of window dressing.*

There were a few moments of complete silence. Nobody rattled a tea cup, nobody took a tiny cake from the crimson-and-gold plate.

Then Adrian said with a touch of anxiety. "Yes, we must begin the campaign soon because—"

"Because what?" Regina looked at him. "The way I see it, although we can discuss clothes now, we can't possibly proceed too far ahead because of fashion. This is merely preliminary."

Adrian rose and rocked a little backward and forward on his heels. He was smiling and watching Eve. "You see, Regina, Eve and I are planning to start a family in the New Year. Eve will be able to work, of course, for the first few months until the new range is safely launched and then . . . " He was looking at Regina, watching for approval.

For a few seconds another silence hung in the room—more tense, more potent than before.

Eve, too, watched Regina. But her expression gave nothing away.

"That's what you want, isn't it?" Adrian asked his mother. "You have always said—"

"So you both want a family." Regina reached for a copy of *Vogue* and leafed through it. "I see that Esmeralda has a double-page spread to publicize her French silks. The coloring is superb. When the time comes we must arrange for spreads to coincide with the promotion campaign. Josh must arrange a liaison with America and Europe. Oh, and I think the Middle East."

Eve got up and walked to the door. *"No,"* she said in a voice that carried through the room with a fierce clarity. *" 'No' to everything you have said."* She had one swift glimpse of Adrian's furious, blazing eyes as she passed him and left the room. She walked very steadily, but feeling as if she were weaving like someone faint or a little drunk. Anger tore at her.

She gave no thought to the fact that behind the door she had left open, they would break into a discussion about a family—*her* family, *her* children . . . The last thing Adrian had said privately to her about that was that he didn't want children yet; that he wanted her all to himself.

"Eve—and—I—are—planning—to—start—a—family." *But we're not damned well planning anything of the kind. Or were you asking Regina's permission, Regina's opinion, Regina's decision?*

Every footstep she took toward the top floor of the penthouse and her own room hammered the words into her mind.

She felt her face burn, felt her legs like slender weapons ready to kick at anything in her way—the great Sèvres urn with its seventeenth-century painted figures; the small, elegant table covered with expensive bric-a-brac, even a Fabergé box surmounted by a gold figure of Minerva driving her chariot of lapis lazuli. She would have liked to smash the lot in rage.

When she reached her room she locked the door and locked the one also that communicated with the anteroom between her bedroom and Adrian's. She was alone. But the anger couldn't be assuaged by solitude.

She had a strong suspicion that the quiet session with Adrian after lunch accounted for what he had said to Regina. He had sensed her halfhearted love and had seen in it the first chink in the armor of their marriage. She kept seeing, as she sat alone in her room, the wild, shocked look on his face when she had burst out in anger at his unexpected announcement to Regina.

She was quite certain that Adrian would find time to come to her before he left for his flight to Brussels, even if it meant a delay at the airport, and she wished she could be strong enough not to go to the door and open it for him. But she knew that she would not be able to keep him away. She had to let him know how she felt in far more detail than just that angry walk out from Regina's study had showed.

When he tried the handle of the door, she got up and unlocked it.

"Why did you do that?" He came in, closing the door behind him. "And why did you walk out of the study as you did? You know we hadn't finished our discussion."

"The discussion as to whether I should have your children?"

"Eve, I can't stop to argue now."

"Then you must go, mustn't you?"

"And take with me the picture of you standing there like some cold, accusing housewife?"

"That's just what I'm not. I rather wish I were—a housewife, I mean."

"I know what's making you so angry and I'll try to explain everything when I get back. I know I've changed my mind rather suddenly about us having a family and—"

"Please just go, will you?"

He reached out to take her in his arms but she jerked herself away from him.

"Don't do that!" he cried sharply. "Don't ever pull away from me when I need you." He forced her close to him, bending his head to kiss her.

She turned her face sideways. "Do you have to discuss with Regina whether, and when, we have a family.?"

"Eve . . . " He put out a hand and forced her face round to his. She pushed fiercely against him and saw that strange wild look in his eyes. He lifted his hand as if he were going to strike her.

For one moment his hand was held rigid in midair, then he dropped his arm and moved away. "Something has gone sour between us and I don't like it—I don't like it at all." His voice was curiously flat, but behind the fairly harmless words Eve sensed an anger that was barely held in check. Then he walked to the door. "Be careful, Eve. Just be careful. Don't try me too far." The door closed very softly behind him.

She had to distract her thoughts from the wretched afternoon. She went to her desk and unlocked it, taking out more drawings of the cosmetic bottles.

She knew she had given Vivian Mote sufficient details to work on those she had discussed with him, but she wanted to create more. The details on the outlined bottles in her sketchpad fascinated her. She started filling in delicate tracery, swirls that could be engraved on crystal by the craftsmen—the veins in the leaves of a rose, the shadow of a down-turned petal, a sea nymph's floating hair, details she had made of Margaret's bottles in her written notes accompanying each sketch because there had not been time for it all while she was at Quintin Street. And gradually, as the joy of her work took hold of her, her anger faded.

At dinner that night, Shari said, "Mama, I saw that amethyst necklace Adrian gave Eve in a shop on Bond Street." She watched Eve as she spoke, her eyes alert for one of the challenging exchanges between the two women she so enjoyed listening to.

"You mean," Regina said, with little interest, "You saw one like it."

"No, Mama, it really *was* that one. I know because Eve said when I told her—"

"Shari is quite right," Eve interrupted her. "I found the necklace too heavy for me and when he saw me wearing it, Adrian didn't like it either. Victoriana doesn't suit me—it's too ornate and heavy. So Adrian sold the necklace."

Regina finished eating, laid down her fork and said, "It was extremely foolish of him to buy it in the first place—he should have had more taste. I thought so when I saw you wearing it at the reception."

Eve said loyally, "It was a very lovely piece and the workmanship was marvelous. I'm sure there are lots of women who could wear it and look very regal."

Regina was frowning, then remembering that her forehead should be smooth at all times, massaged it lightly and deliberately with her fingers. She often did this when Eve and Shari were around, in order, so she told them, to remind them that frowning brought ugly furrows and was quite unnecessary. One could be angry and keep a calm face.

"I must speak to Adrian about this," she said. "I dislike the idea of selling. We don't need to rid ourselves of possessions, even though we have no need of them." She shot Eve her cold, violet glance. "Or did *you* sell it?"

"No."

"I must be reminded, then, to speak to Adrian about doing such a thing."

"I'll remind you, Mama," Shari said eagerly.

"Thank you, darling." She smiled. "And now I'm going to have a really relaxing evening—I think I have earned it after my hectic week. Shari, you and I will watch that film about the great Maria Callas. *She* had flair and a gift for life. Eve, do you want to watch?"

Eve chose not to, realizing that Regina wanted her company that night as little as she wanted hers. The scene that afternoon at tea must still be in her mind.

Eve was in the small private sitting room she and Adrian so seldom used when the telephone bell rang. Margaret Somerset was on the line. "I'm back from my cultural visit to Cambridge," she said. "We've talked and been questioned until, for the first time in my life, I feel I never want to see a piece of ancient history again—though Peru is really fascinating." She laughed. "Now I want to see you and have some real women's gossip. Can you come round now—or does that sound rather peremptory? Should I ask you to look in your diary and make a date?"

"I'm coming now," Eve said firmly. "Or, of course, you could come here. Adrian is in Brussels and I'm on my own."

"Thank you, dear." Margaret's voice sounded amused, "but merely walking through those damned gilded halls of yours is enough to make me rush back to South America. I love my little house here, so do come."

"I'll be with you in ten minutes," Eve said promptly.

Changing into more practical clothes, Eve thought that though Margaret and Scott seemed vastly different in looks, actually his sister's red hair was evident in Scott's, especially when the sun shone on to it—as it had done that time when they had sat, half in the sun and half in the shadow of the oak tree . . .

She would remember that for a long time, like something that mattered a very great deal and yet must not be thought of. And one day the memory would be gone. She would never see Scott again and what had been said in that sunny field would be merely one more link in a chain of small poignant and flattering moments throughout her life. That was all.

XXI

EVE ARRIVED IN QUINTIN STREET in less than the ten
minutes she had promised and entered the little house
with a sense of warm familiarity.

Margaret had made the French filter coffee she knew Eve enjoyed, and there were also some small dishes filled with sweet-
meats—a very authentic Turkish delight; halva and sesame
seeds; crystalized rose and violet petals.

"Fattening, oh, hopelessly so!" Margaret said happily. "But
you and I never seem to put on weight, so why should we
worry?"

Curled up in their comfortable chairs, Margaret told Eve a
little more about her plans to live in the Near East. "Damascus,

or somewhere like that," she said. "I won't be on any 'digs' round there because my speciality, as you know, is South and Central America." She talked easily and fascinatingly about the Inca empire and the belief she and her colleagues clung to—that somewhere near where they had excavated there was a buried city.

Just once they talked of Scott. Margaret said, "He is so essentially British that I can't see him settling down anywhere else. I love him very much, my brother who walks by himself, like Kipling's cat, but we're very different."

"Then you'll both be leaving England, and this lovely little house will go to strangers. I wish I could have it, oh, how I wish I could!"

"From mansion to cottage?"

"Why not?"

"Yes," Margaret said, understanding, "why not?"

"If Adrian and I could have somewhere like this for ourselves—"

"Suggest it to him. But you'd better wait first to see what Scott decides to do. Canada isn't by any means certain. He has gone there to combine a holiday with a kind of ferreting around."

"He seemed so certain that he wouldn't be back—"

"I know," Margaret said lightly. "But stranger things can happen!"

Eve felt Margaret's blue, perceptive eyes on her and avoiding them, leaned forward and took another piece of Turkish delight. Then she said, uncurling her legs, "I really must go. If I'm away too long someone is sure to come looking for me. It's silly that it should matter, but at the moment, everything seems to matter."

"Then come again soon. I want to see a lot of you before I leave England."

"But you're not going yet?"

"You never know with me," Margaret said. "Do you know that old saying that if you sleep with a goose feather under your pillow you develop the wanderlust? I think the goose feather must have been there without my knowing when I was a child!"

She laughed. "Don't look so sad about it, Eve. The world has shrunk—it takes hours not weeks to circle the globe. We'll meet on occasions, wherever I am."

They kissed lightly and parted at the door. Eve got into her car and drove back to Berkeley Square.

She turned down the narrow street at the side of the house. There were three doors. The first led straight into the garden and was used by the staff. It could only be opened to outsiders by ringing a bell which connected it with the staff porter's lodge. The second was the door to the main garage where Regina and Adrian kept their cars. The third was the door which opened into Eve's own small garage.

She slid back the outside garage doors and drove her car in, pulling the door closed. The doors were self-locking, and when she had checked them she picked up her purse from the passenger seat of the Volvo and crossed to the door that led to the main garage. She was surprised to find it closed and when she turned the handle it didn't yield. She tossed her purse onto a shelf and pulled and dragged with both hands; the door remained firm.

"But nobody ever locks it!" She heard her own voice in the silence. Then realism took over. Someone *had* locked it. For the first time it occurred to her that she had never noticed if there was a key to the door. It didn't worry her. The big heavy key to her own garage hung on the wall; all she had to do was to unlock the doors to the street and make her way round to Berkeley Square and the main entrance.

She crossed to the wall where the key usually hung. It wasn't there.

Perhaps Sanderson, Regina's chauffeur, had taken it for some reason and forgotten to replace it. Or Tom Halligon, the night watchman who cleaned out the garages, could have absent-mindedly put it somewhere else. But there were so few places where it could get mislaid. She searched the bench where some tools lay, then the stone floor and behind the fire extinguisher. There was no key. She was shut up in her garage with the strong outer doors locked and the windows far up in the roof and quite impossible to reach.

Perched half in the driving seat of her car, the door open and her arms splayed across the wheel, she tried to think. There was no panic. She would soon be missed.

And then her frank mind asked, *But by whom?* Adrian was in Brussels and Regina would have remained in her suite. She most certainly would not go looking for Eve—they had no shared interests and no real joy in one another's company. And Shari? She would have been sent to bed and be curled up reading a glossy magazine or a novel about the high life she so loved to know about.

Eve's watch pointed to half past eleven. No one would be looking for her.

It had seemed such a soft early May night when she had left Margaret and driven home. Now she felt the clinging cold seep around her. The apricot coat she wore was of light wool and most certainly not thick enough to keep her warm all night. All night . . .

It was ridiculous that here, with occasional traffic passing and servants in the house across the lawn, she should be imprisoned in a small garage with no one to miss her until early morning.

She heard footsteps outside in the street and muffled voices. She shot to the garage doors and shouted and hammered with her fists. If she could hear them, they must be able to hear her. Every time she heard passers-by and there was a lull in the traffic she shouted louder. But nobody was listening for a voice behind closed doors. And if they heard her, they would think whatever fracas was happening inside that place with its high-walled garden was none of their business.

There were car owners who always planned for emergencies— keeping a spare garage key handy somewhere in the car; stowing a rug away. She thought: *I've been spoiled because there are always people here to do things, to take responsibility.* Sanderson would have a spare key to her garage, but he lived in a tiny apartment in a terrace of mews houses not far away that was owned by Regina. Even if he had been living in the staff quarters in the house, she couldn't have called him for help. The telephone was in the other garage.

She went back and stared at the communicating door between the two garages. She had never known it to be locked before, and there was no reason it should be now.

The idea struck her that a sharp draught could have slammed it, causing the lock to jam. But there had been little wind that day, and the door was a heavy one.

She walked backward and forward, not quite knowing where she was going. She was beginning to think the same thoughts over and over again, like someone in a panic.

She tried to steady herself. She would spend a cold and uncomfortable night in her car, but she was safe and at least she had electric light. And a book to read to pass the time? She searched the car and found a map of southern England and that was all. Well then—she managed a false cheerfulness—by morning she would know every village in Surrey and Sussex. She grinned at the map and flung it into the back seat of the car.

One thing she did not dare do. She must not turn on the car's engine for warmth, because the only windows in the garage were closed and there would be no way for the fumes to escape.

She went back to the street doors and banged and shouted again. Then, leaning against the cold stone wall she tried to remember what time Tom Halligon made his nightly rounds. At twelve o'clock, at three and at six. She looked at her watch again. It was past twelve. He had probably toured the house, poked his nose into the garden, and seeing that all was quiet there, had locked up until his next round at three.

It would be impossible to see her small garage from the house because of the larger one on the far side of that locked door. So the lights she had turned on would not be visible. From twelve o'clock until three sounded like time everlasting. But she must think, by then, of some way to attract his attention. She had once been told that she had ingenuity. Now was the time to use it.

She wrapped her coat round her, found a scarf in the glove compartment and put it round her throat; the thin silk would make her just a little warmer.

She curled up on the back seat of the car, kicking the map of southern England to the floor. Somewhere behind the garage doors a girl laughed. For a wild moment she wondered if it was one of the house servants coming home late. She listened for the garden door to be opened when the girl rang the bell. But there was no sound; the girl was merely a passing stranger.

Eve had no idea how long it was before she was aware that the air seeping into the car had changed its quality. It felt thick, and she reached forward and opened the door of the Volvo. Immediately she clapped her hand to her mouth.

The "ample air" she had comforted herself would be sufficient to keep the car fresh until morning, if necessary, was thick with fumes from a car's exhaust.

She tied the scarf round her mouth and nose and scrambled out.

She stood for a moment listening. Then she heard it.

It was the undeniable, soft purring of an engine beyond the locked door where the Rolls and the Bentley were garaged for the night. Someone had switched on one, or both, of the engines and the fumes were sweeping through the space under the door. She stared in horror at the wide gap there.

But she wasted little time in conjecture; she was too aware that her life could be in danger. She tore out the cushioned seat from the car—thankful that they had been specially made for removal for the picnics the family never had. She dragged the bulky seats over to the ill-fitting door, stuffing them against the gap.

It occurred to her suddenly that whoever had switched on the engine might not even know she was there. Sanderson could have returned to make some adjustment to one of the cars and could be working with the doors of the larger garage wide open. But if so, that deadly little cloud of fumes would not be seeping under the closed door.

She looked up and measured the distance to the high glass

windows. Not even by standing on the work-shelf or the car roof could she possibly reach them.

Her thoughts raced, jumbled, falling over themselves.

Regina . . . Adrian . . . Shari . . . She dismissed them all as being in any way involved. She began to think of the staff, of anyone who might have a grudge against the family and had awaited an opportunity for revenge without the least caring which of them suffered. Perhaps someone Regina had dismissed had managed to get into the garden, hide there until it was dark and then planned to harm one of the family—whichever one was unlucky enough to come home late.

It would only be a matter of time before the build-up of fumes triumphed over her puny efforts at blocking up the door crack.

She went back to the car and shut herself in and tried to think. Inaction was impossible. Only seconds after she had closed the car door she opened it again, in a panic that nothing could stop the seeping fumes if whoever had started the car's engine had gone away and left it to run all night.

She dragged the stool with which she had repeatedly hit the garage doors to the street to attract attention, climbed on to the bench, picked up tools that lay there and hurled them at the windows. Each time she missed by many feet—the glass was set at angles in the roof and only an athelete could have reached them accurately and powerfully enough with a throw. But she continued trying, desperation forcing her on although she knew she was exhausting herself without hope of result.

The fumes from the pulsating engine beyond the car door were winning the war against the seats stuffed as near as possible against the cracks. The seeping, evil mist was so strong that Eve had a terrifying suspicion that the engines of both cars had been started.

She got down from the bench, found a nail file in her purse and ripped the covers off the car seats, tearing at them in a fury. Then she stuffed the material more tightly into the cracks, jammed the seats themselves into the folds as close as they would go. Remembering that smoke and fumes rise, she wrapped her coat around her again and crouched on the floor in a far corner.

If Tom Halligon would look out of an upstairs window when he was on his rounds of the house at three o'clock, he would see the light in her garage. In three hours time . . . with fumes crawling through the cracks all round the door . . . She would probably be dead by then. Rage was mixed with terror. Then words came unbidden with a kind of automatic weariness: " . . . Hope till hope creates/From its own wreck the thing it contemplates."

Contemplating safety . . . rescue . . . hollow optimism . . .

It was then, as she remained still, her blind choking fear tensing every muscle, that she heard a shout. It came from the second garage and was accompanied by coughing.

Eve dragged the scarf from her mouth, rushed to the door and banged and kicked it, managing desperate croaking sounds that she was afraid would not be heard.

A man's voice bellowed through coughing, "Is . . . anyone . . . there?"

"Me! Me!" She gave no thought to whether whoever called would know who "me" was. She had no reserves of air in her lungs for more words. She was aware that the deadly fumes were less obvious, or they could have risen upward toward the ceiling of the garage. As if it mattered! She kicked again at the door.

A key was being turned in the heavy lock, the door moved, dragging bits of the torn cloth with it as it opened inward toward the main garage.

Hands grabbed her roughly, dragging her without dignity through the larger garage, thick with car fumes, but quiet now that no engine was running.

The heavenly air of the garden hit her with a mixture of pain and relief. Her throat felt raw and her stomach turned over. She crawled to the seat round the old walnut tree and sat, bent forward, pressing her hand tightly against herself. Eyes closed, she sat gasping and shivering.

"For the love of God," Tom Halligon dragged her to her feet and thrust her to the ground. "Don't sit there hugging those bloody fumes in your stomach. Get rid of them. Breathe, girl, breathe!"

She was not Mrs. Thayer any longer; she was not the Contessa's daughter-in-law. She was a girl who might have died from the prolonged inhaling of car fumes.

The waves of nausea passed and at last, dizzy and feeling that her head was reeling, she sat up. The dark garden danced around her, the grass seemed to come up and hit her, but she fought like a demon to control her brain and managed to say, "Someone— locked—that—door and—the key was on—the other—side."

"I'm going to get you into the house before we start talking."

She rose to her feet and swayed against the big, muscular body. "How could—someone—turn on the engine?—"

"Both, Mrs. Thayer, both! Hey . . . !" He steadied her. "I'll carry you."

"Tom, I can walk—" She took his arm and said, "We've always felt so safe here and none of us ever removes the key from a car. And someone must have known that and—"

"And a bit longer in there," Tom said ghoulishly but kindly, "and you wouldn't be talking to me now! Who, in God's name? . . . Oh, well, that can be a job for the police. Mine is to get you safely back to the house."

"I suppose we will have to—call—the—Contessa."

"You bet we will!" Tom said without a hint of reverence.

Eve crossed the quiet garden still leaning against him. The pain that had wracked her throat and chest were lessening and she no longer felt sick.

Tom was saying conversationally, as if hoping to take her mind off her shaken body, "Funny thing! Could be that Providence was at work, in one of its mysterious ways, because for once I was late on my round tonight. And when I went into the garden I heard a huge thud coming from the direction of the garage."

"I was throwing things at the garage door and then throwing Sanderson's car tools up to the windows to try and break one. But they were too high." Her still unsteady feet trod on a tulip bed. "Oh, look what I've done!" She bent to pick up a broken, flame-colored bloom and tilted forward, giddily.

"The best thing you can do is just don't let go of me," Tom said, matter-of-factly. But he bent and picked up the full-blown tulip and handed it to her. "That kind hasn't got any scent, but it'll smell sweet to you."

She said, holding the flower close to her face, "Tom, the key that locks the door between the two garages . . . I believe I've occasionally seen it in the lock on my side, but I'm really not certain."

"Nor am I. But don't bother your head. It's a police job."

"Oh, Tom, the Contessa will hate that! You know how she goes to great lengths to avoid the police coming to the house."

Tom said a word that was fruity and apt and, although still feeling as if the world were swinging round her and it was difficult to get a foothold, she felt relief at his firm irreverence.

While Tom rang the police, Eve lay back in the deep chair in the staff interviewing room, which was just inside the garden door. Someone had obviously managed to get into the grounds. It could be some father or mother whose beautiful daughter had been passed over for Eve and who had, all this time, carried a terrible grudge. It was far-fetched, but then so was so much that happened in the world. She thought of the letters she had received during the time she was the Contessa Girl—crazy or resenting or threatening. Sick minds at work . . .

She closed her eyes because the room was swimming round her. Then she lost all awareness of time or place. She had fainted.

She opened her eyes to find the room filled with people and Solange bending over her, slapping her cheek gently. "Madame . . . Madame . . . Open your eyes. You are safe."

Eve roused herself, looked up into Solange's dark-brown eyes and tried to smile. It didn't quite come off.

"Ah, so you do wake up!" Solange's voice was gleeful. "It is so good that you did not die in there and—"

"Solange, stop being so stupid and tuck that shawl round Eve. She is still shivering."

They were all there, Regina and Tom, the police and even Shari, staring wide-eyed at Eve, full of avid curiosity, her fingers pulling impatiently at the tassel of her silk dressing gown.

Regina sat stiffly on the chair prospective Contessa staff employees used. She wore a geranium-red robe cut like a monk's habit, the cowl lying softly around her shoulders, a white cord tied at her waist and her hair knotted loosely at the back. The rest of the group stood.

Eve was asked if she felt well enough to answer questions. She nodded at the tall inspector and answered the first question as the sergeant pulled out his notebook. "No, there was no sound except people passing outside, until I heard the cars' engines running—I didn't know then that both were turned on."

"How long did you hear the sound?"

"Oh, it seemed like years. I don't know. I've proved one thing. When you're in a panic you lose sense of time."

"The key to your own garage is missing. Do you think you might have inadvertently taken it into the house with you?"

"I am certain I didn't." She wanted to say: "Someone go and search my rooms." And she knew she couldn't because she would have to let them have the key to the drawer of her desk where the extra sketches she had made for the crystal bottles lay hidden. "I would never take the garage key into the house."

The sergeant was taking notes and in the silence Eve realized the significance of that key—as significant as the locked door between the two garages. *Those two things make it a deliberate attack on me. On me* . . . Not hating someone, *anyone* in the family, but Eve. And that must surely link it to this business of being the Contessa Girl. She heard herself say her thoughts aloud. "Someone must be very unbalanced to do this to me just because—because I'm—"

It was Shari who finished the sentence by asking, "Do you mean that someone hates you? Eve . . . why? I mean—"

Sentences begun, sentences not finished . . . But not for Inspector Masters.

"Your husband is away?" His voice was kind, but firm.

"In Brussels on business."

"You have his telephone number, of course."

"I think he stays at the Hyatt Regency."

"He does," Regina said. "But why bother him? Eve is all right now and he wouldn't be able to help you with any enquiries."

"I'm sorry, Madame. But where is your telephone, please?"

Regina waved with obvious impatience toward the hall and the sergeant disappeared.

They sat in waiting silence. Regina's face was like a mask; Shari's full of almost uncontrollable curiosity; Tom distracted and kind—the kindest of them all. Martha, the cook, was at the door saying she would make Eve some tea. Eve accepted gratefully and there was silence again as Martha went bustling out.

The sergeant returned. The desk clerk at the Hyatt Regency in Brussels had reported that Monsieur Thayer had left. He had stayed only a matter of hours.

So, the inspector's expression conveyed, where was Adrian Thayer?

Regina said tersely, "We have our own plane—he must have flown on somewhere else. What does it matter? I happen to know he gave orders to Sanderson, our chauffeur, that he meet him at the airport tomorrow morning." Eleven o'clock, she thought. She glanced across at Eve, who shook her head. Adrian hadn't told her. She forbore to add that they had parted bitterly.

Sanderson had been called to the house. He arrived from his mews apartment round the corner, correctly dressed, entering with his hands quickly smoothing his hair before approaching the Contessa.

He had been quite certain he had closed the main garage doors earlier that day after taking Mr. Thayer to the airport. The sergeant was sent out to verify this, and returned with the news that the lock on the garden door had jammed. In other words, he explained patiently, the door had been opened and not closed properly.

Shari said, anxious to be noticed and important, "That's the staff door the policeman is talking about, Mama."

"I'm perfectly aware of that." She looked at the quiet inspector. "So someone could have seen the door not properly shut and seized the opportunity to get into *my* house."

"It seems they didn't, Madame. Their objective appeared to be the garage and your daughter-in-law."

Regina nodded. "I suppose I have enemies who would injure one of my family if they could not attack me. And my house is well guarded. That is the danger, these days, in every country, for the famous or the rich. God help us!"

"God helped Mrs. Thayer," the inspector murmured, "or rather, your watchman did!"

There was a coldness in his voice. Eve guessed that Regina had irritated him by bringing the danger to herself, who had been in no danger at all; of seizing the stage like a splendid but ancient actress resenting the attention given to a young newcomer. It was petty, but then those who knew Regina were aware that she was petty. And the inspector, who must have been in his early fifties, had obviously seen such situations many times before.

The silence was broken by Regina saying, "Go back to bed, Shari."

The inspector turned to her as she gave Regina a resentful stare. "Have you been anywhere near the garage?"

Shari stared at him, her mouth a little open—a habit of hers when she could scarcely believe what she was hearing. "Me?" She gave him an incredulous look. "I'm fourteen, I'm not allowed to drive. Though I do on our estate in the Cotswolds. We have lots of land there, you know." She turned at the door and looked at Regina. "Mama, where *is* Adrian?"

"Probably on his way home. Now do what I tell you and go to bed."

Shari fled.

Regina turned to the policeman. "You know, Inspector, what *I* think?"

"I would like to hear, Madame."

Eve sat listening, aware that no word, no glance, no inflection in the voice would be lost to that thin, upright man, Inspector Masters.

Regina's opinion was obvious. Hatred had bred a desire to destroy someone—even someone entirely unknown to the destroyer. Just hatred of all the great, beautiful house stood for.

There would, of course, Regina added, be a staff inquiry in the morning. If the inspector cared to be present . . .

"Oh yes, Madame, I shall be present."

His tone, inferring that he would have been whether she invited him or not, seemed to throw Regina slightly off balance. "Not that," she said severely, "I can for one moment consider the possibility that any one of my staff—"

"—but no stone must be left unturned," murmured the inspector with a deceptively gentle smile, and Eve suspected, a deliberately uttered cliché.

Checks had apparently been made while they had been talking in the interview room for fingerprints on the car and the three doors to the narrow side street.

Eve heard it all, watched and waited, longing for everyone to go so that she could escape to her room and sleep. Her own thoughts were of the incredible fact that something one might read in the newspapers had happened to her. Victims of wanton killings, attacks by people unknown to them. Now she had joined their ranks.

Envy bred hatred. She had been a public figure and a glamorous one. That in itself could make her seem a spoiled and pampered woman to many people. And one of those, resentful of her success and the bally-hoo surrounding her beauty, could have dreamed of some opportunity to avenge, finding it when, in passing down the street, she or he had seen the side door ajar. But that theory was a long shot—far too long for logical reasoning.

Eve gave up trying to work it out by weary conjecture. Leave it to the police, only they never conjectured . . .

Inspector Masters and his sergeant left at last, assuring the unusually silent Regina that they would be returning the next morning. Tom saw them out and locked the great main doors, returning to ask what Madame required of him.

"Nothing," she said.

"But the key—the one missing from Mrs. Thayer's garage—"

"Don't fuss. It will be somewhere around—or probably tossed away in some street by whoever stole it." She gave a heavy sigh. "It's nearly two o'clock and I have a meeting in the morning. Tell Solange if there is anything you want," she said to Eve. "Anyway, you seem to be practically yourself again. Good night, my dear. There's absolutely nothing to be scared of now. You're safe."

"I wonder for how long?" Eve heard herself ask with a sudden sharp foreboding.

Regina paused on the way to the door, "From now on we will turn this place into a fortress at night. The wave of crime is appalling—and I'm afraid it's only to be expected that we, because we are in the public eye, must suffer more than the ordinary man in the street."

Eve watched her disappear, and then got up and walked steadily to the door. Solange was waiting to help her to her room, but once there Eve's legs felt strong again and her head was almost clear. Only inside herself the shaking continued.

She thanked Solange and sent her away, saying that she could undress herself. She couldn't hurt the Frenchwoman's feelings by telling her that the last thing she wanted was a tirade of words and questions in mixed languages, however kindly meant.

Later, while Eve lay sleepless, the terror that had gripped her when she was in the garage wouldn't loosen its hold. She watched the light from the moon permeate the chinks in the curtain and knew that the next time her life was threatened there might be no one near to save her. It shook her that she was accepting the fact that there would be a next time . . .

She turned restlessly, plunging her face into the pillow. Adrian had not been staying overnight at the Regency, nor had he arrived home. Where was he?

Immediately on top of that question, a tremendous sense of relief swept over her that he was not there, a complete disinterest in his whereabouts. All she cared about at that moment was being alone. It was a shattering realization when she looked back on all the longing for him that, until recently, used to overwhelm her whenever he was away, even for one night.

Was this marriage—the frantic need to be together, to touch, to fondle and then gradually to find passion—easing, becoming less urgent? But, of course, she knew that. What she had always believed, though, was that in place of the high emotion would come a sense of security, of pleasure that Adrian would be there, near her. This relief at the thought that the room next to hers was empty was not as it should be between two people so recently married and in love. The sense of failure hurt. She slept badly that night.

XXII

WHEN ADRIAN ARRIVED BACK in London the following morning he explained that he could not be reached at his Brussels hotel because he had flown across to Paris to see Philippe Gros.

He came to the small sitting room where Eve, in an effort to force her mind away from the previous night's terror, was at her table working on more crystal designs. She had made no effort to hide them from him since telling him her intentions, and now the sketches were scattered over the large table.

Adrian didn't even glance at them. He stood and held out his arms and when she went to him, held her close.

"I heard. Regina told me. Darling, I'm sorry . . . I'm so sorry you had that horrifying experience. There are too many madmen about!" He held her away from him and searched her face. "You don't seem badly shaken. *Are* you all right?"

"Yes. A bit squeamish inside, but nothing that won't settle."

"The police are coming here again, so Regina tells me. Though I can't imagine what for. They questioned you last night—Regina told me they were here for some time."

She saw the sudden flash of suspicion in his eyes. "I wonder—"

"What?"

"If all this is connected."

"All—what?"

"The gossip paragraph, your visits to Quintin Street. Someone watching you—and"—he tilted her chin, looking hard into her eyes—"men do mad things when they think they are being made fools of."

"I haven't any idea what you are talking about!"

"Some man in love with you."

She stifled laughter that had no joy in it. "Oh, I see. Some man I don't even know prepared to kill me because I visited a friend's house? Adrian, really, what wild idea will you think of next?"

"Read the newspapers, darling, and you'll know then that truth is crazier than fiction."

"Well, if you suspect such a thing, then I can't help it. But it's utterly improbable."

He seemed content to leave it at that, and put up his hand, smoothing back her hair. "You look very pale—"

"So would you if you had been inhaling car fumes. Don't worry, I'll put on some makeup before I show myself in salons, though I suppose by now most of them will have heard how Eve Thayer was locked up in a garage. I'll just have to assure them that, since the staff side door was left open, someone who was quite insane crept in and that it's all in the hands of the police. It would be useless to deny anything. They'll all know now. The Mayfair grapevine . . . "

214

Adrian's suspicion and his questioning of her had been curiously brief and she could only imagine that Regina had already told him every detail. Even so, aware of how like his mother he was in wanting to thrash a subject into endless repetition, she was surprised that he had asked so few questions. Also, she was vaguely hurt that he had not insisted on hearing the story as only she could have told it to him.

Then, as if he understood a little of how she felt, he reached for her and laid his face against her hair. The affectionate gesture was worth a hundred questions. It was comforting. He said, holding her lightly, "Just let me give you a piece of advice. Eve darling, listen to me. Don't go to Quintin Street again."

She drew away from him. "You think whoever was watching me on those nights was the man who last night locked me in my garage? But Adrian, surely that's too far-fetched . . . "

He was fondling her smooth body. "Let's stop conjecture, shall we? It leads nowhere. Leave it to the police. And to hell with work! We'll lock the doors, take the telephone off the hook and go back to bed. I've had a tiring time flying back and forth, anyway. And a boring one. I need sleep—but I need love more. Come—"

"Adrian," she reminded him gently, "you have an office and a staff awaiting you downstairs, and Regina could be calling you at any moment." She pulled away from him, needing all her strength to free his hold.

"What *is* this? The Fire Queen turned into an Ice Maiden?" It wasn't said charmingly; in fact it was a mockery of the playful words, as if Adrian were covering anger with spun sugar.

She tried to keep the conversation on a light note. "I don't think it would be very comfortable making love when office staff could be running round looking for you. Locked doors wouldn't keep their voices out. Go on"—she gave him a little push—"go and deal with your mail."

To her surprise he gave in, went to the door saying, "So we take a rain check on love," and walked away.

She went to the window and looked down at the old walnut tree with its limbs propped with two heavy supports.

Don't go to Quintin Street again. Why not? Scott isn't there and Margaret is my friend . . . Why warn her? She had no answer and she didn't try to find one. Although she would never see Scott again, Adrian's jealousy remained.

She turned from the window and sat down at her desk. Work had to be her panacea. She picked up her pencil and her sensitive fingers drew light curves on the glass bottle shaped like a rose.

On the afternoon of the day following Adrian's return from Brussels, his secretary, Jeanette Roth, laid his midday mail in front of him and commented on a cheap ink-printed envelope.

"Begging for something," she said succinctly.

But it wasn't a begging letter.

A snapshot fell out. Adrian's taut fingers had creased it as he had slit the envelope, but in spite of the obvious shadows flung across the lens, the snapshot was only too recognizable. Eve, standing at the door of the little house in Quintin Street, the soft light from the hall lamp streaming out and Scott's hand on her shoulder.

Well, for God's sake, why not? Saying "Goodbye and thank you." How many times had he laid a hand on a woman's shoulder—and more, much more? But that had been in the days before Eve became his wife. Since then he had been "faithful to her in his fashion," and his fashion had been complete and untarnished. He tried to steady his thoughts.

Eve had told him why she went to Quintin Street and he knew, because of that bloody gossip paragraph, that she had been watched. So why was he shaking inwardly as if he had received another shock?

Because he had. Because, seeing the enchanting house, seeing the two of them standing close together, it had hit him that the major question was what had happened between them before they had come to the street door. He must have been away at the time, for he and Eve were always together in the evenings when he was at home, and the snapshot showed a light in the hall. But then it was one of those small period houses where walls were oak-paneled and dark even when the light outside in the street was fairly bright.

It had never occurred to Adrian to want to see where Scott, or indeed any of the Contessa's employees lived, but now he longed to see that house, to see the room where they had sat together, where Eve had sketched and then, when she had closed her sketchbook, talked and drunk martinis together . . . And made love?

Red flashes seemed to burst in his brain. He felt his heart thud with the pictures his imagination was conjuring. He remembered how Regina had discussed the gossip paragraph with him and had decided to ignore it. How she had said: "Of course Eve isn't having an affair—especially with a man like Scott."

Then, when Adrian had raged on, insisting that he was going to take the matter up and sue the newspaper, Regina had said sharply, "Never fan a dangerous flame, Adrian dear," and then had softened her inference by telling him that of course the whole thing was malicious newspaper gossip, but that it was always more dignified to ignore such vitriol. She had seemed to regret her impulsive comment about the "dangerous flame," and because he wanted to believe and trust her with her great wisdom, he told himself that she had spoken without thinking and that, as she had assured him, the whole thing was just a matter of malicious gossip.

But the snapshot had brought all the tensions back. His impulse was to rush and find Eve.

The telephone bell rang and automatically he picked up the receiver. It was a call from Philippe Gros in Paris. It was a long call, and when it ended Adrian was more or less calm again.

He wondered whether he should tell Eve about the snapshot and decided that it would only reopen old arguments. He looked at it again and told himself that it was so dim and out of focus that it might not be Eve at all, but some woman of her height with her fair hair. But he knew, by the clothes she wore, that it was Eve. He tore the snapshot in half and threw it away. Then he retrieved the pieces and locked them in his desk.

The day was completely disorganized for the family. The police came again. The two garages had been inspected by experts and now the police collected the names and addresses of dismissed domestic and office staff. Nothing significant emerged.

Regina had been calm and very reasonable. "We are exposed to risks as a family," she told Inspector Masters. "In these lawless days we need to look over our shoulders all the time." She agreed that of course they must complete their investigation—after all, her daughter-in-law's life had been in danger. Her dear daughter-in-law . . . her smile was sweet and superficial. But please, if they would, just keep it out the newspapers.

The police had even investigated Merlin Saturn's gossip paragraph. But all they could find out was that it had been sent anonymously, handed in by one of his society "spies" and paid for by him in cash.

And the "spy"?

Saturn was so upset at the distress he had caused the dear Contessa that he had sacked his informant for giving such outrageously wrong information. He believed the man was now abroad, "doubtless searching for libelous gossip for some journalist who had far fewer principles than he." Saturn washed his hands of such people.

Hearing all this, Eve gave one half-flippant thought to the fact that Saturn must be metaphorically tearing his dyed blond hair in fury that he did not dare use the attempt on her life in his column, perhaps with the titillating heading, "What has a certain famous beauty done to deserve to die?"

Before her marriage to Adrian, she had been aware of the power of money and position, but had never fully felt it for herself. Marriage had made up for that ignorance.

All kinds of irrelevant thoughts went through her mind as she sat at the conference table with Inspector Masters and his sergeant. They had been courteous, but their questions were penetrating. Regina, insisting on being present at the interview, watched and felt an impotent fury. *She has charmed them. Dear heaven, that girl has only to smile and a jury would free her from a murder charge!* Damn Eve. Damn her for breaking into their lives, disrupting them and surviving . . .

She had had words with Adrian just before the police had arrived for the interview. "You see how she disorganizes our lives?"

"For heaven's sake, Mother, you can't blame this on Eve . . . "

"My dear, she has been rash and foolish and has ignored the fact that in her position here she can't behave just as she likes without some unpleasant repercussions. There are always neurotics and psychopaths ready to take advantage of a public figure's slightest indiscretion." Regina had worked herself up to what was really in her mind. "You tell me you plan to have children. It will make no difference. Eve will never conform."

"Mother, you want grandchildren."

"But not by Eve."

"Oh God! Between you, you are—"

"I know! I know, Adrian dear, it's all so hard for you. But please just be patient. Difficulties solve themselves in so many strange ways. I understand that you won't let Eve go. But just wait and let—well—call it fate, if you like, make *its* contribution to our dilemma."

"What do you mean?"

She smiled at him. "Darling Adrian, only fate and the gods know!"

XXIII

Regina was seated in one of the deep, comfortable chairs in her private sitting room. Her solicitor, David Tindall, sat facing her so that the spring sunlight fell on his lined, cautious face. The positioning of chairs in Regina's presence disconcerted many, but not that wise, middle-aged man.

Regina was saying, "But my dear David, of course I have a case against Scott Somerset! He is intending to leave me a month after this holiday of his is over. He is, I believe, in Canada at the moment. But we are in the middle of planning the very important launching of our new range of cosmetics. I want to know if his contract allows him to do this. It is vital for me to be certain."

"I'm afraid that he can, Contessa. I've brought his contract for you to see."

She snatched it from him, flicked through it angrily and said, "I think it's up to you as my lawyer to find a way round it."

David shook his head. "The condition of his remaining with you, after his actual contract is completed, refers to his part in finalizing the formulas for the cosmetics. Once he has done that you have no jurisdiction over him. He is free. Neither the promotion nor the marketing, which is all that I gather is now in question, is his responsibility. Tell me, though, he surely warned you of his plan to leave?"

"No." Regina fidgeted under the cool, shrewd eyes.

"No letter?"

"No."

"Are you sure? You see, if you decide to take him to court over this, which is what you are hinting at, you must be absolutely certain of every factor."

Caught by the implacable demands of a legal mind, of the necessity for a straight "Yes" or "No," she waved a ringed hand and said crossly, "Oh, he did write some sort of letter warning me that his contract was almost completed. But that was two or three months ago. I was just leaving for Rome and I really hadn't time to be bothered—I felt certain that all Scott was really implying was that if I wanted him to stay, then I must increase his salary . . . a kind of blackmail."

"But was it? You will have to produce the letter in court because I feel quite certain that Scott Somerset would have kept a copy, probably lodged with his solicitor. So I would ask you to have that letter you say he wrote you found before you enter a court case."

"I tore it up."

The lawyer sighed. "Contessa, I'm sorry, but I think you have no grounds for suing Scott Somerset for breach of contract. And you know, court cases are ugly things and very unpleasant for those who lose."

"As you say," she snapped, "I know that perfectly well. I haven't been in big business all these years without learning something of the ways of the law." She sat for some moments, her eyes narrowed, her fingers tapping the silk upholstery of the chair arm. Then she said very quietly, "No, I shan't take Scott to court. But, if he leaves me, then I shall see to it that he regrets it later."

David gave her a quick, alarmed look. "Please be careful, Contessa. Don't act hastily." He picked up his briefcase and rose.

She looked up at him, smiling slightly. "Oh, I'll be careful."

She remained seated and alone after he had gone. Her thoughts were entirely practical. Had Scott intended to remain with her she would have given him the daunting task of finding some way to make the cortisone byproduct so safe that the health authorities would have passed it. As it was, Scott obviously had no intention of remaining at the Contessa laboratories, and Regina had wanted the matter made clear by her lawyer. Had he told her that there was some loophole by which she could hold Scott until the new range was launched, she would have forced him to remain. But Scott was free of her by the third week in June. That made her next move clear. She would hold up the order to go ahead with the production of the new moisturizer until the very day Scott left. She had a fanatical belief in her own formula but if, by any disastrous chance, its use was followed by a spate of skin troubles, then Scott—as head of her laboratories at the time when the formula was worked out—would be held responsible. She had safeguarded herself by creating the formula while Scott was still responsible. If trouble came, it would be her word against his—and her second man, Robert Chase, had been sworn to silence. That there were snags in her thinking didn't occur to her. Her mind had reached a state of excitement beyond all reason. Achievement, pride, success—in a self-willed woman, that was a dangerous combination.

While David Tindall made his way out of the building, word was speeding round the executive offices.

"Scott Somerset is back. He can only have been in Canada a few days. He's here, with the Contessa, and he looks in a devil's own temper."

And that, behind the heavy closed doors of Regina's office, made two of them. In answer to her blazing question, "And who gave you the right to come storming into my office unannounced?" Scott replied, "No one. But you know damned well why I'm here—or if you don't you can make a guess."

"I will not be sworn at."

"When I'm in a temper, I'd swear at a saint."

Regina let it pass, recognizing his icy fury. "I'm busy. I've just been seeing my lawyer. And whatever you have in mind, I had expected the courtesy of a request for an interview."

"Which I knew perfectly well you wouldn't have given me. What I didn't know was that I'd been working my guts out this past eight years for a woman who finally gave in to criminal intent."

"How dare—"

"I? But I *have* dared. I'm here because of one word—one name which has a mere medical meaning to the public—but which can have a far more sinister meaning if you let that new formula of yours go through—that one, Regina, which you slipped in for the second batch of what should be, like the first, a perfectly harmless and excellent moisturizer. Yes, that's right. The byproduct of cortisone."

Regina was like a woman turned to stone. "*Who told you?*"

"Only one man could. Robert Chase."

She had been holding her breath and now she let it out in a long, harsh hiss. "He dared—he actually dared—to tell you of a conversation he and I had in confidence in the laboratory office?" The word "dare" kept raging round in her mind, concerned with Scott, with Robert . . .

"He found that reasoning with you was useless and you intended to go ahead."

"The disloyal, double-crossing fool! He is out; from today, he is *out*!"

"He is prepared for that. But he wasn't prepared to lose his reputation as a good chemist."

"Very well. You can now have the pleasure of telling him to go."

"He'll get another job right away. He's an excellent chemist and he's honest. When he tried to point out the possible danger of this new formula—"

"—I told him I would give him a generous increase in his salary—"

"That's right, but he refused to be bought and you refused to listen to his warnings. So—"

"So he let me make my plans, take him completely into my confidence in telling him that I would produce something that would revolutionize moisturizers and then, behind my back, telephone you in Canada. You must have had a very long conversation and he'll probably wish he hadn't rushed to tell tales when he gets his telephone bill—or did he call you from the factory on *my* time and on *my* telephone?"

Her acid question went unanswered.

Scott said, "I came straight to you hoping that you might realize the sheer craziness of jeopardizing the good name of Contessa Cosmetics for the sake of one commodity—one bloody moisturizing cream. *You* read *The Lancet, you* know of the warnings and yet . . . *you* know that drugs can be taken through the skin as well as by mouth and injection. All right! Cortisone can often be used to good effect when prescribed by doctors. But you are introducing it in a beauty product—in God's name, how can you be so insane?" He got up and stalked across the room.

Regina sat very quietly. She watched him brush past a low table and accidentally sweep a priceless Fabergé patch box to the floor, pick it up without apology and replace it. Her reaction showed only in the ice of her voice. "What happens between my staff and myself is confidential. I can sue Chase. His contract states that he must divulge nothing that takes place in the confines of my laboratory."

"And if you sued, Regina, the Safe Standards Council of the

224

cosmetic industry would be most interested in the case. Especially now that the government is tightening up on cosmetic ingredients."

Regina gave an uncharacteristic shake of her shoulders like a petulant child. "I know more about the beauty business than any of them. Nothing is absolutely proven. *I* read what was written about corticosteroid, for instance. I will quote you. My memory is excellent. 'There could be dire consequences in *prolonged* use.' Note where I stress the word, Scott. But there are dangers in many things if the public doesn't follow directions."

"Clients need to trust manufacturers."

"You cannot legislate for people with allergies."

"This is not a case of allergies."

"I've already had Eve try it out and—"

"YOU—WHAT?" He had been half turned away from her. He swung round in sudden fury. "You tried it on Eve, with her almost transparently delicate skin? For—"

"You've had your quota of swearing, Scott, so please control your temper. I promise you, if I chose, I could out-shout even you. Yes, Eve is testing it for me and it has done her no harm."

"Did you make her use the sensitivity test first?"

"No. Anyway, Eve is perfectly capable of doing it if she had any doubts. She might even have done so—using some on her forearm and waiting twenty-four hours for a reaction, if *that's* the test you are talking about."

"You know perfectly well that that would not, in this case, be sufficient time. It would have to be done at weekly intervals for at least three weeks before an allergy reaction showed. And you let her use this stuff directly on her face!"

"She has come to no harm."

"*Yet!*" Scott shouted at her.

"Would I allow my own daughter-in-law to risk damaging her skin?"

"Yes, you would. And please don't start to try and justify your actions to me. But I tell you this, Regina. I intend to see Eve—and alone, without your or Adrian's interference. I shall tell her about the cortisone byproduct you have introduced into *my* original formula, and I'll see that she stops using it."

"As far as telling Eve what to do and what not to do, I'm afraid you are in for a shock." Her full lower lip curled in bitter derision. "My daughter-in-law doesn't take kindly to being told anything."

"Ah, but there are ways and ways of telling. There is your way, which is rather on a par with the ancient divine rights of kings. And there is the human way."

"Perhaps we could leave Eve out the discussion."

"Fine. As long as you realize that I intend to see her." He noticed the tightening of Regina's mouth and warned, "You can't stop me, you know. You can bar me from entering your house, but sooner or later she'll go out, to shop or just to walk"—he paused and a faint smile broke over his face—"especially if there is a rainstorm." The thought turned his dark gray eyes to silver flame.

Regina said testily, "Will you please sit down—I dislike people standing over me."

"I don't think there's any point in remaining." He moved to the door.

"But I haven't finished. Frankly I doubt if the ingredient you and the authorities are so anxious to warn the public against would have any ill-effects used, as I plan, with a counteracting ingredient."

"You know as well as I that there isn't one."

"I can always try. And if what I plan proves not to be, then"—she paused and watched Scott.

"Make your point, Regina," he said and sat down again.

"If such a time should come when the authorities discover that a byproduct of cortisone has been used in the new batch of moisturizer and is having an adverse effect on women's skins—which I most decidedly doubt unless they misuse the product—then I shall state that I dismissed you when I discovered that this was your formula and that you were doing this on your own without my authority. I shall state that I had my suspicions and went to

226

the laboratory on some evenings just to inspect, on my own, exactly what you were doing. That will take care of the fact that I was known to visit the laboratory occasionally. Remember, Scott, you are still responsible for anything that goes out of that factory."

Scott looked at her with alarm. "What in heaven's name has moved you to imagine that you could get away with that? I could rip the whole evidence to shreds in a court of law."

She said softly, "Please don't be too sure, Scott. I may have put the matter a little too simply to you, but believe me I shall make my evidence stick!"

"There's an old Spanish proverb," Scott said. " 'Glory on horseback, misery riding behind.' You see, Regina, there is one thing you have forgotten. Robert will not remain silent. He has integrity. He could be your 'misery riding behind.' "

Regina sat back and studied Scott's quiet face. "Yes, Robert has integrity. But you know, Scott, in all my years of tough experience, I have learned that in the very last analysis, you cannot be certain which way a man will jump. If it's a choice of integrity with you or financial security with me, I'll win. I'll see that I win."

Scott looked at his employer in amazement. "You know, you almost make me believe in reincarnation, Regina. You're like one of the women of history, who severed the heads of those who displeased them or used poison they kept in rings to destroy their rivals."

No one else dared speak to her as Scott did. She hated him for it and yet it intrigued her. She told herself that as he would not be remaining in her employ, he could say what he liked. She preferred not to waste her energy in fighting him when he would so soon be gone. She turned on him a small, one-sided smile. It gave her face a vicious look. "We are all devious at heart. Some more than others. How else do you think I built my empire?"

"Let's get one thing clear." His voice had sharpened. "I am still your chief chemist and I will not pass anything that even you may have slipped into possible production behind my back. You should thank God I came back in time to stop the processing."

"You are on holiday."

"I've cancelled it. Adding those three weeks to the last month of my contract means that I still have another seven weeks before you can get rid of me." There was a calm and an absolute absence of anger in his voice that alerted Regina to the difficulty ahead.

But her dogged defiance rose to the occasion. She drew a memo pad toward her. "I will have Marion type my formal notice of your leaving my employ tomorrow morning."

"Which I will take straight to my solicitor."

"I hope he's a good one."

"The best."

She frowned, her mind seeking a weak point in his armor. "Why are you so anxious to remain in my employ until the very last moment of your contract? Was the interview in Canada a failure? Did they turn you down and has that shaken your faith in yourself?"

"No. And I'm not proud. I'd have admitted it if they had sent me away with a 'No damned good' pinned to me. But they didn't. In fact I was being seriously considered. But instead of waiting for the result I packed up and came home." He got up. "It must be very obvious to you, Regina, that you will, for a short while at least, be taking orders from me." He leaned against her desk and bent his head to meet her cold, wary eyes.

She rose quickly and walked across the room, standing at the window with her back to him. "You seem to enjoy being insufferable, but you can't threaten me. I am head of Contessa Cosmetics—I am answerable to no one; no board of directors, no shareholders—and certainly not to you."

"*Just listen,* Regina," Scott said quietly. "Unless you want to be in dire trouble, you will most certainly listen to me." He paused, sensing the moment when he would receive her whole attention. He knew he had both shaken and intrigued her.

When he saw the slight turn of her head he said. "For the next seven weeks, I accept no salary from you and if you attempt to pay me I shall give the money to a charity. Now, to the point. You will rescind the order you gave while I was away for the next batch of moisturizer and allow the old one to go into production. *There will be no additive of any sort.* If you defy me, I shall report to the authorities that while I was in Canada you changed the formula and introduced a byproduct of cortisone that they have banned. Robert won't back you with any lies—I'll see to that. And now"—he pushed himself away from the desk and went to the door—"if I stay, we shall merely go round in circles, and I dislike repetition." He looked at his wristwatch. "They'll be surprised to see me walk into the lab nearly three weeks before I'm due back. But that's where I'm going."

"Wait." Regina swung round and faced him. Sunlight and shadow chased each other across the rich carpet and ivory, silk-covered walls.

Her voice held a shaken intensity. "I've planned a large investment in this product as I see it, the answer to the dream I've always had of finding a way of giving a radiance to a woman's skin. Scott, there will *always* be people with allergies; we can't be certain, *ever,* that someone won't suffer ill effects from—well, from using some innocent face powder, for instance. You know that."

He looked at her across the length of the room. "I warned you we'd go round in a circle if I stayed. Let this bloody argument about cortisone have its swan song and get it over. You know perfectly well that the government has tightened up on ingredients used in cosmetics—I reminded you of that once before. I've always thought that the States was more aware of the risks than we, but we've caught up fast. Cortisone is a danger in certain cases and I won't touch it. I have a duty to protect the public— it sounds pompous but it's true of us all. If you don't rescind that order of yours, then, as I have threatened, I will report it to the authorities."

She said softly, "Be careful, Scott. If you try to make trouble, I promise you, you won't ruin me, you'll ruin yourself."

"I accept the challenge." He closed the door quietly behind him.

Regina strode to her desk, picked up an ivory paper knife and stabbed her memo pad violently. Then she called Marion. "Fetch me coffee. Strong and black." She leaned back in her chair and stared at the painted ceiling.

XXIV

Since the event of a few nights ago, Eve now always entered her garage from the street.

The police were still working on the case and she knew that the general idea was that hers had been one of those odd and terrible instances where the innocent had suffered for a psychopath's unreasoning hatred. The difficulty was, as always in such cases, to find the man before he struck again.

Now, as she swung the garage door open, she saw Scott's car drawn up alongside her short driveway. She stopped and stared at it and then turned and saw him coming down the street. Her heart began to pound with a wild excitement she couldn't understand and didn't want to try.

"I thought you were in Canada."

He looked down at her and smiled. "I was. But I came back."

"So soon . . ."

"Plans change quickly sometimes," he said vaguely. "But you—this thing that happened to you . . . I've already heard about the attempt on your life in the garage. Someone here told me. I'd have thought the newspapers would have seized on it."

"Regina wanted it kept quiet. You know how she hates ugly publicity."

"Ugly be damned!" he said violently. "Quite often the solving of crime can be helped by a newspaper report—a casual reader knowing something, seeing something he thought at the time irrelevant."

"The police are working hard."

"They have any leads, any suspicions?"

"Scott, I don't know. I wish to heaven I did. But British detectives seldom give their theories public airing unless they can prove them. So, I'm still in the dark." She laughed, slightly shamefaced. "I'm still nervous of entering my own garage, even in daylight. Isn't that rather idiotic? I come in this way, from the street, rather than go through the garden and the main garage to get to mine. I feel safer closer to the people and the traffic passing."

"Go on feeling safer," Scott said and reached out and touched her cheek.

She stared back, her eyes flashing nervously over his shoulder and up to the windows of the great house on the other side of the wall.

"It's all right," he said. "I'd do that even if the whole staff and the family were watching me. Your skin—"

"What about it?"

"I believe Regina gave you some of the new moisturizer to use. Hers—not mine."

"Yes."

He touched her face again. It felt smooth like silk and cool like shadowed water. "Have you got it on now?"

232

Her eyes danced. "Don't tell, will you?"

"Tell what?"

"Regina gave me her trial flask and I've lost it. In all the chaos we've been having, I forgot about it. You've just reminded me. So I'm afraid the skin you see is me, not what comes out of a bottle."

"Keep off it. And when you find that flask, will you make me a promise?"

"It all depends."

"Let me have it."

"Oh, Scott, dear Scott!" She burst out laughing.

He laughed with her. "It's all right! The only beauty product—if it can be called that—I use is a razor and maybe I'll throw that out one of these days and grow a beard. I'll see what the girl I'll marry has to say about beards."

"Are you thinking of—"

"Marrying?" He shook his head. "The girl I want is married already. Why the devil didn't you wait for me? And don't tell me I could never have stood a chance against Adrian. My morning mirror doles me out that piece of information. At the same time, even a scientist sometimes dreams idiot dreams. But let's talk realities. Will you try and find that flask and let me have it with the rest of the lotion in it? Don't go washing it out as though I need it to take the milk home in."

"Scott, why do you want it?"

"Ask Adrian. He just may know. If not, Regina does."

"Suppose *you* tell me."

"The lotion she gave you to test contains an ingredient I refuse to use."

"But it must be safe, whatever it is. No formula can be changed without being submitted for government analysis."

He lifted his eyebrows. "You are reckoning without Regina's will to do what she likes."

"She would never risk the good name of Contessa Cosmetics."

He shook his head. "Oh, my dear, sometimes the brain, even a brilliant one, goes berserk. Something, heaven knows what, sets in motion some wild idea and the mind does a kind of somersault and can't find its steady level again—in fact it doesn't even realize it's lost. It happens—"

She stared at him. "You mean—you are trying to tell me that—"

"That Regina has gone a little mad? Perhaps. But don't be alarmed. She's not mad in the general sense of the term. You could call it the madness of ambition. And now, I have to get back to the lab and show them that I'm in harness again. But Eve"—his expression had a deep seriousness—"I want that test flask Regina gave you."

"Of course. I'll look for it this morning."

"Good." He turned to his car.

"And Scott . . . "

He waited, hand on the car door, as Eve said, in a sudden burst of words, "I've heard everything you've said—everything. And how glad I am you're back!" And then she swung quickly round and fumbled with the garage, embarrassed and shaken at the emotion in her voice.

She got her garage doors open and heard Scott's car rev up behind her, heard the purr of the engine as the Mercedes swung onto the road and sped away. She didn't look round.

Eve was on her way to the Tamarisk Glassworks. She had with her the extra batch of sketches she had made from her own ideas. She decided that there would probably be a call for modern designs—clear-cut lines with perhaps the only ornamentation being a spiral base or a scroll lip on an exquisitely clear glass bottle. Unlike the designs taken from Margaret's collection, her ideas were based on purity of line, of an almost intangible quality as if water had been caught and held by magic into a shape. Eve knew exactly what she wanted and she knew that Tamarisk could produce them.

Peter Lerner and Vivian Mote were delighted with her new sketches. Seated at a table by the sunny window where work was always inspected, both men had the imagination and the sensitivity to see that Eve had great creative gifts.

Peter said, "I'd give a great deal to employ you, Eve. If you can think up ideas like this—"

"I'd never have even tried if Margaret's scent bottles hadn't started me off."

"There is room, if the scheme can ever get going, for both styles—the antique and the modern."

Vivian was sketching lightly over a vase-shaped bottle Eve hadn't been quite pleased with. He said, "This one needs some kind of break in the line. You see, it's too solid as it is. If the glass blower will give it a thickness at the base and then sweep it to a thin edge at the top where the neck of the bottle is, it can create a subtle optical effect. . . " He swung the sketch round so that Eve could see what he meant.

"But that's lovely!" She traced the delicate lines with her finger.

Vivian said, "Then again, you could use the basic idea another way. By air-traps. It's done by blowing a great bubble of glass and then laying strips of glass in a pattern on to it. Then a larger bubble fits over the first. That's what gives the air-trap its unique design."

Eve turned to Peter. "And then you congratulate *me* on my simple ideas!"

"Simplicity of design for modern glass is the first requisite. You're a trained artist, Eve. You have the eye and the imagination. That's what I congratulate you on. Vivian has the experience as well."

"I'd like to come and watch when you make the two trial bottles we've planned for Regina to see."

"Of course. I'll take you into the blowing room and you can meet the gaffer. He's the master craftsman. But then you know that, don't you?"

Eve drove home in a kind of singing happiness. The designs were safely in trusted hands at the Tamarisk Glassworks and the whole scheme was in the process of becoming a reality. Even Regina would surely not be able to resist a combination of originality and challenge.

When she arrived at Berkeley Square, she went straight to her bedroom and searched for the flask of moisturizer. It was not on her dressing table; she must have put it away and forgotten where. She was worried not only because she had promised that Scott should have it, but also for an even more sinister reason. There was danger of commercial espionage even in the cosmetic industry. If the flask got into the hands of rivals, Regina's rage would be terrifying for everyone until the culprit was traced. But it wasn't possible. Only the family, Solange and the maid who cleaned her room and had been working at the house for nearly six years, had access.

She was still searching when Adrian came through the ante-room. "You haven't changed, and you know that Regina has guests tonight."

"I can change in ten minutes flat," she said.

He watched her take a long gown of titian-colored silk from a hanger and put it on. Then, as she opened her small jewel case and took out a plain gold necklet, he said, "Just this once . . . " He came and stood behind her. "Just this once, darling, will you please me by wearing the emerald ring—the one I showed you? It would be wonderful with that dress. I won't ask you to accept anything more from my love store—that's a good expression, isn't it?" His laugh was forced.

Eve twisted out of his arms and faced him. "You mean it's all still *there*?"

"Well, yes. What time have I had to sell the stuff? Meetings . . . Brussels . . . "

"Don't you think you had better make time, Adrian, since the auditors will be here soon and I can't see how you are going to explain any discrepancy they'll obviously find in the books? And"—she turned away from him and began brushing her hair—"please get that casket out of the safe. I asked you and you promised—"

"All right! All right! I'll do it tonight after everyone's gone to bed." He left her abruptly and closed the doors between their rooms.

This was an occasion when Eve knew she should have used the moisturizer. With two foreign executives as guests, Regina would expect them to be shown her new product. But it was useless to repeat the search in places where she had already looked and she tried to think when she had last seen the flask. It took her only a few minutes to recall that Shari had been in her room on that last occasion. Always avid to try new makeup, she could have taken it to try.

Eve went along the thickly carpeted corridor to Shari's room and knocked on her door.

The thin, imperial voice called, "Come in."

The girl was at her dressing table. She actually had the flask in her hand and when she saw Eve's reflection behind her in the mirror she swung round and stared at her.

"I'm waiting for Solange. She is going to do my hair. What do you want?" Her tone, like her expression, was hostile.

"That." Eve nodded toward the flask.

"Why shouldn't I have some of it?"

"Because Regina gave it to me for a long-term test."

"Oh, of course, *you* must be the one to have it; *you* must be the one to look marvelous . . . "

"Shari, don't be childish!"

"Oh, I see. If *I* want to look good, I'm childish. But you've got to look beautiful all the time."

Eve said patiently, "If the moisturizer is ever put on the market then you'll be allowed all you want."

Shari studied her face in the mirror. "It's simply gorgeous; it'll make a fortune for us and I'll use it every day." She smoothed her skin and Eve watched her, remembering Scott's censure of Regina's formula. She couldn't explain this to Shari who would refuse to believe her. But as Shari turned toward the light Eve saw the small red blemishes that had appeared on her face. It was as if she had rubbed the places raw.

Eve recalled, then, that Shari had the type of skin that was highly allergic to many cosmetic ingredients and obviously to whatever concoction Regina had used for the moisturizer.

237

Dismayed, she said, "Shari, give me that flask."

"No." She held it against her side, laughing.

"I promise you—and I mean it—that as soon as production is approved, you shall have quarts of it. Isn't that fair enough?"

"*I* want to look good *now*—I don't want to have to wait. Eve, why won't Mama let *me* try these new things out sometimes?"

"Because in test cases it has to be an adult who is the guinea pig; your skin is too sensitive yet. If there is a bad reaction to anything that is tested, then I can take it better than you."

"But there's nothing wrong with the moisturizer. Look, Eve"— she held her face to the light—"it's hiding these blotches I've suddenly got."

Eve couldn't tell her that it was an allergy to the moisturizer that was probably causing them. She just went to Shari and held out her hand for the flask. "Please—"

"*What have you got there?*" The voice from the door interrupted them.

Shari turned swiftly. Regina was standing in the doorway, her purple eyes black with anger.

"Your new moisturizer, Mama. Eve gave it to me."

"Now *that*—" Eve began furiously.

Regina stopped her. "Be quiet!" She swept into the room, seized Shari and tilted her face, examining it. "I thought so! Go and wash that stuff off at once—with soap and water. Do you hear? And only use that special soap I gave you. Do as I tell you."

"But Mama—"

"Go." Regina commanded, and then more gently, "Go, darling. Do what I say."

Shari burst into tears. "But Eve uses it."

"Eve has a less delicate skin than you and is less liable to allergies. Don't ever use that moisturizer again, do you hear?"

"But Mama, if you are going to put it on the market it must be good and—"

"Don't argue. Now, go into your bathroom and wash your face—gently, mind. Don't rub. Just pat your skin. And tomorrow

238

I'll find you a lotion that will take those blotches away. Run along now. And Eve—we must talk." She went out of the room, her dress rustling, her scent delicate and subtle.

Eve followed her as far as the staircase. Then she stopped and half turned toward her bedroom. "I'm going to finish dressing."

"Not until I've talked to you," Regina said and then called over her shoulder to Shari who was in her yellow bathroom. "Solange is coming to make you up, darling. So just wait. She won't be long."

Eve was already on her way to her own room. The rustle of silk followed her. Regina stood tall and regal, gowned in orchid silk, and seeming to guard the door against Eve's possible escape.

"I suppose Scott has told you about his aversion to my own formula?"

"Yes."

"I am a trained chemist; I know what I am doing. That moisturizer is a masterpiece, but you know perfectly well that Shari's skin is sensitive to almost any makeup—and yet you gave her that flask."

"I didn't. That was her story, but it isn't true. She took the flask from my dressing table at some time or other and when I looked for it this evening, it occurred to me that she might have it. I just went to her room to ask her."

"You are saying that Shari lied?"

"Yes. But it's not important. People lie out of fear."

"Maybe *you* are lying out of fear."

"But I'm not afraid of you, Regina. I have nothing to fear."

"You must have missed the flask days ago. And during that time Shari has been using it. You saw the result for yourself—those purple blemishes. Surely it occurred to you that only Shari could have taken it—it's natural for the child to be curious about any new beauty preparations."

"If you want the truth," Eve said defiantly, "I stopped remembering to use it. That experience in the garage drove everything out of my mind. Shari hasn't been using it long enough for permanent damage, surely? But doesn't what that moisturizer has done to her skin prove to you that Scott is right?"

"Shari is exceptionally allergic, as I've told you."

"There must be many women with skin like hers."

"Few with such drastic sensitivity," Regina said impatiently.

"But because of those few," Eve said gravely, "you can't put this moisturizer on the market!"

"What I do is entirely my affair." Regina walked to the door. "But I have guests and I cannot argue with you anymore now. And use that moisturizer—it's not going to harm you and I want Nikos and Guido to see the effect it has."

Eve said coldly, "Very well, I will. And take the risk."

"There is no risk. You have no allergies. And the men must see it."

"They'll be shocked when they see what it's done to Shari's skin—only you won't tell them, will you?" Eve spoke clearly and angrily. But she spoke to an empty room. Regina had disappeared.

XXV

EVE USED THE MOISTURIZER, did her hair and chose a plain gold bracelet to match the necklace. She moved round her room mechanically, choosing high-heeled sandals, touching her throat and wrists with a Givenchy perfume. Then, after locking away the moisturizer, she went down to the drawing room.

The guests were again from Europe—Regina's chief marketing manager from Greece, Nikos Spiridakis, and Guido Carvalli from Italy. Regina was always wise enough to allow her representatives abroad the freedom to market cosmetics according to the particular needs of the women of their particular country, but she kept a sharp eye on them.

It was not an easy dinner party. On the one hand, Regina was insistent that neither country was marketing Contessa Cosmetics with sufficient energy and imagination. On the other hand, she protested that women used too much makeup. She watched their incredulous expressions and laughed.

"I'll tell you what I mean. Women need makeup, but they must not be seen wearing it pasted on the way some artists slap color on to a canvas—in great ridges and weals. They must learn to use it so that they appear to be wearing scarcely any. I've said this all before—and you know that I have. Your young women," she turned to Nikos, "have such magnificent bone structure that you must concentrate mainly on their eye makeup. You"—she addressed Guido—"should let your women highlight their marvelous hair and accentuate their mouths. Study your own countrywomen, not those whose color, skin texture and contours differ from theirs. Sell . . . sell *all* my products, but keep an eye on those in which you should specialize."

Then, handsome, smoothly elegant and completely mistress of the conversation, she changed the subject and asked how the Cool Lily lotion, which had been so popular for the past two years, was selling now that summer was coming.

Ten percent increase on last year in Greece; fifteen percent in Italy, they told her.

"It's not enough," she retorted. "You know how tourists, especially the British who are used to cool skies, bake themselves in the sun when they go abroad. Then they dress up in the evening and spray their skins with scent. *You* both know the result: burns, caused by the combination of the oil used as a perfume base, and long exposure to the sun. There are products on the market to counteract the danger, but mine is the best; you know that. Scott Somerset went to enormous lengths to bring out just the right formula to enable women to sunbathe heavily *and* use perfume on their skin. I don't approve of prolonged sunbathing for anyone—I'm too aware of the dangers of ultraviolet rays— but if people must bake themselves, then sell them Cool Lily lotion. Sell it! And while we are on the subject of sun, just teach your demonstrators to warn women about using soaps or cosmetics that contain other chemicals dangerous to sunbathers. We have to educate the public, and you two are in tourist countries where the sun can do great damage. Well, advertise the fact. But subtly."

Dinner was over and coffee was being served in the drawing room. Adrian and Guido were laughing at a gimmick someone had thought up: advising women to determine their kind of makeup by referring to their astrological signs. "You are Taurus and you should use X makeup because it will project your particular personality." It was supposed to be scientific, worked out as if Venus or Saturn or Jupiter knew a hormone from a steroid.

Shari said, "You are just making it up, Guido."

"I'm not. It would surprise you, *cara,* to know what people will believe if you make enough fuss about it." His English was careful and beautiful.

Regina had been silent for some time. She said suddenly, with faint irritation, "Shall we dispense with trivialities? There is so much we have to discuss." She began twisting a marquise-cut diamond ring, watching its flashing fire.

"For the moment we continue with our present products, but next fall the campaign will be well underway for the new range. I may as well tell you," she added, looking from Guido to Nikos, "that we are not altering our basic ingredients—we will still use honey for its softening effects and yellow beeswax rather than paraffin. There is, however, one addition to our range—a very expensive one, but exciting." Like an actress holding the stage, letting her audience wait for her important line, she looked at each of them slowly.

Outside the great house, the traffic slid by with tires hissing softly on rain-wet roads. There was the scent of cigar smoke in the room.

Regina smiled. "We shall, of course, use our sapphire porcelain containers for general sales. But it has occurred to me that the very rich might be tempted to spend money on luxury bottles for their lotions and creams. I have decided to discuss my plan

243

next week with the Tamarisk Glass people and then to start a very individual and costly range of crystal containers. Each piece, like the sculptures in my salons, will be signed by the artist. They will be very exclusive, but that will be their selling attraction to the woman who already has everything else. Well?"—she glanced at them one by one, avoiding only Eve. "What do you think of my idea?"

Eve sat absolutely still, her eyes fixed on Regina's face with such intensity that in the end her mother-in-law was forced to look at her. Regina's smile widened, showing her fine small teeth. "And you, Eve dear? Tell me, don't you think it's a rather enchanting idea of mine? Luxury *in excelsis.*" She half closed her eyes, adding dreamily, "Parisians, Romans, and the Arab women in their palaces—all of them will, I am convinced, rush to buy my super-luxury items—those beautiful crystal bottles! When the contents are finished, they can, of course, be replenished and eventually those pieces will become collectors' items."

Blind anger shook Eve. She had been sitting quite still while Regina dropped her bombshell in that pseudosweet, confiding voice. Now she felt herself trembling. No one at the Glassworks, surely, would have betrayed her secret plan; nor Scott; nor, of course, Margaret. So . . .

She looked across the room at Adrian. And she knew.

She pushed back her chair and rose to her feet, holding on so hard to the carved back that the acanthus design dug into her palm. She was sufficiently in control of herself to know that, with guests seated around, this was no time for attack. But she could not let Regina's insufferable announcement go unchallenged. She heard her own voice speaking so calmly that she might have been uttering the lightest of social niceties.

"How strange, Regina! I think there must be something in telepathy after all. Because, you see, I've already gone ahead with the same scheme. But before I told you about it I wanted to have everything clear—designs, costings, ideas for promotion. When you contact the Tamarisk people, you will find that they are already working on some of my ideas." Her control was on the point of snapping, but she managed to add, "Or maybe you already know about it?" She turned a forced smile on the Greek and the Italian. "Please forgive me. I have some very urgent letters to write, and I am sure there is much that you have to discuss with my mother-in-law and Adrian."

She walked quickly to the door, giving none of the men time to get up and open it for her. She went down the stairs, feet flying over each step as if she knew that, whatever her speed, she wouldn't fall. Anger gave her an instinctive sure-footedness on the elaborate twisting staircase from the penthouse.

She went to the garden door on the ground floor next to the small interviewing room where she had sat, dizzy and aching after the incident in the garage. She turned the heavy lock and went out, crossed the lawn and leaned against the old walnut tree. It was very quiet down the side street, away from the traffic of Berkeley Square, and the late spring flowers, sweetened by recent rain, gave off their subtle scent.

Her sense of betrayal was acute. Love? Adrian loved her? She now knew that whatever love he had for her did not include loyalty, and strangely, that was not the shock it should have been. Her months of marriage had shown her that where the good of the business was concerned, love for her came second. For some reason, Adrian had been afraid that his mother might discover Eve's plan of creating crystal containers. And so, rather than having to admit, later, that he had known about it but had not told Regina, he had betrayed Eve's confidence.

There was a light stir above her in the old tree. A bird, perhaps, watchful of predators even in sleep. She was aware of the cool, damp night seeping through the silk of her sleeves. But ahead of her, the house shone with light. The lovely Georgian lines and Corinthian columns seemed almost nostalgic, caught between the high blocks of apartments and offices that stood where other great mansions had, for two centuries, entertained the Prince Regent, the King of Prussia and the Prince of Orange . . . Great names . . . noble families. And now, so little left except Regina's lovely home—and within it, the canker of an obsession.

The outside iron stairway that led from the conservatory gleamed wet with recent rain. She would never again walk down it to the garden, never again risk those wisteria-shadowed steps . . .

Love? Was there any love at all between the three who had lived there for so long? A quotation slid into her mind. "No creature was ever loved too much; but some in a wrong way and all in too short a measure." She tried to remember who had said it. Traherne? Not that it mattered. The truth lay in the words, and that truth, she saw with clarity, applied to her.

Adrian has loved me in the wrong way. But I have loved him in the wrong way, too . . .

For she saw now, in this moment of her betrayal, that the sexual attraction had been strong; enjoyment of his violent feelings for her had been irresistible and flattering. It occurred to her, for the first time, that she loved Adrian most when she was not with him. But they were not companions, not two people who could laugh and be happy in silences together. She had loved being loved by a man obsessed . . . Adrian had blinded her. And that time ago, before her marriage, her mother—wise and noninterfering—had seen it all.

So they had nothing but their strong sexual emotions and their physical beauty in each other's eyes.

The time had come for the break.

She got up and went into the house, locking the door. She went up in the elevator to the executive floor and then climbed the staircase to the penthouse and her bedroom. Then she sat down and waited for Adrian. He might come to her in half an hour or an hour or longer. It didn't make any difference. She was not even planning what she would say, how tactfully to put it to him.

Women with the same anger she felt often just packed and left. That was not her way. She had to face Adrian and tell him. That much she owed him.

As she waited, she heard Shari come up to her room and turn on the television. A clock struck the quarter after eleven. Eve went to the window and looked over Berkeley Square, watching

246

the lights slant onto a charming little statue of a girl pouring water from an urn. The plane tree—two hundred years old and still rich with leaves—shadowed one of the girl's pale arms.

I shall never see the view from this window again . . .

She suddenly realized how much she loved it.

There was a tap on her door and Shari entered. She still wore the deep pink dinner dress Regina had chosen to give warmth to her sallow skin. Although she had put on the two silver bangles Margaret had brought her from Peru, she hadn't considered them grandiose enough on their own but was wearing, between them, the pink topaz bracelet Regina had given her on her last birthday.

Shari leaned against the door, holding it half open. "I'm sorry, Eve, really I am. I didn't mean to scream at you about the flask. Only it does seem unfair that everyone else can use gorgeous new things on their skin and I can't."

Eve tossed away a tissue she had been using to clean off some of her lipstick. "You may grow out of these allergies you have. People do. I don't pretend to understand them, but don't worry. Marvelous things are being discovered for people with allergies. All you have to do is to let Regina advise you. You're lucky that she knows so much about skin care."

Shari was fingering her bracelets. "Wasn't it odd that both Mama and you had the same idea about those crystal bottles?"

"Very."

"Don't you hate someone else having some lovely idea you thought was all yours?"

"Perhaps."

"They're still talking about it downstairs. Nikos thinks it's a wonderful idea—but then lots of Greeks are very rich, aren't they?" Her eyes were bright, watching Eve. "Shall I go back and then come up later and tell you all the things they are saying?"

"No, Shari. Thank you."

"All right, then, I'll go down and listen to it and keep it all to myself!" She flung round toward the door. "As you had the same idea as Mama about those cosmetic bottles, I thought you'd be interested."

"If I had been, I'd have stayed."

Shari gave her a shrewd look. "Would you? Oh, Mama didn't think so. When you left the drawing room she apologized to Guido and Nikos. She said, 'I'm afraid Eve has moods. And she is obviously upset because I had an idea for those crystal bottles before she could suggest it to me.' Or," Shari said with a quick shrug of her shoulders, "words like that."

"Shari—I'm very tired—"

"Which means you want to get rid of me. All right, I'll go." She flounced out of the room and slammed the door.

Eve sank into a chair and put her face in her hands. The more contact she had with Shari, the more she felt that her aggressiveness was a cover for hurt. Downstairs in the drawing room she would have listened to adult conversation but would not have been part of it or even noticed, except perhaps to have been reprimanded for slouching in her chair.

Eve thought: *I should have done more for her. But how could I?* Regina had never encouraged a friendship between them—she had made it very clear that Shari was not to be drawn into Eve's own circle of friends. Nor had she any hobbies except her passion for the beauty products that surrounded her. She was not easy to amuse or entertain, and there always seemed to be too many tensions blotting out any effort to understand that strange, charmless child.

And now it was too late.

XXVI

THE HOUSE WAS VERY QUIET. Eve's door was closed and Adrian supposed that she was probably asleep. Later he would go to her, wake her and tell her that he had done what she wanted and taken the casket away from the anteroom where it seemed to haunt her. And there would have to be his explanation, too, as to why he had told Regina about her plan for crystal cosmetic bottles. He had to make Eve understand. But first, he must get the casket from the anteroom safe to the one in his office.

It was after twelve o'clock. After being well fed and briefed in what they had to do, Nikos and Guido were gone. There had been tremendous discussions about marketing and Regina had sent Adrian to her office for some papers connected with British marketing. It had been the last thing they had discussed before the two men left, and Adrian realized that he had forgotten to return the papers to the filing cabinet in Marion's office. But it would do in the morning. The papers would be quite safe in the drawing room overnight.

He took the casket out of the safe, moving very quietly because he didn't want to disturb Eve until he could assure her that it was no longer too near to disturb her peace of mind.

The corridors of the Berkeley Square house were always softly lit all night, and he went down the curving staircase to the executive floor so that the sound of the elevator would not reach Regina's sharp ears.

His footsteps made no sound on the thick sapphire carpet of the floor leading to his office. To the left was the curving passage that led to Regina's office. He walked purposefully forward, carrying the beautiful casket carefully so that the loose jewels inside would not scratch against one another. It had been part of his joy that they lay there glittering and not enclosed in their leather cases, which he had piled at the back of one of the filing cabinets in his secretary's office.

And suddenly he heard the swish of silk. He stopped dead. It was too late to go back or to race forward.

Regina had come round the curve in the passage and was standing in front of him.

"What are you doing with that casket?"

"It's useful for keeping some personal things in. After all," he added, with a touch of self-justification, "the casket was doing nothing, simply standing on that table outside my study."

"It was placed on that table by *me*; the casket, which as you know is very valuable, isn't yours to use for whatever it is you want to lock away. What *have* you got in it, anyhow?"

"Oh, just a few—"

"A few what?" She reached forward and turned the tiny gold key which was in the lock.

Adrian held the box tightly against him. "Mother—don't!"

"Don't what? Open something that happens to belong to me? Oh . . . " It was a long-drawn sound. "Oh, my God!" She stared down, her body tense and riveted. Then she put out a hand, picked up a diamond necklace and let the jewels slide through her fingers and fall with a silken rustle into the box.

"Mother, please understand—"

She gripped his arm and pulled him into the nearest door and switched on the light. Three empty desks and chairs, three covered typewriters and some filing cabinets were all that the room contained. She took the casket from Adrian and set it down on a side table, pushing some orange and blue files aside. Then she faced him. "Now! Perhaps you'll explain."

"They're mine," he said, with a touch of defiance, "I bought them and I don't have to explain—"

"Oh, but you do, Adrian, you do!" She dug her hand in and scooped up sapphires and the great emerald ring. "There is a fortune here—and, Adrian my dear, you don't *have* a fortune— you lost the right to dip into Contessa funds many years ago. So, how is it that on the salary I pay you, for all its generosity, you can have acquired—this—this hoard?"

"Mother, I'm not a child, nor am I any longer a young man. I don't have to account to you—"

"I'm afraid you do, because, you see, it is very obvious that the money didn't come from any saving of your salary. And you haven't sold the yacht; we still have the family plane; we still have the Cotswold house. So, dear, just don't prevaricate. Give me a straight answer."

"The straight answer," he said with spirit, "is that I work damned hard all day and every day—we seldom have our weekends to ourselves without entertaining some executive or other; we have amassed a fortune and so I think I have a right to some of it to spend as *I* wish."

"All this—what you call—hard work you have always seemed to enjoy."

"I do. Mother, I *do*! But because I work as hard as you do, I have a right—"

"To spend your salary, yes. But you could never have bought all this with what you earn, my dear." Her tone was harsh. "And, it would be interesting to know *why* you bought it. Against inflation? Or—"

"Eve." he whispered her name.

"Ah-h-h-h-! So once again your infatuation for a woman has led you into trouble. But unless you wish to deck her out like a Christmas tree—"

"I give her presents when I wish!" he said angrily.

"On borrowed money. Tell me, where did you borrow the money from? Or do I need to ask?" She saw his face go gray with fear. "Of course. From my profits. That's it, isn't it? Just as last time. And what do you imagine is going to happen when the auditors come?"

"There'll be no discrepancy."

"Then you are either a magician or a fool."

"I'm selling the jewelry."

"Yes," she blazed at him, "you damned well are. And tomorrow morning. Do you hear? Don't let me find you in the office. You obviously know your way round the most expensive jewelers in London, so take that journey again and come back with some good large checks. And while you are doing that, I will deal with Eve."

"Eve has nothing to do with this. In fact—"

"On your admission, she has. You didn't buy that . . . that hoard for some mistress—you're not the type of man to have a mistress, you're too besotted with what you've got. So, I will deal with Eve."

He said with spirit, "If it hadn't been for Eve hating the lot and loathing the idea of them being kept in my personal safe in the anteroom, you would never have set eyes on these tonight, Regina. It's because I was fool enough to show this box to Eve and make a promise to get them away from that safe that I'm here now."

"How loyal you are, my dear! I could have wished you were as considerate of this business, which keeps you in great comfort! And if you weren't my son and I loved you, you would be in dire trouble over trying to use *my* money without my knowing. You fool . . . oh, you fool! And all for what? A little upstart beauty."

"I've promised you that I'll get rid of the lot tomorrow!"

She said, "It would please me so much more, my dear, if you would get rid of Eve."

For a moment there was dead silence. Then Adrian said very quietly, "That will never happen."

"Or," she said softly without taking her eyes from his face, "it might."

"Eve won't leave me." He said it with violence and yet, in his heart, not knowing whether it was true. He felt himself trembling and tense, reaching out with one hand to grip the table. The jewels mocked and glittered under the light.

"Two women—" Regina spoke slowly with a new weariness in her voice. "Two women in your life who have nearly broken you—*would* have broken you had I not been strong. Will you never learn your lesson?"

"Not if it's one that rids me of Eve."

She regarded him through narrowed eyes. "Get out of my sight! And take that." She pointed to the casket. "Tomorrow, I shall have to rethink your position in the business."

"For God's sake," he burst out, "I'm 'family'! You can't demote me. What I did I did for love of Eve. I give you my word nothing like this will ever happen again. It was—it was just that Eve loves beautiful things and I love to give them to her . . . "

"Greed!"

"No, she's not greedy." He saw that, in trying to ease his own position in his mother's eyes, he had placed the blame on Eve. "She's beautiful and she's a woman—naturally lovely things attract her. I know . . . I know I've been a fool. But I give you my word that the books will be straight when the auditors come."

"My dear Adrian, *I* give you *my* word that they will!" she snapped back.

"Please don't talk to Eve about all this. Everything will be put right and there will be no need—"

"I shall do precisely what I think best. Don't give me orders in my own house."

"Isn't it mine, too?"

"Not yet. It's your home, but that is a different matter. Now, *get out of my sight!* Or do I have to tell you a third time?"

Adrian picked up the casket and walked out of the room without a word. He had no idea how long Regina remained in the room. He went straight to his office and put the casket in the safe. He knew he could sell the jewels, but he dreaded the thought that he would probably be known at each jeweler's shop he went to, even though he would sell the necklace where he had bought the emerald and the turquoise and diamond earrings where he had bought the sapphire brooch. The jewelers knew him too well to try to offer low prices. Adrian Thayer of Contessa Cosmetics was probably selling because things were not going well between himself and his wife. But Adrian knew perfectly well that they would buy whatever he offered because they would know that one day he would return for other diamonds, other emeralds.

Far more important was the anxiety as to what Regina might do to punish him. It could not be too drastic because he was her only son, and strong though she was, she could not run the business without him. One thing she had said stood out in his mind.

I will deal with Eve.

He saw another confrontation and dreaded it. A wild thought crossed his mind: If only he had never met Eve he might have met and married a girl he could never love obsessively but who would have fitted into the world of Contessa Cosmetics, have got on well with Regina, borne children quickly and easily. There would have been no great obsessive love—but there would have been peace in his life . . . It was too late now. He thought: Dear God, tomorrow Regina will send for Eve and the three of us will be on a collision course—and there is nothing I can do to stop it . . .

254

He went out of his room, along the softly lit corridor to the penthouse stairs. Shari was sitting halfway up, her dressing gown tucked round her, hugging her knees.

"Hullo, Adrian. I couldn't sleep."

"As none of us seem to have gone to bed particularly early," he said curtly, "you aren't an exception in that!"

"Are you angry with me?"

"Yes, if you decide to sit on the stairs at half past twelve at night. You were told to go to bed some time ago, so go."

She got up as he reached her and slid her arm through his. "Eve was very angry tonight, wasn't she?"

"Was she?"

"Oh, don't pretend! You know she was. And it would have been much worse if Nikos and Guido hadn't been there. It was about those glass scent bottles they both had the same idea for, wasn't it?"

"Suppose you go to bed and stop being inquisitive about things that don't concern you!"

They had reached the top of the staircase. Shari traced the delicate lines of the wrought iron with a slow, thoughtful finger. "Mama doesn't like Eve, does she?"

"Of course she does. Now stop probing." He was angry and tired, and those small, dark-brown eyes were far too penetrating. He heard himself saying, "When people marry and families live together, there have to be adjustments. But everything works out in the end for most of us. When we have a family of our own, Eve and I—"

"Are you going to?"

"Of course." He tried to push past her.

She was still holding his arm and she lifted her head, her face a blank. "Oh . . . "

There was a sad, forlorn look about her as she stood there, thin and small in her blue dressing gown. It moved Adrian to say reassuringly, "It'll make all the difference, having our own family—Eve and I—"

"Yes," she said. "Yes, it will, won't it?"

"And now, off you go to bed."

She reached up and kissed him and went quickly away toward her bedroom.

Adrian entered Eve's room. It had been a strain trying to keep the lightness in his voice while talking to Shari. Now, facing Eve, he shed all pretense.

She was seated in a low chair, a green robe wrapped tightly round her as though she were cold. He leaned against the dressing table and said in a tight voice, "Regina knows."

"She made that very obvious. You broke your word to me. You told her about my plan—" She saw the flash of bewilderment that crossed his face, and said quickly, "Adrian, don't lie, please. No one else who knew about the plan would have done this to me."

His face cleared. "Oh, you're talking about that scent bottle idea of yours. So far as that's concerned, darling, please don't make a fuss. You must understand, nothing can be secret in this house, nothing must ever be. We work as a team and so I had to tell Regina. After all, she would have known sooner or later."

"And I," Eve said icily, "planned for it to be later."

"You must believe me over one thing. I didn't dream she would take the whole plan out of your hands and pretend that it was her own. I couldn't have imagined—"

"It doesn't matter any longer." She cut him short, her voice slow and spiritless. "I have something far more important that has to be said."

"So have I. Eve, when I told you that Regina knew—I had something else in my mind, not your crystal bottles. Regina knows—about the jewels."

She made no movement but asked in a small, disinterested voice. "How?"

"I took the casket down to my office tonight—I thought it would be a time when no one would see me. But Regina was coming out of her office—she had been returning some papers I had brought her earlier. She saw the casket and she made me open it. Eve—she knows." He paused and added bitterly, "There was a scene—"

Eve looked across the room at him. "Of course, there would be."

"I had to give her my word that I would take the whole lot out and sell them tomorrow—go around from jeweler to jeweler with that damned hoard—"

"It's what you promised me you would do days ago," she reminded him, without reproach or interest. And then, with sudden curiosity, added, "What reason did you give her for having bought them in the first place?"

"I told her the truth—that I did it all for you. I said I couldn't refuse you anything."

"*Refuse* me?" She became suddenly alive again. "You said *that*? You blamed me and *my* demands—"

"Eve, it's really true. Not the demands, but the fact that you are really responsible—through being loved so much. Or that was how it was until I realized what a goddamned mess I was getting myself into."

"You mean what a mess *I* told you you were getting yourself into." All the previous deadness of feeling had fled. She shook with a new anger. "It's a pity you weren't truthful as well when Regina found you out. I didn't want those jewels—you knew that! You bought them, you tell yourself, in order to keep my love. That, in itself, is humiliating enough to me—the thought that all this time you have known me so little that you were sure that, if there was any risk of trouble between us, a few diamonds would buy me back into the Contessa fold! And if you think that then you are deceiving yourself. You bought those jewels because *I* was linked with your idea of possession. 'What I have I hold.' That's the general motto here, isn't it?"

"Eve, stop!"

"I can't! I won't!" Dismay, disillusion gave her new and flaming energy. "So there was a scene between you and Regina and I was made the greedy scapegoat. And I suppose you told her that all you have done has been done out of love for me . . . love . . .

257

love. The word gets bandied about so much that it ceases to mean anything but 'I want to possess.' Well, it's over. You don't possess me, Adrian. *It's over.* It has to be over. Nothing can keep me here now."

There was not a quiver of change in his expression. He said in a whisper, "Oh, but Eve, you must realize that I can't let you go."

The fire that had suddenly swept her, left her with a heavy weariness. "Just let me be, will you, Adrian? There's nothing more to say tonight. Please go." She reached up and undid the slender gold chain round her throat.

He snatched it from her and threw it roughly onto the floor.

"Please don't do that," she said, "It was my stepfather's wedding present to me. I love it." She picked it up and then stumbled a little as he grasped her arm, dragging her round to face him.

"You aren't leaving me. That's not the way things are ever going to be between us."

She said as quietly as she could to calm the sudden wild look in his eyes, "When one of two people says, 'It's over,' then I'm afraid it is. Adrian, don't let's break with bitterness. It would be a far more terrible thing for us to stay together. We aren't making each other happy and in the end we'd destroy one another. We're worlds apart."

"To hell with all that nonsense! All right, then, we're worlds apart—and the worlds have come together and like it or not, it's going to stay that way."

"Blame me, if you like. If you could, then perhaps you would find it easier to let me go. Because I *am* going. And I *am* half at fault because I believed we had a real love affair. And it was, in its way, but it didn't last. So—"

His hand came down and struck her sharply across the face.

It startled her, but she didn't reel from the stinging blow. She shut her eyes, turning her head away and waiting, expecting another. If it came, then it would merely mean that she would not wait until morning but pack and leave immediately. Her cheek burned with the stinging blow, but she didn't put her hand up to touch it.

Adrian asked, in a whisper, "Who is he?"

"There is no one." She sat down on the bed and rested her head against the carved post. "I'm leaving you for the reason I have already given you. We no longer make each other happy, and I believe that happiness is more important than clinging to some abstract idea of duty. I shall go back to the life I had before I met you. I want nothing from you. I shall probably study design and I'll make a good living for myself. We're making a break at the right time, Adrian, before too much suffering takes place."

In a single spring he was on her, his face so near hers that she turned her head rather than look into those fierce stranger's eyes. She tried to wrench herself away from him but he fought her and ripped her fragile dress at the shoulder. And all the while he imprisoned her, he was gasping words that were forced from him almost as though he hated her.

"Get one thing . . . clear. No other . . . bloody man will ever have you. Not Scott . . . if he's on your mind. But he isn't, is he? You could . . . never be a . . . poor man's wife . . . And by our standards he is poor. And *your* standards, my darling . . . your high, rich standards that I brought you . . . can only be matched by . . . some bastard with millions. You may find him, but I won't let you go."

He was speaking with his lips against her throat. She cried out. "You're hurting me—" and pushed frantically as his hands pressed hard against her ribs.

Taken unawares by her sudden strength, he fell away from her and she got up from the bed and went to the far side of the room. She tried to think of words to say that could sound reasonable and steady him.

"Perhaps our worlds are so impossible to merge because mine was very free and casual and yours here is—well, to me anyway—claustrophobic. So many women would be content to live your way—" she stopped speaking. She had so nearly said, *But I doubt it unless they were devoid of any individuality.* Instead, she added tiredly, "Please do as I ask you, Adrian. Please go now."

She had her back to him, staring out at the darkness broken only by the oblong lights from the windows of the tall buildings and an occasional car's headlights. Her hands were clenched and she scarcely dared to break the silence, even by breathing. She was willing him to go. But there were no receding footsteps, no closing of doors between the two rooms. No sound came. Tension rose in her again so that her heartbeats were wild and irregular. *He has got to go. We can't remain here like two silent, inanimate objects . . .*

Then she heard it—that most alarming of sounds—a man's wild sobbing.

Pity swept over her. Through it all—the arguments, the tensions, the attempts to break down her resistance, to mold her—she had seen too clearly the weakness that lay in him and in Regina: the inability to accept defeat. Then the need to comfort overcame her aversion to prolonging the ugly scene.

She turned and went to Adrian who was leaning against the wall near the door, his hands over his face. She said gently, "We do terrible things to one another in the name of love, Adrian, we all do. I have hurt you, but you have hurt me. You broke a confidence; you gave Regina a chance to defeat the one thing I could have done that might have saved our marriage, given me an interest, given me back my faith in myself, in my ability. I needed work, creative work. But between you, you and Regina put a stop to any hope of my being useful in life. *That* was how *you* hurt me. I hurt you because I couldn't give up everything for Contessa Cosmetics. And because neither of us could compromise, it is obvious we don't love one another the right way. That's why it has to be over."

He took his hands from his face. It was blotched, but no tears showed. She wondered if the sounds she had heard had, after all, been sobbing or hysteria.

Still leaning against the wall, he said without raising his voice.

260

"*Won't* you understand? No other . . . bloody man . . . will have . . . you."

The words and the voice held an extraordinary quiet menace that made her shudder as if she sensed a threat without knowing what form it would take. She said again, desperately, "There *is* no other man."

She saw his eyes narrow in disbelief. He began speaking softly, as if to himself. "The pattern never changes. Oh heaven, dear heaven, the pattern never changes!" His hands moved convulsively, clenching, twisting, and his fine Viking-blue eyes seemed to blacken. For the first time since she had known him, Eve was afraid. He stood there making those strange sounds that were not exactly sobs and yet were torn from him. His eyes, his skin, even the bone structure of his face had suddenly collapsed. He was Adrian and yet not Adrian. It was as if, when there was no more hope, no more seeing someone through the haze of illusory love, her mind was so clear that she saw reality. She saw Adrian, no longer proud with love but thwarted.

She had heard of primitive fear, now she understood it. In those moments, when they stood there like enemies stalking one another, she tried to rationalize her fear. Somewhere at the back of her mind was something Regina had once said. At the time she had passed it off. If she could—if she only could remember . . .

She heard Adrian say, "At least, Eve, grant me one thing."

"What do you want?"

"Just one more night together." He had come close to her and drew her into his arms, his eyes watching her too closely.

She said quietly, without resisting his hands held tightly round her. "It wouldn't work . . . it couldn't. It would be just what so much has been—a fantasy; not real . . . "

"One last magnificent love night!" he said softly.

It was all out of character. Adrian was never inclined to use pretentious words, nor was the voice in the least like his usual modulated tone. It had the curious hazy pitch of someone talking in a dream.

She pulled away from him. "Adrian, we can't!"

He was trembling violently. But it wasn't that which frightened her; it wasn't anything she could explain. Fear raced like a fire through her; she was as terrified as she had been in the locked garage. But this time it was not of an unknown enemy.

XXVII

SHE RACED TO THE DOOR and out of the room, hearing him call her name. She ran down the passage and, without any real awareness of where she was going, ran down the semicircular staircase, past the executive floor, the salons on the floors below and down the double staircase that led to the columned hall.

Her crystal profile in its glass case was turned her way as if watching her, the subtle lighting giving an almost unearthly beauty to the sculpture. It flashed through her mind that its serenity isolated it from her; it was no longer her face lit with soft, calm luminosity like moonlight.

She fled to the great doors leading to Berkeley Square, then changed her mind and ran the other way, through a passage, past the staff interviewing room to the door that led to the garden.

When she unlocked it and stepped outside, she glanced upward, drawn by a light in the conservatory. Without stopping to remember the last time she had stepped onto that outside stairway, she raced up it to the conservatory door. Then she paused and looked in. Regina was inside, seated in one of the cane chairs, head bent, hands limp, as if she were asleep.

The door was locked and Eve hammered on it.

Regina gave a great start, lifted her head, rose slowly to her feet and came and unlocked the door. Eve almost fell in, breathless from her panic race from Adrian.

She leaned against the thick glass by a great palm as Regina locked the door again.

"Really, Eve, do you have to come rushing in here like—" she stopped, peered more closely at Eve and asked sharply, "What is the matter?"

Eve shook her head. She was still breathing heavily and her legs shook.

Regina asked again, more sharply, "What is it, Eve?"

There was only one way, and that was to tell the truth briefly and starkly. Regina was no sensitive, gentle mother whose feelings must be tenderly considered.

Eve said, "I have just told Adrian that I am leaving him."

"*And?*" The word came swift as a shot.

Eve said, still leaning against the cool glass wall, "I'm frightened." She waited. Regina didn't speak. Eve said again, "Regina, I'm frightened—and I don't know why. But I've got to get away. I'm not fitting into your world and although I've tried, I know I never will. It's best for everyone. But I know—I know—that Adrian—"

"Go on."

Eve said on a soft, scared breath, "I'm frightened of what he might do."

"Oh, my God!"

Regina reached back and felt the arm of a rattan chair behind her. She sank into it, and watching her, it seemed to Eve that she saw nothing of the scene around her, that her eyes were looking inward—or back into the past—and that what she saw terrified her. And Regina terrified was, in itself, shocking.

Eve couldn't bear the deadly silence of that green and scented place. "Why are you looking like that? It isn't because I've said I'm leaving Adrian—it's not that, is it? Something is wrong, something that has *always* been wrong only nobody has told me what it is."

Regina remained silent, sitting with her fingers gripping the arms of the rattan chair so hard that the fibers creaked under the pressure.

"*Regina!*"

Eve's desperate, compelling tone roused the older woman. She got up and walked slowly to the little fountain and looked down into the water.

Eve moved away from the wall and went to Regina's side. "Why didn't you laugh at me when I said I was frightened? Why didn't you tell me I was a fool to be scared of my own gentle husband?"

Regina asked, "Where is Adrian?"

"In my room. Or he was. Why?"

The fierce dark eyes met Eve's. "Go back and tell him it was all a mistake. Go back and say you will not leave him."

"That isn't what *you* want!"

"God help me, I'm not thinking of myself."

"Because you want me to go—of course you do. I don't fit in with your schemes and I understand. Then why are you asking me to go back to Adrian? *Why?*"

Regina said in a strained voice, as if every word were forced reluctantly from her, "You think you understand, but you don't. You can't. And why should I tell you? Adrian is my son—what happened in the past is between us and nobody else."

"If whatever it is affects my relationship with him, then you must tell me. And it does, doesn't it? *Doesn't it?*"

Regina had risen from her chair and they faced each other, for a moment or two neither speaking, the only sound being the water dancing into the green marble of the fountain basin.

"You have never understood Adrian," Regina said.

"In the beginning, no. But then we all make mistakes in people, don't we? Something about them touches a chord no one else has touched and from there we begin to see just what we want to see. It's different now. Reality always catches up in the end. The blinkers are off, Regina, I have seen what I never dreamed I'd see. I have to leave Adrian and he has convinced himself that he can never let me go. It isn't love. It's obsession. I know. I know. *Adrian cannot lose what is his.* He is determined to hold me and that's what frightens me. Regina, what is it about him, about his character, that ties in somehow with something that happened in the past?"

"The past is dead . . . It has to be dead . . . " Her voice had the flatness of defeat. She sank down on the wide rim of the fountain basin.

Eve saw her suddenly as old, the vitality stripped from her like a skin; the eyes, lifted momentarily to Eve, empty of light. In that flash between them Eve suddenly felt herself to be the strong one, the one who could demand. She said with a new firmness, "No, Regina, that's just it. The past isn't dead. What I want to know is—what *is* the past? What *is* it that I have never been told? The secret . . . ?"

Regina's spirit rallied. She said with sudden firmness, "Eve, you must not leave Adrian."

"There is no 'must' about it, and you know that. Why stall? Why 'mustn't' I leave Adrian—as if something terrible will happen if I do? Because that's it, isn't it? From your point of view there is nothing you'd like better than for me to leave him, leave your house. You know, as well as I, that there is no meeting place for us. I anger you and I can understand. You want a daughter-in-law who will merge with the business, who will make it her life, as you do, as Adrian does. So why . . . Regina, *why* do you tell me I must not leave Adrian?"

266

"Oh God, what have I done?" Regina cried, lifting her hands like a supplicant. "What have we all done?"

"Yes," Eve asked quietly. "What?"

"It was so long ago." Regina sat, head bent, watching the diamond sparkle of the water. "I thought it was over—that it was a young, terrible brainstorm. I thought, after all these years, Adrian was cured; that such a thing would never happen, *could* never happen once he learned to be adult in his behavior. But all the time I watched and was . . . yes, *I*—my dear Eve—was afraid."

"Why, Regina, why?"

"Youth is so impetuous and I told myself that Adrian was a late developer. He was only twenty-one when it happened. The courts are full of cases of the young doing terrible and foolish things. But they grow out of it. They—"

"*What—happened—?*"

Regina didn't lift her head. The light shone on her carefully tinted bronze hair, her crimson robe swirled round her as if it had been arranged by a photographer for a formal portrait. But, for all her elegance, Regina's expression was pitiable.

The swift compassion that was part of Eve's nature but which had never before been manifested where her mother-in-law was concerned, softened her voice as she said, "I think the time is past for hiding things, don't you? Please, let's talk like adults. Adrian is my husband. I know it's said that when two people marry, their past lives should be left undiscussed if that's the way they want it. I can see that to open up the past indiscretions and mistakes that we all make asks for recriminations. But this is different, isn't it? This is very serious."

"Yes."

"What is it *you* didn't tell me and Adrian didn't dare?"

There was a sound in the great dim ballroom beyond the conservatory. They both stiffened, listening. It was only Benson, obviously puzzled at the lights in the conservatory at that late hour. They saw him glance toward them and then go quietly out.

But to Regina and Eve, he seemed a thousand miles away.

"Perhaps I should have told you," Regina was saying. "But how could I? And if I had, how could I believe that you would respect it as a confidence?"

"Then you must risk it now. The truth, Regina . . . Because it's too late for anything else. I'm leaving Adrian."

Regina met Eve's eyes with blank resignation. "When you came rushing in here tonight in a panic, I knew then that you knew."

"But I don't. I'm waiting for you to tell me. What is it that I should have been told a long time ago?"

Regina met question with question. "What did Adrian say to you tonight that frightened you? Or—what did he—do?"

"All he said was that if I planned to leave him, at least let us have—what he called, 'One last magnificent love night together.' I don't know why that made me afraid—perhaps it was because he doesn't go in for flamboyant sentences. But it was more than that. It was something about the way he looked at me—I've seen that look before, in a play I think, I can't remember, but it was the same—and in the play they were . . . I remember . . . they were . . . "

"Go—on—"

"The eyes of a madman."

Regina's despairing cry broke through. "Oh God! He said it to you, too? As he said it to Olivia after I had paid her to leave him."

"Who is—was—Olivia?"

"A girl he loved many years ago, when he was only twenty-one, the one girl out of all those who threw themselves at him that he wanted to marry. I stopped it. She was wrong for him. I paid her off."

"Just like that!" Eve cried. "Well, if she was the kind of girl to be paid off—"

"She was, but Adrian refused to see it. He loved her—in his way."

"You mean he was obsessed by her?"

268

"Yes. She was so lovely. But in her heart she had one word written indelibly. Money. The good life was all she wanted."

(Money . . . success . . . Oh, Regina, she was one of you!)

"So what happened?"

"Adrian appeared to accept the fact that it was over. But he pleaded with her for 'one last magnificent night' together. She agreed. I knew later that she believed it would not be the end of the affair, that that night would result in their marriage. It didn't. Adrian"—Regina was finding the words difficult to say, but they came, strangled and painful—"Adrian tried to kill her. That was his idea of a —"

A last magnificent love night . . .

"But he didn't kill her?" Eve asked faintly. "Regina, he didn't?"

"No. Olivia screamed, she screamed so loudly that the man who was then our night watchman heard her. He saved her and we managed to hush it up."

"With money."

"Of course. Olivia had planned that she would be such a lover to Adrian that night that he would defy me and marry her. They had their 'wonderful night,' but she never dreamed what the aftermath might be. Adrian did not dare to go against my wishes—he was so young, and in those days he always ended by doing what I told him. But he couldn't face the thought of some other man possessing Olivia so—he tried to strangle her. She escaped in terror. I paid her off, but she held a sword over our heads. She came to our Cotswold house one weekend and told me that she was pregnant and that it had happened on that last terrible night."

"You believed her?"

Regina nodded. "I had to. I dared not let her take the matter to court."

Eve sat down weakly by her mother-in-law's side on the fountain's rim. "Where is Olivia now?"

"I don't know." She put her hands to her face. "I thought it was all over—that madness. But now you—"

"Regina, help me. Please . . . You understand that it's impossible for me to remain here. Make Adrian see that. Find him, please, and keep him while I pack a few things."

Regina rose. "Stay here until I return." She went swiftly out of the conservatory.

Eve remained where she was, the warm, sweet smell of the hothouse plants enclosing her in a world that had suddenly become unreal. It was ironical that Regina, who had been her enemy, should now perhaps be her rescuer.

XXVIII

THE SOUND THAT BROKE the stillness came from inside the house. Something crashed with the long-drawn, splintering sound of breaking glass. Immediately the alarm that was attached to Regina's crystal sculptures rang loudly.

Eve started up and began to run, pushing through the conservatory door, racing across the great room beyond and down the Grand Staircase to the hall from where the sound had seemed to come. The alarm had stopped ringing, but the hall was full of people—Regina and the domestic staff—Benson and Martha the cook, and Solange and behind them one of the penthouse maids. Adrian was racing down the stairs, taking them two at a time.

271

Regina was pointing to a carpet that glittered in the light from the chandeliers. Her face was gray and her body rigid.

The plinth that stood between the two curves of the double stairway was bare. Contessa Cosmetics' prize sculpture no longer dominated the great columned hall. Eve's wonderful likeness lay in glittering splinters on the sapphire carpet.

Regina broke the stunned stillness. "*Who—did—that?*"

Silence greeted her words.

"Someone speak," she thundered, her voice ringing round the high marble hall. "Who came past and knocked into that plinth?"

Cook spoke, sounding indignant. "None of us were up here, my lady. We were watching late television—"

"So that's what you do when you should be asleep and resting for your work tomorrow! But, since you were up and awake, then I suppose you were too carried away by some foolish movie to be aware that someone was breaking into my house."

Tom Halligon, arriving from the passage leading to the garden, said, "No one has broken in, my lady. All the outer doors are locked and bolted. I have checked."

Regina swept past them to the small interviewing room. "Send for the police, Tom. And all of you come in here and wait."

Solange, who feared no one, said stoutly, "Madame, you cannot send for the police because something in your house has been broken and there is no evidence of forced entry." Her English, when she was sufficiently resolute on a subject to use it, was perfect. "Someone must have knocked over that beautiful piece and dare not own up." She looked about her, her black stare arrogant because of her favored place in the Contessa establishment.

Suddenly, unexpectedly, the doorbell rang. Tom went to answer it. Voices sounded in the hall. Tom's and another man's. Footsteps crossed the marble hall.

Scott Somerset walked into the room.

Regina looked at him as though she could not believe he had

materialized in front of her. "What are you doing in my house at this time of night? And—uninvited?"

"I have something very important to say. But first, let your staff go." He stood aside for them. "What I have to say is just for the family."

"Don't give orders in my house."

"Let them go," Scott said very quietly.

Regina made a gesture of dismissal, warning them, "But all of you keep yourselves free to come when I call you. You will be interviewed by me later, one by one. Solange, you stay."

They slid out of the room, silently.

Regina said, "Do you realize what time it is?"

"Yes, it's coming up to the early hours of tomorrow. But you were entertaining and so I waited outside until your guests had gone."

"Since you did, then perhaps you will say whatever it is that you have on your mind. If it's to do with the business of the moisturizer, I fail to see why you disturb my whole household in this outrageous fashion."

"It seems your household is already badly disburbed. Who smashed that magnificent sculpture of Eve's head?"

"We are in the process of finding out."

"Are you? I wonder if you could ever guess? What I have to say is, I believe, linked with that smashed crystal in your hall. You see, I know who made that attempt on Eve's life in the garage and who surely was responsible for this act of vandalism, too."

The silence could have lasted for a flash of time or a matter of minutes. Eve couldn't tell.

Then Scott broke the silence. "I think we might have Shari here. She is 'family,' after all. She has a right to hear—"

"Hear what?" Adrian demanded. "At this time of night, too! A child needs her sleep—"

"Child? These days, fourteen is not childish, I'm afraid."

Regina turned to Solange, "Fetch her." Then she said to Scott, "So you think you know who tried to harm Eve! Well, you seem to be wiser than the police. That's strange, since their investigations indicate that it must have been some casual passer-by, probably just hating the rich. But *you* say you know."

"Yes."

"I will congratulate you when you can prove your extraordinary statement."

"Oh, I can prove it."

"And can you prove, also, who broke my most valuable piece of sculpture?"

"I think so."

"Then you must be a remarkable man."

"No. You may perhaps say that I'm the watcher on the outside. You are all too close, too claustrophobic here. You can't—or maybe you won't—see what has stared you in the face. Ah, Solange. Where is Shari?"

"I've searched everywhere, Madame—oh, but everywhere—and I cannot find her. She is not in the house."

Regina gave a strangled half cry. "Oh, dear heaven! You see what has happened! Someone has got her . . . There must have been a struggle—Shari would fight—and that's how the sculpture got broken. But who took her? Oh, the child would fight but none of us heard! Get the police; get—"

"No one has 'got' her," Scott rapped.

Eve had been staring down, dismayed and fascinated by the glitter of the smashed sculpture. Among the diamond-white pieces were chips of deep mauve, the color of amethyst. She darted forward and picked up some of the pieces, holding them in the palm of her hand.

"Look." She showed them all, Regina and Adrian and Scott, "they are amethyst chips and"—she spoke to Adrian—"do you remember when I fell on the night of the reception, I hurt my leg because something tripped me up on the outside stairway? And I found chips of amethyst and the gem rock was missing from the table near the conservatory door. And now, *just look,* chips of amethyst again, here. So someone threw that gem rock at the sculpture." *At my likeness . . . wishing it were me . . .*

Regina said, "Solange, the amethyst should be by the azaleas in the conservatory. Go and see if it is there and if so bring it to me."

Adrian had gone to the window. "There's someone outside. It's too dark to see, but it's someone small—it could be Shari. What in heaven's name is she doing at this time of night—?"

Scott moved like an Olympic runner. He shot out of the room, Eve and Adrian racing after him. She heard Regina's slower footsteps on the parquet floor of the narrow hall that led to the garden door.

It was open, and Scott had disappeared into the night. Eve raced across the garden to the staff door that led to the street. It was securely locked with the extra burglar-proof lock Regina had had put on after the experience in the garage. Then she turned and saw Scott at the foot of the old walnut tree.

"Shari!"

Looking up, they saw in the lights from the house a white face and the hem of a blue robe.

Regina's voice carried clearly. "Come down at once, Shari."

There was no reaction. Regina's voice carried powerfully for a second time through the dark garden. "Scott is here and he has something important to tell us. He knows who made the attempt on Eve's life in the garage. Surely, you want to know, don't you, darling?" Her voice softened and became caressing. "But we can't shout it up to you. Come, please, don't play games. It's very late."

Shari broke into a wild fury of sobbing. "I won't! I never want to come down again." She parted the branches and looked directly at Eve. "Why didn't you *go*? Why didn't you get scared when things happened to you and got out of here? You don't belong . . . Mama said so. But you just stayed and stayed. And tonight I heard—I listened and Adrian was angry with you, too. He shouted at you. And you just went running to Mama instead of leaving us. We were happy till you came. Oh, I could kill you. You've taken everything—you've taken Adrian—"

"Shari, stop it! You're hysterical." Regina called in a voice sharp with agitation. "And come down here."

"She'll never belong . . . you said so, Mama, *you* said so. And *I* do! Or I *did*!"

It was a child's ranting but it was also a woman's hatred. Eve moved to escape the tirade against her, to hide from that frantic little face among the walnut leaves.

Scott held her arm. The lights from the house cast the garden in a vivid chrome yellow light.

Adrian said, "Shari, please come down and let us talk to you. It's silly to stay up there."

"I won't come down till you promise to send her away. I was happy before *she* came because I belonged. Now I don't."

"Talk sense!" Regina's voice was hard, her scant patience had snapped. "Get down from that tree and talk sense."

Scott moved closer to the twisted walnut trunk. "She *is* talking sense," he said quietly. "That's the tragedy. *Her* sense."

"Why didn't you fall on that stairway? Why didn't you hit your face and never have been beautiful again? Adrian wouldn't have loved you then. I watched you fall, but you didn't see me, did you? I hated you because you only hurt your leg. I wanted it to be your face; I wanted you to be scarred for life . . . for all your *life* . . . " She was so far in hysteria that everything poured out.

"That's enough!" Adrian said sharply. "You've got it out of your system. Now come down."

"It isn't enough and I won't come down! Why shouldn't you know *all* I did? I wanted Eve to die in the garage when I turned on both car engines—people in films die that way. I knew exactly what to do and I did it. I've been in the cars so many times that my fingerprints would be all over them, but I wore gloves when I turned on the engines. *And* I opened the garden door to the street so that everyone would think someone from outside had killed her. You see, I thought of everything . . . " A burst of weeping stopped her wild speech.

276

In the momentary silence when no one, it seemed, knew what to say to this child dominating the scene with her hate and her misery, Eve thought, "All those thrillers she reads and the violence on television—"

"I can't think you know what you are saying." Adrian's voice broke through Eve's thoughts. He was leaning against one of the staves that propped up the old tree. "It's all terrible and I've got to make you see *how* terrible. But this isn't the kind of talking we can do with you up there and us down here. Come into the house and—"

"What's terrible," Shari screamed, "is that since *she* came, I don't belong anymore—"

From where Eve stood she was aware of the light from one of the windows streaming out and illuminating her as if she were the center of some nightmare stage scene. She drew back so that she was in the shadow. The silence that had fallen again over the group around the tree was suddenly broken.

"Shari . . . Shari . . . " Regina's voice came in hard, jerking sobs. "Listen to me . . . listen. You belong . . . more than . . . anyone except Adrian. You always have and you always will. Nobody can take your place. You belong, Shari darling. Listen . . . stop crying and listen . . . You are *my* girl . . . my own . . . my real grandchild . . . *Adrian is your father.*"

The garden seemed to Eve to take a somersault; from behind her came Tom's cockney voice. "Oh, holy heaven above us!"

Adrian lurched forward, clutching the gnarled trunk of the tree, thrusting his forehead against the rough vertical fissures as if desperate for one pain to compensate another. "Oh, God in his mercy . . . my child . . . Of course, she has to be Olivia's—"

His cry rang round the garden. For moments that stretched out for too long, nobody dared obtrude on that intense shock. Adrian continued to beat his head against the tree until Regina uttered a loud, wailing cry. "Adrian . . . oh my dear . . . my dear, don't! I saved you from years of mental pain, can't you understand that? She was wrong for you; she would have destroyed you."

"Shari is—*my* child. Mine . . . " he choked on the word.

Eve went forward and then checked her movement. She didn't belong to this shocking private scene; she was as much an outsider as Scott and Tom. She ached with pity for Adrian's pain, but she knew that going to him would not help. She knew, too, that what stunned him now was not the knowledge that for fourteen years Shari had lived in his home as someone unrelated. It was something far more fundamental; his grief was not for the love he might have given and received as much as for the fact that Shari was his daughter, something owned by him without his knowledge of ownership. Had he thought of her as someone he might have loved, he would have reacted differently. He would have gone to her, spoken to her with latent love. Instead, his pain was for himself . . .

It was Regina who broke the awful silence, and her voice had that terrible strength of some fatal regret that nothing could rectify. "How could I? After all these years of silence, how—could I? But I have . . . Shari, I've spoken for your sake, to prove to you how deeply you belong—by blood, by law . . . Darling, understand. Adrian—your father now—*your father*—must love you more than anyone else in the world. Fathers do care for their daughters in a very special way. Now that you both know—"

"What *you* always knew." The branches of the tree quivered. "You let me think you took me out of—out of what, *Grand*mother. Pity? Thank you very much! I thought my mother and father were dead. Well, they aren't. And, *Grand*mother, what happened to my mother? Didn't she want me? Am I illegitimate? Well, that's no stain these days. I'm as much Contessa Cosmetics as *you* are . . . But you let me think . . ."

"Shari, what I did, I did because I believed it was for the best."

Adrian swung round on his mother. There was a gash on his forehead where he had deliberately thrust it at the tree. "What did you do? What did you do to stop me knowing that Shari was my daughter?"

"I paid Olivia off."

"You paid! Almighty heaven, we can always pay, can't we? And—"

"*And what about me?*" The voice from the tree rose to a hysterical scream. "*What about me?*"

Eve was standing back, near Tom. Like him, she was tense and alert and very still. The cool leaves of the peony bushes against the side wall felt soothing, like fingers steadying her.

Scott spoke. "Whatever your birth, my dear Shari, you had comfort and security—you had so much more than millions of young people. You've never known poverty or cruelty. So stop being sorry for yourself. Have you forgotten why you're up there?—which is a damned silly place to be, anyway. You ran away because you were hiding and listening somewhere and you knew when I arrived that you had been found out. You're very quick-brained, Shari, but you're also tainted with the need to have your own way, come hell or high water. *You* sent that malicious piece of gossip about Eve coming to my house to the newspapers; *you* arranged for that man to follow her. And with your quickness of mind you knew tonight that *I* knew. And now you can come down from that ridiculous position in the tree and behave like an adult."

She cried in the same high, wild voice, "At least I'll never have to look at Eve's face again in the hall. Mama will never have another sculpture made of her . . . Mama—ha!—I'm calling her 'Mama.' I mean, of course, *Grandma.* She didn't want me to know that I really belonged. She wanted me to think I was some . . . some charity child." Her voice had lost its hysteria and held the pathos of a defeated adolescent.

Scott's anger was too great to feel pity. "Shari, just stop dwelling on your own hurt and face a fact. You're old enough to take the truth, and you must. You tried twice to harm Eve—you could have killed her, and you know it."

"But I didn't hate her—not really. I only hated that she belonged here more than me and I wanted her to go."

"Without caring how!"

Adrian cut in. "Shari, I'm coming to fetch you." He reached

up and caught at a branch and swung himself onto the tree. They saw it sway and heard menacing creaks.

Scott cried, "That tree won't take your weight."

Adrian ignored him. He was making a tacking climb from branch to branch.

Shari cried excitedly, "Come on, Adrian . . . Father . . . that's funny! *Father* . . . Let's go away together, let's go over the wall."

"Stop playing at melodrama," Scott called.

Shari had reached the branch which hung over the wall. She scrambled onto it and the branch dipped dangerously with her weight. She sat astride the wall and turned and looked down into the street on the other side. "Come on . . . come on . . . " she was urging Adrian in a high, overexcited voice. "Let's run away together. We're rich. We can go to Bermuda and live in the sun. Father—"

She stopped suddenly as a branch Adrian had grasped gave a loud cracking sound. Regina cried out, Tom dived forward, his great bulk encompassing half the tree. Shari reached back wildly to grab Adrian's arm.

There was a rustle of leaves and a thud. One of the two thick stakes driven into the ground to hold up the ancient tree had collapsed.

Shari screamed. Tom shot forward, but Adrian fell at an angle, wide of the great arms. He didn't even cry out as he fell, but Shari gave a heartrending moan.

Adrian lay on the grass with one leg under him and his neck twisted; his body was inert in the shadow of the walnut tree.

Scott and Tom were by his side.

"The doctor . . . an ambulance . . . " Regina shouted high-pitched orders. "Go on, Tom . . . Get to the telephone . . . "

No one took any notice of Shari who was trying to find a way down from the wall, weeping in loud terrified wails.

"Fetch some rugs. Don't move him. Nobody dare move him!"

Eve, kneeling by his side, said his name softly. "Adrian . . . "

Regina hissed. "Take her away. Somebody, take her away. Get her out of my sight! She was leaving him—*now let her leave him.*"

Hands guided Eve, leading her to the house. The lights that had been switched on to illuminate Shari up in the tree, dazzled Eve. Behind her in the garden there was screaming and confusion. Eve saw Solange racing ahead of her for rugs. Tom had already vanished inside the house to the telephone.

Eve walked rather as she had done after the incident in the garage, weaving as if she couldn't find her balance.

She was aware of walking into the house, into the first room she came to, which was the little interviewing room. Cook was already there, wrapping something warm and soft round her shoulders, understanding that even on such a warm May night, shock can chill. All the servants must have formed a tight little group of watchers at the awful drama in the garden, huddled at the windows, not knowing what was expected of them. Eve could visualize them still there, still not knowing what to do, still afraid of Regina.

XXIX

SHE WAS ALONE. No one came near her for a long time after Cook had gone out of the room. Or maybe there were people there and it was just that she saw nothing, heard nothing—wrapped in a fog of limbo.

Regina's voice still seemed to hiss in Eve's mind. "Get her out of my sight!" 'Her' . . . Adrian's wife . . . *Me* . . .

She thought: They belonged—Regina, Adrian, Shari. And the same taint touched them all. *I want. I must have. If I cannot, then I will destroy* . . . Only the business, their god, was sacred.

Her eyes closed, lying uncomfortably back in the chair, Eve heard someone come into the room, then Scott's voice said, "They have taken Adrian to the hospital."

"It will be too late. I saw—the way he looked. He died—out there in the garden."

Another voice spoke, kindly, coaxing. "Here, dear Madame, drink this. A good cup of tea—"

Just as before , when she had sat in that room enveloped in shock . . .

Eve opened her eyes and saw Cook. She reached out gratefully and said, "Thank you. Oh, it's hot!" She felt it burn her throat and welcomed the pain if it would kill the greater pain of tragedy.

Scott was perched on the corner of the table watching her.

"Where is Shari?" she asked.

"The doctor has given her a sedative. It'll knock her out for hours."

"And—Regina?"

"Has gone to the hospital with Adrian in the ambulance."

Simultaneously with his answer, Eve heard Regina's voice outside in the hall, and protested. "Oh Scott, she didn't go! And *I* should have gone. What happened? Why didn't they call me when the ambulance came?"

"Regina went—and now she is back."

"But there's been no time."

He said gently, "It's nearly two o'clock."

"Then what has happened since we were all in the garden? I came straight in here and waited—"

"You were in shock and you lost count of time. Don't be scared. It can happen." He turned as Regina entered.

She held her dark, heavy cloak round her and her head was high as if she were forcing herself into a position of undefeated pride.

"Adrian—?" Eve's voice was scarcely audible. But it was unnecessary to ask. She knew.

Regina sank into one of the hard interviewing chairs. "My son is dead." She looked across the room at Scott. "*You* did this to him." Her purple eyes were full of hatred. "Why did you interfere? If you hadn't, none of this would have happened. But you

283

came into my house; you accused. And Shari heard you—she listened and she heard and knew there was no way out for her. She panicked."

"Perhaps when you are less shocked, Regina, you can think of an alternative to what I had to do, though I doubt it. While Shari ran loose, hating Eve who was to her a ursurper, your daughter-in-law's life was in danger."

"From a *child?*"

"From an adolescent who had never been taught the right values. Your grandchild. If anyone is at fault in all this, look to yourself, Regina. But this isn't the time for recriminations."

"Oh, it is . . . oh, it is! A-d-r-i-a-n-," she found it difficult to say his name. "is dead. I can take it as well now as I ever will." She was sitting up very straight, her manner defiant and arrogant and yet infinitely tragic because the defeat and the emptiness showed through. "You criticize me—you blame *me*. Very well, tell me why; tell me what I have or have not done. Enjoy attacking me and my sins because you will never have another opportunity. You will not enter this house or my laboratory again."

"I think it's best if I go now. Later—"

"Oh no. I have fought all my life. I can fight now—I mean, fight my own aversion to hearing what *you* have to say!"

"Be kind to yourself, Regina, please," Scott said gently. "You are trying to force me to hurt you more in order to change the pain. But it doesn't always work. Just wait—"

"There's nothing now to stop anything being said, so say what you wish. That's the way I want it. Then, after that one starts afresh."

Starts afresh—with her son dead. Eve's tired mind marveled. Ruthlessness or courage—she guessed the latter. Regina possessed a formidable courage that could face adversity, battle with it and win.

Scott understood. He did what Regina sat steeling herself for. He plunged straight into the truth. "Shari never knew who she was. A child living a happy, normal family life probably would give it very little thought. Shari had no such life here. She probably thought she loved her life, but deep down she was insecure and uneasy. You couldn't bring yourself to tell her the truth. I can guess why. You were afraid that if you told Adrian that Shari was his child, he would go to this woman, Olivia—and she was obviously not the material for the heir to Contessa Cosmetics. You were determined not to have her in your world. So, the lying and pretense began, and Shari lived in a paradox of spoiling and neglect."

Eve rose from the comfortable interviewer's chair. "Regina, please come and sit here."

Without raising her eyes, the offer was waved aside. As though speaking to herself, Regina said slowly, "I have told Eve; but I don't have to tell anyone else the whole story. It's over. I did what I thought was best. Olivia was beautiful and dangerous. Money was her aim and I gave it to her. I could not bear the whole ugly business to become a matter for the courts . . . " She was rocking herself backward and forward as if in pain. "Olivia would never have belonged, but Adrian could not bear to lose her. She was his . . . But the shock of what he so nearly did brought him to his senses—I hoped, oh God! I hoped for good, forever." She looked at Scott. "You tell me that Shari felt she never belonged. But she knew she did!"

"Here? In a house entirely dedicated to the beauty business, to such obsessiveness that neither you nor Adrian ever saw the damage you were doing to the child?" Scott's voice was angry. "And when Eve married into the family, Shari's world seemed to her to collapse. She wanted just the three of you—a little triangle of belonging."

Regina asked, "How do you know all you seem to know about Shari? I mean, how did you know about Shari's involvement in Eve's experiences?"

"It was simple. I went to see the gossip columnist who printed that paragraph about Eve visiting my house. Did you imagine that your staff knew nothing about it? Surely not! You are 'news,' Regina, and so is Eve, as you're only too well aware. So, like everyone else I heard about the paragraph. But I let it go because it was beneath contempt. That is, until I learned about the attempt on Eve's life. That was when I began working things out for myself. Someone was wishing her ill—someone who hoped that that paragraph would have had repercussions that could destroy her marriage. That failed, and so other means were tried. It didn't need any brilliant deductions—just a visit to a man called Saturn. I frightened the hell out of him and so he told me the name of the man who had watched Eve and supplied the information about her visits to Quintin Street, with a few scurrilous guesses thrown in."

"Saturn told me that the man was out of the country," Regina said faintly.

"Oh, but he wasn't, as you would have known had you pursued the matter as I did. I learned who had told him of Eve's visits—it was someone who lived here and had listened in to a telephone conversation. Shari."

"That is utter nonsense!" Regina showed her first flash of anger since she had returned from the hospital. "Shari doesn't know any newspapermen so how could she contact a gossip spy?"

"Oh, you'd be surprised what the girls at her school know. A friend of mine has a daughter there. Society gossip is their food and drink; they know all the twists and turns of rumors and how to spread them. It's one of what they call their 'fun' hobbies.

"Even so," Regina's voice was less certain. "Shari wouldn't—"

"Look at the truth, Regina. You heard what she said out there in the garden. It wasn't difficult for her to contact a man; someone at the school must have put them in touch. Shari would have offered him money—you do keep her well supplied. So, she got him to watch Eve; she even demanded a snapshot. Wherever it is now, I have no idea, but it was of Eve and me at the door of the house. We were saying goodbye after she had been sketching some of my sister's scent bottles."

Regina shot a covert glance at Eve. Then she rose and pulled herself together with an effort. "Of course . . . the school. And Shari has always had a gift for prying. I've tried to stop her doing it here, but she loves this place so, and all it stands for. But that she went to those lengths merely out of jealousy for Eve—"

"Oh, no," Eve heard herself say clearly. "It wasn't me personally, nor jealousy. My marriage to Adrian was to Shari the first split in that perfect, safe triangle. I was the threat from outside, because by marrying Adrian I 'belonged' as she would have put it, more than she."

Regina had seemed not to be listening. She had an uncharacteristic look of indecision on her face as if she had no idea how to hold onto her command before Scott's cold analysis and Eve's quiet insight. So she chose to escape. She said, "I must go and see if Shari is asleep." She managed to walk from the room with her usual firm step, but once out of sight, she drooped, drawing the heavy cloak round her bent shoulders.

She pressed the elevator button and the gilded cage opened. The motor hummed softly as it bore her up to the beautiful staircase to the penthouse. She leaned her head against the sapphire upholstery.

I wanted something to break up the marriage; I wanted her out of our lives. It was true that if one went all out for what one wanted, regardless of everyone else, everything else, the dream became a reality. But at a price . . . at such a price!

Retribution. The word came into Regina's mind. She tried to dismiss it, but she could not.

She entered Shari's bedroom and looked down at the sleeping child, remembering how desperately she had prayed that Eve would go out of their lives. But she had prayed to *her* gods, who had neither heart nor compassion. They had answered her prayer and in doing so had exacted the most terrible price of all. Her son. And the same warped violence of his character was in her granddaughter.

She turned from the bed and went to the window. The lights of Berkeley Square drew her as they had drawn Eve, glittering and winking through the swaying branches of the trees.

Her great mansion stood solid on its corner; her empire was safe while she still lived. The brief time of madness and irresponsibility that had lured her to risk her business integrity for a beauty preparation was gone. There would be no magic moisturizer. Hating him for his strength, Regina admitted, in the quiet of the sleeping Shari's room, that she owed Scott a debt of gratitude for saving the vast edifice of beauty that she had built. Regina's courage was as great as her ambition.

There was only Shari now, but Regina faced the fact that the heavy task ahead of her was no longer just the business—she saw that she might have to turn it into a company. But Shari was her other problem. At fourteen, it was still possible to mold her character—and it was very possible that this terrible night had taught her that the world was not just for her own pleasure. Regina had a solemn task ahead: to mold that young character—it was her debt to her dead son.

Eve and Scott were still in the little interviewing room. "I don't know what else I could have done," Scott was saying, "how else I could have handled what I had to say. Regina doesn't ask for gentleness and I believe that, if she had to hear the truth, my way was the only way she could have faced it. All that concerned me was that every moment you spent in this house was dangerous for you."

"I think you were right. Regina has to be hit hard for anything to register."

Scott got up from the windowsill and came to where Eve sat. She reached up and touched his hand. "Thank you, Scott."

He bent and put his lips to her forehead. "I doubt if we shall ever meet again. Good night, dear Eve."

She didn't speak. She was aware that he had left her, although her face was turned away from him; aware too that he had said something else so softly that it had been as if he hadn't intended her to hear.

The door closed behind him and in the silence around her she sensed a kind of quivering alertness, as if everyone in the house, except the sleeping Shari, was awake and listening. Not even the servants, who had no blood ties to the family, would find it easy to sleep that night. She knew what they would be asking. *What will the Contessa do now? What will happen to this house . . . to us . . . to the business?*

Eve could have told them. Regina would pick up the shattered pieces of her life and carry on.

She made no effort to find her mother-in-law. Regina had not wanted her around during these past difficult months; she would want her even less now, seeing her as a reminder of her terrible mistakes and failures. Regina would seek out Solange who, although not really liking her mistress, was tied to her in the strange way of such relationships.

Eve was aware of an inner chill in those gentle, windless early hours. Facing the truth, she knew that she had loved impulsively, married impulsively; she had been enchanted by charm, by enormous physical attraction, by the unreal world into which she had plunged. She had made that common error of mistaking a physical ideal for an ideal in character.

Only Scott had been real. Scott. Her emotions gave a small lurch.

"I doubt if we shall meet again." She had heard those words clearly. But he had said something else, and she had thought she hadn't heard. But she had. She had listened with some inner ear that had nothing to do with physical hearing.

"Goodbye, my love."

When the shock of Adrian's death was over and the sadness became faded in her mind, she would rebuild her life.

"I doubt if we shall meet again," he had said.

Oh, but we will, Scott. We will . . .

About the Author

ANNE MAYBURY is a full-time writer very well known among readers throughout the world, the author of such popular books as *Jessamy Court, The Midnight Dancers, Ride a White Dolphin, The Jeweled Daughter* and *Dark Star*. She lives in London, and has traveled extensively, which, with "the stimulus of great cities," had been an indispensable inspiration for her work.

7

Mary Welsh Hemingway

HOW IT WAS

Weidenfeld and Nicolson · London

Hail to R.A.G. and his tribe

First published in Great Britain by
Weidenfeld & Nicolson Ltd,
11 St John's Hill, London SW11
1977

First published in the USA by
Alfred A. Knopf Inc.
1976

Grateful acknowledgment is made to Warner Bros. Music for permission to reprint
lyrics from "Somebody Loves Me" by George Gershwin and B. J. DeSylva, lyrics by
Ballard MacDonald. Copyright 1924 by New World Music Corp., copyright
renewed. All rights reserved. Used by permission.

The author also wishes to acknowledge the Executors of the Estate of C. Day-Lewis
and Jonathan Cape Ltd for permission to reprint two lines from Book 1 and twelve
lines from Book 2 of *The Georgics of Virgil*, translated by C. Day-Lewis (1947).

Photographs on pages 1, 2 and 3 of the illustration section following page 440 by Earl
Theisen. From the LOOK Collection at The Library of Congress.

ISBN 0 297 77265 1

Printed in Great Britain by Cox & Wyman Ltd, London, Fakenham and Reading.